The
NINE LIVES
of
Christmas

FLORENCE McNICOLL

TRAPEZE

First published in Great Britain in 2019 by Trapeze
an imprint of The Orion Publishing Group Ltd
Carmelite House, 50 Victoria Embankment
London EC4Y 0DZ

An Hachette UK Company

1 3 5 7 9 10 8 6 4 2

A CIP catalogue record for this book is
available from the British Library.

ISBN (Paperback) 978 1 4091 9265 7
ISBN (eBook) 978 1 4091 9266 4

Typeset by Born Group
Printed and bound in Great Britain by Clays Ltd, Elcograf S.p.A.

www.orionbooks.co.uk

For the cats who make our houses into homes.

And in particular, for our beloved cat, Booby.

Author's note: While the novel is inspired by the fantastic work of Battersea Dogs and Cats Home, it is a work of fiction and I have taken some liberties with exact rehoming procedures. What is I hope reflected in the novel is the great care that Battersea takes in finding new homes for their beautiful cats. For more information on this process, and to register for rehoming enquiries, see www.battersea.org.uk

Chapter 1

What would a cat do? thought Laura Summers blearily, through the beeps of her alarm clock. She reached out a hand to hit snooze, Rob grumbling beside her before he fell back asleep.

A cat certainly wouldn't be dragging herself out of bed at 6 a.m. on a cold, dark, winter morning. No, any cat worth her salt would curl right back up under the duvet and sleep until at least ten, probably eleven, before surfacing and demanding food and cuddles and finding the perfect spot by the radiator to keep cosy for the rest of the day.

Laura smiled. The thought of all the cats waiting for her at Battersea was more than enough to get her out of bed, pull on her dressing gown and pad through to the kitchen for a morning cup of tea, and to crack open the very first door on her chocolate advent calendar. Who said chocolate wasn't an acceptable breakfast? In Laura's book, in December, all normal dietary rules were off.

Mornings hadn't always been like this. When she'd been working as a PA at Nimbus, one of London's top advertising agencies, she'd often been lying awake already before the alarm went off, a tight knot of anxiety in her stomach, worrying about whether she'd sent off those invites, or booked her boss's taxi for the right time, or any number of other potential disasters. She'd left the agency about two years before, following a particularly vicious dressing-down from her boss after she'd asked if 'anyone needed a hug' in a tense client meeting. Pulling herself together in the office loos afterwards by watching some of her all-time favourite cat videos, Laura had seen an advert on Battersea's Facebook page for a welfare worker in the cattery. It had felt like a sign. Laura had decided she'd go somewhere where her talent for looking after people – well, cats, who were pretty much her favourite people anyway – would be appreciated. And she'd never looked back.

She'd loved her time in welfare, caring for the cats right from the moment they came in, ensuring that they were safe, well-fed, happy and healthy in preparation for their new homes. Just a month or so ago, she'd changed job and was now on the rehoming team, helping prospective owners find their perfect match, and the cats their forever homes. She'd spent time shadowing the rehoming interviews, before practising taking pictures of the cats for their online profiles, and answering phone and email enquiries. Her experience in the welfare team had been a great help, but it had still been a steep learning curve, and Laura was keen to prove herself in this new role – as well as being more than a little nervous. She'd always struggled with her confidence. She often felt like she was the one in the room who didn't have much of a presence, the one who wasn't heard, or who muttered and was asked to repeat things. It was one of the reasons she often felt more comfortable being around animals than humans – and, specifically, around cats. She never felt tongue-tied or silly when she was chatting to a cat. Their presence relaxed her, and the flick of a tail, the twitch of an ear, the rumble of a purr all assured her that she was listened to and understood.

Laura finished the last of her tea and tiptoed into the shower, hoping it wouldn't wake Rob. He'd got in late last night, slightly tipsy, having celebrated landing yet another new client. Rob was the one great thing she'd taken with her from her time at the ad agency. He was a hot-shot account director at Nimbus, charming, confident and completely gorgeous, with his blue eyes and dark-brown hair that flopped over his forehead in a way that still made her stomach flip. Laura had admired him from afar, their conversations generally extending only to him requesting meetings with her boss and sometimes asking her to arrange coffees – she'd always taken special care thinking what biscuits Rob might appreciate – and so she'd been amazed when he'd asked her out for a drink at the company's Halloween party two years ago, coming over to find her where she was standing in the corner, twisting her fingers and wondering how on earth everyone else found so much to say. Laura liked to think it had been because her biscuit offering that day – a zingy chocolate Bourbon and pink wafer combo – had finally convinced him they were meant to be together, but Rob said it was more to do with the Catwoman outfit she'd been wearing.

They'd been together pretty much ever since. She'd left the agency and joined Battersea shortly after they started seeing each other, which Rob had been supportive about. He thought she'd be happier in another role, and that it would be better for them not to work together if they were going to be serious. Then, about a year ago, she'd moved into his beautiful home, in fancy Chelsea. She felt like she'd hit the jackpot, really, especially when she'd been sharing a grotty flat in the outer reaches of north London with three other girls who were big on partying and low on tidying. Rob's place was an oasis of calm, exquisitely designed in an array of neutral colours.

After a boiling-hot shower and dressing proudly in her Battersea polo shirt and fleece, Laura slipped out of the house, shivering a little in the frosty air, hopped on a bus and began the journey to Battersea. She was determined to be a star rehomer in her new role. Insecurities couldn't get in the way. She couldn't bear to think of cats alone for Christmas – they would be well cared-for on Christmas Day by the amazing army of festive Battersea volunteers and staff, but nothing compared to knowing you were *home*, for good. And there was one particular cat she had in mind.

The bus pulled up outside Battersea's famous gates and Laura felt a thrill of pride as she buzzed her way in, waving hello to the security team and the receptionist. She crossed the courtyard, taking in the mix of old and new that she loved so much about Battersea. There was the old cattery building in the middle, named Whittington Lodge after the famous Dick Whittington and his cat, with its tiled roof and pretty blue staircase. It was a wonderful reminder of the history of the place. Laura always thought about the many feet – and paws – that had crossed this piece of ground since 1871. What stories they could tell! She got goose bumps at the thought of it.

It was just before eight, and Laura had enough time to pop up to the cattery before the morning meeting – the perfect representation of 'the new' in Battersea's history. The cattery was warm and cosy, with each cat living in an individual 'pod', large enough for a cat to exhibit its natural behaviours with lots of places for hiding – and they even had heated floors!

In anticipation of their breakfasts, most of the cats were now at the front mewing – the dawn chorus, as Laura liked to call it. She strolled past the pods, filled with cats of all colours, shapes, ages and personalities, to see the one cat she had a particular soft spot for. Laura's emotions rose up at the thought of Felicia. It was one of the most amazing, and most difficult, elements of working at Battersea – the emotional attachments you formed with the animals. And there Felicia was, running to the front of her pod as soon as she saw Laura. Laura couldn't resist opening the door and slipping inside, joy rising in her heart as she heard Felicia's loud purr of greeting. Laura sat down and Felicia clambered onto her knee for a cuddle.

Felicia had been one of the saddest cases during Laura's time in welfare. She'd been brought in emaciated and very sick, found by a dog walker in a nearby park. It had been touch and go on those first days as to whether she would survive, but thanks to the care of the veterinary team, Felicia had started to put on weight and recover physically from whatever ordeals she'd been through. Indeed, thought Laura as she held Felicia in her arms, they might have to start watching she didn't get a little *too* plump.

But the damage with animals was often so much more than physical. Felicia had been withdrawn and completely untrusting of humans, cowering at the back of her pod and responding with hisses and the occasional nip to those who came too close. Laura had been assigned as Felicia's 'consistent carer' when she was in welfare. Alongside the daily tasks of feeding and cleaning, Laura had started to build up Felicia's trust, working at the cat's pace, and often simply spending time sitting at the front of the pod, quietly reading or catching up on emails, to get her used to human company. Laura vividly remembered the day when she'd felt a touch on her leg, and had looked down to see Felicia's outstretched paw on her knee. The cat had blinked her golden eyes up at Laura, and Laura swallowed, a lump in her throat, elated and moved at this breakthrough moment.

From there, Felicia quickly gained in confidence and was soon climbing onto Laura's lap for cuddles, bumping her head against Laura's hand when she felt she was slacking off with the under-chin rubs. Laura would talk to her in a low voice and, even though she knew she'd sound crazy, she could have sworn Felicia understood. Occasionally, a playful side to Felicia would emerge – as an older cat at the ripe old age of eight, she was a rather stately lady most of the time, but she could be roused to action by a carefully twitched catnip mouse. Of course, other staff spent time with her too, but it was Laura she had a special bond with. Felicia took time to warm to people, that was for sure. Choosy, Laura thought, but she knew some would see it as unfriendliness if they didn't give her a chance. Then, one proud day, Felicia was assessed to be suitable for rehoming, and was moved to the first floor where she could meet her public.

'You're not tempted to take her yourself?' Jasmine had asked. Jasmine worked between intake and rehoming and was Laura's best friend at Battersea. Best friend full-stop, really.

Laura had shaken her head sadly. This was a major point of contention between her and Rob. He just didn't like cats, he didn't want one in the flat, using all his fancy mid-century furniture as a scratching post and getting hairs in the vinyl collection. Laura knew they could provide a perfect home for a cat – they had a small garden too – but Rob was adamant. He had a beautifully kept tank of tropical fish, and he'd said Laura could name a few of those. She hadn't had the heart to explain that it wasn't the same, much as she'd tried to bond with the newly christened Flotsam and Jetsam.

'How are you this morning, missy?' whispered Laura into Felicia's fur, receiving a louder purr in response. 'Ready for your breakfast?'

That received a small 'Miaow!' and Laura laughed, sure that Felicia understood. She put the cat back down and carefully let herself out of the pod, making her way to the morning meeting, where her team would go through all the cats on 'The List' who were currently up for adoption, as well as checking with the welfare team to see if there were new cats who were now ready to be rehomed. As it was 1 December, Laura made a mental note to get some Christmas decorations up in the cattery – Christmas songs had already been playing on the radio for weeks.

'Still no home for Felicia?' said Laura's boss, Sally, when they came to the cat's name during the meeting rundown.

Laura shook her head sadly. 'It'll have to be the right person. She's a special cat, she just needs someone to notice her, and who'll understand she needs the time and space to settle in. Plus someone who can cope with her medical needs.'

This was another element that had to be considered for Felicia. She'd tested positive for FIV – feline immunodeficiency virus. The virus was a slow-acting one, and many cats went on to enjoy normal lifespans with minimal health implications, but that wasn't always the case. There was the possibility that a FIV cat would have a weakened immune system, and be more prone to infections and other diseases. In order to protect other cats from contracting the virus, and an FIV cat from being exposed to illnesses from other cats, Battersea required that gardens were enclosed in any prospective new homes. This was simple to do with the right fencing, but understandably people could be reluctant to take on a cat with extra needs, and FIV cats took the longest to rehome. The staff always bonded with these cats, as they were in the cattery for so long, and when they finally did find their forever homes, they were given a special send-off with everyone gathered to say goodbye.

Sally nodded. 'Well, she'll be safe here with us for as long as it takes. But let's hope she finds her home soon. She's looking at being one of our longest-ever stays, poor girl.'

Laura did some mental arithmetic and realised that Felicia had been at Battersea for almost one hundred days. With cats counted as a 'long stay' after thirty days, she was already at more than three times that. Laura swallowed. Some cats just couldn't catch a break. Felicia was a bit older, and she was black and white – which for some reason proved to be an unpopular colour. As well as her FIV, she also had a heart murmur that could potentially lead to veterinary treatment, and people were understandably wary about extra costs, but Laura just knew the right match was out there. Felicia could bring someone a lot of joy. All Laura had to do was to keep believing and keep trying. This was to be her Christmas wish, then. Or, rather, her Christmas challenge: find Felicia her forever home, by Christmas Eve.

*

After the meeting, Laura was soon caught up in the flurry of emails and enquiries she received from potential rehomers. A huge part of the job was responding to these, as well as offering support and aftercare to new owners as the cats adjusted to their new homes, and the morning flew by. She hurried over to meet Jasmine for a quick sandwich in the on-site café.

'The first mince pie of the season!' Jasmine said, as they moved on to dessert. Last year, she and Jasmine had tasted pretty much every mince pie going from every major retailer, from the cheapest to the poshest, under the excuse of scientifically finding the best one. 'Shall I get the mince pie spreadsheet going again?'

'Absolutely,' said Laura, through a mouthful of pastry. 'The world needs to know the truth.'

'We're scientific pioneers, really,' said Jasmine.

'They should give us the Nobel Prize!'

'Nobel Pies!' said Jasmine, causing Laura to groan.

'Jas, we're not quite close enough to Christmas for me to cope with your cracker jokes just yet.'

Jasmine held up her hands in surrender. 'All right, all right. So, tell me how things are with you. How's rehoming?'

Laura took a breath. 'Well. I love it. I'm proud to be doing it. But I'm a bit nervous, I have to admit. The thought of doing a lot of interviews on my own – it's intimidating.'

'You will be completely fine,' said Jasmine. 'You've done all the shadowing and the training, and you won't be alone – you know we're a team effort and there will always be help if you need it.'

Laura nodded. It was easy for Jasmine to say – she could chat to absolutely everyone. She was just one of those people who lit up a room with her presence and her raucous laugh.

'I can tell you're stressing,' said Jasmine, reaching out a hand to pat Laura's arm. 'But don't. I've seen you with people – you've got that talent of getting people to open up to you, so you can find just the cat that suits them.'

Laura smiled. 'Thanks, Jas. That's really kind. What about you? Any hot gossip?'

'Not really. Just enjoying a bit of routine before the next foster rescue mission arrives.'

Jasmine was one of Battersea's foster carers, taking in cats who needed special care, or who were too stressed by life in the cattery.

'And are you ready for Christmas?'

Jasmine grimaced, and her face fell. 'As I'll ever be. Not my favourite time of year, I have to say. I've signed up to spend the day here, can't think of anywhere I'd rather be.' Laura knew that Jasmine had had a rough year, splitting up with her husband after she'd found out he was cheating on her last Christmas. She'd declared herself 'quite happy to be a crazy cat lady, thanks very much', but Laura knew this

Christmas would be a tough time for her. Jasmine was strong and proud, but Laura knew how deeply she'd been hurt.

'We can't tempt you to spend Christmas Day down here?' asked Jas. 'It is pretty amazing. Santa comes to visit, and there might even be a drop of prosecco at lunch.'

'I doubt Rob could be persuaded,' Laura said, with a sigh. They were scheduled to go to his parents in Surrey for Christmas, which she couldn't help but feel a little nervous about. Malcolm and Izzy were perfectly pleasant, but were from the Very Confident School of Life, just like Rob. They were a family that liked an occasion – there were many photos of Rob's boisterous childhood birthday parties in the house. He loved to reminisce about those days and how much fun they were, and Laura admittedly loved looking at the pictures of Rob as a cute kid, his delighted face smeared with chocolate cake, a grin from ear to ear. Christmas would be a noisy day of playing charades and commenting with great expertise on wines – just like last year. She'd struggled to recognise most of the films and plays that had come up in charades, and had overheard Izzy saying to Rob in the kitchen, 'She's as quiet as a little mouse!' 'Just give her time,' Rob had said, but the comment had thundered in her ears and she'd become even more quiet, retiring to bed as early as possible and wishing she was different.

'You know he's not keen on cats,' said Laura, breaking out of her reverie. 'So he's probably not going to be up for cleaning litter trays on Christmas Day.'

Laura had frequently tried to persuade Rob to come and see the cats at Battersea – she was convinced that if he'd just get to know the right one, he'd realise what a wonderful addition to their little household a cat would be.

'Ah yes, Mr Perfect,' grinned Jasmine. 'Apart from that one little oversight. What are you going to get him, then?'

'Not sure,' mused Laura. 'I want to get him something really special.'

'You two are just the perfect couple,' teased Jasmine, but when Laura didn't respond, her tone became more serious. 'Hey, I'm just messing about. Everything's okay, isn't it?'

'Yeah, it's fine,' Laura said. Why did she suddenly feel like everything *wasn't* okay with Rob? Why was she suddenly anxious about Christmas Day at his parents'? 'I suppose we're not seeing much of each other. He's so busy with work, so when we do spend time together, it's more collapsing on the sofa and staring at the telly rather than into each other's eyes.'

'Sounds completely normal to me,' said Jasmine, reaching over to squeeze her hand. 'What you need is to make time for each other a bit. Date nights! Do something fun, surprise each other. You'll get that spark back in no time.'

Laura nodded, liking this idea. Jasmine was right – she and Rob just needed to get that sparkle back. And what better time than in the run-up to Christmas? She remembered their first few months together: a whirlwind of romantic dinners, trips to the theatre, and lazy Sundays in bed. Then, as they'd become more established as a couple, endless holidays with Rob's glamorous friends, or freebie trips that Rob could somehow make happen through his advertising connections. He'd whisked her off for a night or two at the end of a shoot in some amazing location more times than she could remember, often refusing to tell her where she was going and simply saying what kind of wardrobe she needed to bring. She'd always buzzed with excitement to get to the airport and find out where she was going. Right then, that was mission number two – a little bit of Christmas magic.

Chapter 2

Laura stood in front of one of the posh make-up counters in John Lewis, Oxford Street, and looked doubtfully at herself in the mirror. She'd been mad to come up here after work in the first week of December. All thoughts of a leisurely festive shopping trip to browse gifts for Rob had been elbowed out of the way – quite literally – as soon as she'd had to force her way out of the underground station, carried up towards the fresh air and glittering lights by a wave of determined shoppers.

She'd seen a few nice shirts in John Lewis, but nothing that stood out enough. On her way out, she loitered briefly by the make-up counter, wondering about treating herself to a new look. She barely wore make-up at Battersea, and jewellery could be more hassle than it was worth – a pair of dangly earrings made perfect playthings for kittens.

'Can I help you?' said a harassed assistant, looking as if she'd like to do anything but help Laura. The girl must have been only about twenty. She was skinny and dressed in black, hair scraped back into a tight bun, her face carefully done up with thick dark brows and red lips.

'Well, yes please, if that's okay? If you've time, I mean?' said Laura. 'I'm just thinking of a new look, really.'

The shop assistant – Lucie, said her name tag – sighed heavily. 'Fine. Sit down.'

Laura perched on one of the bar-style stools, and Lucie scrutinised her face.

'Well, first signs of ageing are there,' she announced.

'Oh, really?' Laura had always thought her skin was quite nice. Yes, there were a few laughter lines and wayward freckles from the odd week in the sun, but she was only thirty-one – hardly over the hill.

Lucie nodded grimly. 'So, what do you use as a daily protector? Do you cleanse, tone, moisturise?'

Laura shook her head and Lucie let out another enormous sigh, before attacking Laura's face with a variety of potions and lotions.

'Right, there's a terrible lack of definition around your cheekbones,' she said, 'so I'm going to have to go in heavy with the contour wand.'

Laura opened her mouth to protest but was barked at to keep still, then to open her mouth, then shut her eyes.

'Honestly, do you *ever* do your eyebrows?' said Lucie.

Laura bristled. This was just getting rude now, and if the whole point of the exercise was to make her feel good, it was doing precisely the opposite.

'Yes, I do, and I like how they are, thanks all the same,' said Laura, mustering up her steeliest glare – or as much as she dared when Lucie was still poking around her face with a variety of implements.

Lucie snorted. 'Fine then. Well, I'm almost done so you can have a look.'

She held up a mirror in front of Laura's face, and Laura almost fell off the stool. The look was heavy, to say the least. Thick stripes of blusher ran across her cheeks, and her offending eyebrows had been heavily pencilled in. This was not what she had been expecting. The red lipstick could be quite nice, she thought, if she wore it in a different way, and the mascara made her green eyes stand out, but overall, this just wasn't her.

'I was thinking . . . really, of something a bit more natural?' Laura ventured.

'This is *fashion*,' Lucie snapped. 'But honestly, don't worry about it – it doesn't go with all the cat hair on your jumper.'

Laura gasped, lost for words. 'Well! You can forget about me buying anything!'

Lucie shrugged, scowling, as Laura hopped down from the stool and marched out of the department store. So much for Christmas cheer! The crowds flocking by looked grim-faced and determined, clutching their bags and keeping their heads down.

The Nimbus office was nearby in Soho, and Laura had the idea of meeting Rob for a drink, to calm her nerves, and to kick-start the spontaneous, fun December that she was determined to make happen. They could have a nice cocktail somewhere, that was sure to cheer them both up. She called him and got his voicemail. Then she rang the main office number and was told by his PA that he was in a client meeting.

Laura sighed, her mood plummeting. Fine then. She was typing him a text to say she'd head home and get dinner on, when she became aware of someone sobbing quietly near to her.

She turned her head and saw Lucie, her arms wrapped around herself, wiping tears from her face.

'Hey,' said Laura, walking over to her. 'Are you okay?'

Lucie looked at her, mascara streaking down her face. She suddenly looked even younger below all her make-up. 'Oh God, it's you,' she said, voice trembling. 'I'm sorry. I was such a cow to you in there. I'm really sorry.'

Laura was taken aback to see Lucie so distraught – she couldn't believe how she'd crumbled from her formidable demeanour during the makeover. Her heart instantly went out to her. 'Well, we all have our moments,' said Laura, kindly. 'Do you want to talk about it? Whatever it is that's upsetting you?'

'It's my granny. She's really ill. They're not even sure she'll make it to Christmas.' At this, Lucie collapsed into sobs again.

Laura got a tissue out of her bag and put her arm round Lucie's thin shoulders. 'Here, have this. I'm really sorry to hear it.'

The girl nodded. 'She's everything to me, I just love her so much.'

They talked for a while longer. Lucie explained that her mum lived overseas with her stepdad, and so she was closest to her grandma. Laura could relate a bit to that. She often wished she had more of her own family around her. Laura was an only child, and her parents had moved away from Portsmouth, where she'd grown up, to live in York. They were real adventurers and spent much of the year abroad on different escapades. Laura knew they loved her, and would be there for her in a heartbeat, but she was just more of a homebird than they were. Sometimes, their absence affected her more than she let on in their brief phone calls from Thailand, Mexico, Australia or wherever they were. If Lucie's grandma was her lifeline, the prospect of losing her must be awful. Laura just listened to everything she said. Sometimes, there simply wasn't anything you could say to make it better and she just encouraged Lucie to let it all out. Finally, Lucie sniffed deeply and said she would have to go back to work.

'Is my make-up all down my face?'

Laura hesitated. 'I mean . . . it's smudged a bit, but you can pull it off.'

Lucie smiled through her tears. 'I'll try to convert it into a smoky eye. You do look really nice, you know. The lipstick.

Suits you. And sorry for being so rude about the cat-hair jumper. Lucky you, having a little cat!'

Laura explained that she didn't have a cat herself but worked at Battersea.

'What's that, then?' said Lucie.

'Well, we're a charity and we work to rehome dogs and cats. We look after them until we find the perfect new owner for them.'

'That's cool,' said Lucie. 'So, they get, like, a second chance?'

Laura nodded, pulling out her phone and loaded up the homepage. 'They get as many chances as they need. Here, look – there's the website, if you ever want to read more about what we do. Or just have a look at some of the cats, always cheers me up.'

Lucie smiled, more broadly this time. 'Thank you.' She gave Laura a brief hug before turning around and heading back through the doors of the department store.

You never knew what people had going on, thought Laura. Lucie reminded her of a spiky cat, all claws out and ready to nip, but, underneath, simply feeling scared and vulnerable.

Chapter 3

Almost as soon as she'd got in and popped a ready-made lasagne in the oven, Laura had made the mistake of lying down on the sofa and resting her eyes for a moment. She was woken up by the sound of the front door closing, and hit by the smell of burning cheese.

'Hello, gorgeous,' Rob said, greeting her with a kiss. 'Love the new look!'

She wriggled upright, wondering if he'd found a new appreciation for her polo shirt, and then remembering Lucie's artistry.

'Oh, thanks. Thought I'd try something a bit new.'

Rob dug out the lasagne from the oven, putting it on two plates. 'And this smells incredible. Did you make it?'

I should have made it, Laura thought. This was all about making an effort. Surely she could have whipped up a béchamel sauce without too much hassle? She opted to dodge the question.

'Sorry about the burnt bits.'

'They're the best bits!'

Rob gave her a peck on the cheek before settling down on the sofa and flicking on the TV.

'So how was your day?' Laura asked.

He shuddered. 'Complete nightmare. Honestly, Gerry – the new account director, remember I told you? – completely messed something up. And I had to sort it out, the client wouldn't deal with anyone else, which meant I was completely and utterly behind, and had to try to sign off on the creative for that beauty brand in about five minutes.'

God, agency life. Laura winced at the thought of it. She didn't know how Rob could stand it – he liked the excitement of it all, but she had found the atmosphere incredibly stressful. And, at the end of the day, did it matter that much? She didn't voice that opinion, of course. She tried to gather her thoughts to tell Rob about her date-night idea.

'*Game of Thrones*,' Rob said.

It was a statement, not a question. He found the latest episode and pressed play.

Laura took a deep breath. She shouldn't feel nervous. This was about them making time for each other, falling back in love a bit. Shame that the mutilated bodies on screen weren't exactly a romantic backdrop, but she persevered nonetheless.

'Rob?'

'Mmm. Yes, pea?'

'I've been thinking.'

'Uh-oh.'

'About us.'

He turned to look at her. 'This sounds suddenly serious.'

'No, it isn't! It's just, I want us to spend more time together.'

Rob gestured at the two of them on the sofa, the lasagne, eyebrows raised, corners of his mouth turned up in a way that made her stomach flip.

'I know this is time together,' Laura continued, feeling tongue-tied, 'but *good* time, like we used to.'

Rob grinned. 'Back when I was pursuing the gorgeous Catwoman who took my breath away!'

Laura smiled, relieved. 'Exactly. It doesn't have to be fancy breaks away, just . . . doing thoughtful things. Kind of like a date night.'

Rob rolled his eyes. 'Sounds a bit cheesy to me, but anything to make you happy, pea.'

And, with that, he turned back to the TV.

'When can we do the first one?' Laura pressed on.

Rob groaned. 'I need to check my diary. I'll do it tomorrow. These next weeks are just crazy, and you remember we've got the dinners in? With Alex and Jamie? And hopefully Liz and Helen as well?' These were some of Rob's friends from uni. Laura envied their tight-knit group. They were always arranging to see each other, reliving the antics of their student days. Rob was a few years older than her, but somehow his gang of mates seemed a lot more solid than her handful of friends. She'd never been one for a big group, she was too shy for that, and preferred to get to know people slowly. She had a couple of good friends from university, and even one or two from school, but they saw each other less and less these days. Life seemed to get in the way. So much of their time was taken up with work, and, increasingly, a partner and baby, so it became harder and harder to pin down dates. Weeks slid into months, and Laura knew she was also guilty of sometimes preferring the sofa to trekking across London, telling herself there'd be another opportunity to see everyone.

All the more reason for making sure the same thing didn't happen to her and Rob, and that they didn't start taking each other for granted. Laura wasn't exactly bowled over by his enthusiasm, but perhaps raising the subject when Rob was knackered from work hadn't been the best idea. Later that night, she lay awake for a while in bed, before deciding that she would have to lead from the front and take Rob on a really good date. He was fiercely competitive, she knew that from their Scrabble matches, and if she could tap into that side of him, he'd be up for the challenge.

She'd had no time to even contemplate a good date the next morning at Battersea. Rehoming requests were flooding in, thick and fast. Laura was just getting up to make a cuppa when Sally popped her head round the door.

'I know you're due a break, but could you do a "meet and greet" for me?'

Laura stifled a groan, and banished thoughts of chocolate digestives for a bit longer. It was all worth it if they managed to find a cat a new home. One of the features of Battersea's rehoming process was that different welfare advisers carried out the interview and the 'meet and greets' – the magical moment when cat and human met for the first time. Often, they would show a potential rehomer a couple of cats, as it was important for people to see just how different cats' personalities could be.

'Is there no one else around?' Laura asked, hopefully.

'Sorry, Laura. She was asking for you, specifically. I thought she might be a friend, or something.'

Puzzled, Laura went out to meet the client.

It was Lucie, the girl from the make-up counter. Today, she was dressed in jeans and a baggy jumper, her hair pulled back and her skin scrubbed clean.

'Hello,' said Laura. 'What a surprise to see you here!'

'Wasn't sure you'd recognise me on my day off,' Lucie replied, with a smile. 'Look, I wanted to bring you something.'

She held out a small, beautifully wrapped package, and Laura took it.

'Should I wait until Christmas, or . . .?'

'No! Open it now!' Lucie said eagerly, her hands clasped together.

Laura began to open the little packet, savouring the pretty gold paper and pink ribbon, and found a beautiful lipstick, in a heavy rose-gold tube.

'The one you tried on yesterday,' said Lucie. 'It really did look lovely, and I felt awful for being so nasty to you.'

Lucie looked so young and sweet, standing there with her face bare, shifting from foot to foot as if she was nervous. Laura gathered her into a hug.

'This is so kind of you, and more than makes up for anything yesterday. You're going through a tough time, don't be too hard on yourself.'

Lucie nodded, pressing her lips together and looking down at the ground. Laura sensed she was getting tearful again.

'But you didn't have to go through a whole rehoming interview to give me a lipstick! You should just have asked for me at reception!'

Lucie shook her head. 'No, it was for real. I'll tell you.'

Laura much preferred to listen than talk and that was an element she liked a lot about the rehoming role: the stories she heard. People really opened up when there were animals involved, she tended to find. And she was always happy to provide a listening ear.

'So last night, I did end up leaving work a bit early,' said Lucie. 'Almost took someone's eye out with an eyeliner, and realised I was just too stressed out.' She smiled ruefully. 'And I went round to see Granny. She was awake, bless her. She's being looked after at home now. She told me . . .' Lucie wiped her nose and took a deep breath. 'She told me . . . that she wants me to have her little flat, after, you know.'

Laura nodded, keeping a hand on Lucie's shoulder.

'And I told her not to be silly, she's not going anywhere. But I said I'd move into the spare room and keep her company for a bit. I spend so many nights round there anyway, and I'm a bit sick of my current place. Then Granny told me, it's a cat that makes a home. She's always had them. Her last one was a rescue cat, actually. Tintin. He was a real sweetheart. She didn't want to get another one if she wasn't sure she could look after it for the whole of its life. That's typical Granny, see. But she was pretty insistent I should get a moggy of my own. And when you'd mentioned Battersea, well, it just felt like fate. So, I found myself looking at the website last night – couldn't sleep after all that emotion, and there was one little cat that stood out, so I just thought, why not? I'll come and see. And so the plan is, to get a cat now, if that's possible, and I'm sure it'd be a help to Granny too. And then, well. At least I'll have company.'

Laura took a deep breath. 'Lucie, let's see what we can do.'

Lucie could clearly offer a wonderful home to a cat. She'd shown Sally pictures of the flat – it was on the ground floor, so had garden space, and she and her grandma were experienced cat owners. She'd initially thought she wanted a kitten, but then revised that expectation – an older, calmer cat would be much better. Her grandma needed a calm animal around, and a kitten couldn't be left while Lucie was at work. Laura's heart began to beat faster. Felicia could be a perfect match here.

'So, there're a couple of cats you might want to meet,' said Laura. 'I'll let you into the pod, and if you just stay at the front, that's best. The cats need to know they can retreat into their beds – their safe territory. But they should come forward and say hello in a bit.'

She brought Lucie to Bumpkin's pod first, a stately tabby cat.

Lucie beamed. 'That's him! That's the one I saw!'

Laura nodded. 'Well, let's just see how you get on.' This happened frequently – people saw cats online that they were convinced were the perfect match, only to find differently in reality. Just like online dating, really, Jasmine had said, during one of her forays into that world.

Bumpkin was snoozing when Laura carefully opened the door, and Lucie slipped in. She crouched down low, gently drumming her fingers on the floor. Laura smiled. You could always tell a cat-lover. She'd put money on Lucie having a well-established 'cat voice'. She certainly did, which Rob teased her for whenever she deployed it. 'You sound bonkers,' he'd laugh, as she befriended any cat who happened to stroll in their direction.

Bumpkin's ears pricked up, and he came forward to greet Lucie, tail in the air. He'd been brought in by a lovely family, whose youngest child had developed a severe allergy. This meant he was well-socialised and confident, and he wasted no time in plonking himself on Lucie's lap, purring to his heart's content.

'He's wonderful,' whispered Lucie, tickling under his chin. Laura was conflicted – they were getting on tremendously, but she would love to see Felicia go to a loving home like this.

'Let's meet another cat, just in case,' said Laura when Lucie emerged, beaming from ear to ear.

They arrived at Felicia's pod. 'Now this lady hasn't had the easiest life,' said Laura. 'She's a bit less confident than Bumpkin. But let's see.'

Lucie entered the pod, and crouched down again. Laura could see Felicia in her bed. She was watching Lucie wiggle her fingers, but showing no signs of moving. Lucie glanced back to Laura.

'Give her a moment,' said Laura, but Felicia wouldn't budge. *Come on, Felicia,* Laura willed her. *Just show her, show her that soft side of yours.* But it wasn't to be. Felicia allowed Lucie to stroke her gently, but remained in her bed.

Lucie emerged.

'She's beautiful, Laura. I feel awful leaving her behind, especially as she's had a tough time. But I think Bumpkin is the one for us. Granny needs a cat who'll just . . . radiate love, if that makes sense.'

Laura wondered if there was anything more she could say, if she could have fought Felicia's corner a bit more, but she knew that Lucie had to make the right decision for her – and that she needed to keep her own emotions out of it. 'It does, Lucie. I'm thrilled you've found Bumpkin. And, don't worry, Felicia will stay here with us, until we find her that perfect home.'

Soon, with the necessary paperwork completed, Bumpkin was heading off with Lucie in a snazzy new cat carrier.

'Please stay in touch, won't you?' said Laura. 'We'll check in, anyway, but do let us know how your first Christmas is together!'

Lucie nodded. 'Absolutely. Thank you for everything. And happy Christmas, all of you!' She turned and walked out of the Battersea gates, turning to wave goodbye.

Laura felt emotional. She felt sure that Bumpkin was going to be an enormous comfort to Lucie with whatever lay ahead, and a blessing in her grandma's final days. Christmas could be a hard time, as well as a joyful one. It was full of ups and downs, expectations, fears and hopes. She was lucky to have Rob, lucky they were both well and happy, lucky they would spend the day with his parents – she resolved to appreciate it all more. Laura took a moment to pass by Felicia's pod again. This time, the cat ran straight to the door, even standing up on her hind legs to paw for attention. *How could anyone resist that face?* thought Laura, as Felicia gazed adoringly up at her.

'Oh, Felicia,' said Laura, 'it'll be your turn soon, don't worry. You'll have a home for Christmas.'

Chapter 4

Mark Turner finished making his dinner and sighed. Spaghetti bolognese for one. He stared down at the plate, resting between a knife and fork on the kitchen table. He always made the kids eat at the table, so why should things be different when it was just him?

But it *was* different. He glanced up at the fridge, at the scrawled drawings they'd made for him to try to brighten up his new flat. 'Bachelor pad', wasn't that what the estate agent had called it? Mark hated the phrase.

He'd accepted that things were over between him and Jess, that they were better off apart – and grateful that they'd managed to stay on good terms, more or less. But coping without the kids was something else altogether. They spent alternate weekends with him and their mum, and the weeks without them were really hard. Mark mostly spent that time thinking of ways to make their time together special – dinners he'd cook, TV they'd watch – and counting down the days until Tilly and Ben arrived at his door, a tumble of noise and life. Mark worked from home as a freelance designer, so he didn't get much social contact through work. If he wasn't careful, and didn't have social invites from his pals who kept an eye on him, he could go days without much human contact at all. And, worst of all, this would be the first Christmas he'd spend without the kids.

They were heading down to Jess's parents for the day itself, and, though they would spend Boxing Day with Mark, he was dreading Christmas morning alone. He adored Christmas. He'd never fallen out of love with it like so many adults had – no, the enchantment had always remained for him. He loved everything about it – the traditional carols mixing with the ridiculous pop songs the kids liked, the boozy pub nights, the occasional snow, stuffing yourself with food, cheesy TV – and, when he had a family of his own, it was an excuse to go even more crazy. From the start of December, and even before, preparations started. Days spent writing letters to Santa, nativity plays, making decorations and putting them up, a trip to get the tree – the kids begging to be put in a net of their own, and the garden centre obliging – not to mention planning, practising and then cooking an enormous, elaborate Christmas dinner. There'd not been much of that this year.

His phone pinged.

'Sure you don't want to spend the day with us?'

It was a text from his pal Simon. Mark really appreciated the offer, but Simon had a young family of his own and Mark didn't want to intrude.

'Thanks, mate, but I'm going to enjoy a day of complete control over the remote and watch exactly what I want on telly.'

'Okay, but you're welcome to just pop in.'

Mark smiled and put the phone to one side, before it buzzed again.

'Sammia thinks you should get a dog. Keep you company instead of rattling around.'

Mark stifled a groan. Sammia was Simon's wife, and liked to fix things. Including him, it would appear.

'Not a big fan of them! Plus all the walking . . .'

Another buzz.

'Sammia says a cat, then.'

He had to laugh. There then followed a stream of picture messages of adorable kittens and cats, playing with their toys, snoozing, miaowing for food. It was true, he had always liked cats. They hadn't been able to have any pets as a family because Jess was allergic, but was it completely mad to think of getting a cat now?

'Sorry, mate, Sammia had my phone there. But think about it! She's now going on about how good they are for stress relief. I'll leave you to it . . .'

*

Maybe it was the text messages, maybe it was waking up on another day without the kids jumping on his bed, maybe it was having no packed lunches to make. But, somehow, Mark found himself standing outside Battersea's gates the following morning. He'd always had a soft spot for the place – one of his happiest childhood memories was of going to Battersea to pick out their beloved family cat, now sadly long gone. Was there any harm in just looking and asking a few questions? They'd probably think he wasn't suitable anyway.

He took a deep breath and went through to the cattery reception.

'I'm . . . I'm interested in rehoming a cat, please,' he said to the smiling woman. 'I mean, if you think it's a good idea.'

'Well, take a seat here and I'll see if one of our rehomers is available for a chat.'

Mark didn't know why he suddenly felt nervous. *Calm down*, he told himself sternly. *It's just a bit of research.*

'Hello! I'm Laura,' came a quiet, but bright, voice, and he stood up to shake the hand of the woman in front of him. She had dark-blonde hair, pulled up in a bun, and friendly green eyes – not unlike those of a cat, he found himself thinking. They passed into an interview room, and began to chat.

Was it just him, or did she also seem a bit nervous? Every time she had to ask him a question, she prefaced it with, 'Sorry about this,' and then glanced down or gave a little smile.

'Please don't worry,' he said, time and time again, until she paused for a moment, gave a small laugh and said, 'I'm a bit new at this. I'm sorry, why don't we both just relax a bit?'

Mark laughed too, his nerves vanishing.

'That sounds good to me. This is one of the first things I've put myself forward for in a while, so I'm overthinking things a lot as well.'

Laura nodded. 'Oh, believe me, I get that. From what you've shown me, the flat looks lovely. Great that you've got a little garden out the back.'

'And a catflap already there,' said Mark. He was lucky – his landlord was a reasonable kind of person and said pets were allowed.

'Is it just you at home?'

Mark paused. The question stung. 'Um. Well, I'll have my kids with me some weekends, and hopefully during the weeks a bit. Me and my wife recently split. It's been . . . a bit of a transition for all of us.' He swallowed.

'How old are the kids?'

'Tilly's twelve and Ben's nine.'

He couldn't help but smile when he thought of them. He told Laura how great they were with animals – that they were both gentle, responsible kids – and he felt his heart swell with pride.

There was a moment of silence while Laura scribbled down some answers on a form. He didn't know quite why, but he suddenly found himself wanting to open up to her. It was something about the way she listened, her head tilted to one side.

'And do you have any ideas about what kind of cat you're looking for?' she asked.

'I suppose,' began Mark, 'I'm just looking for a cat that *needs* me.' He swallowed again. He hadn't been expecting those words to pop out, but they had, and that was exactly how he felt. 'It's hard at the moment. I miss having someone – *someones* – to look after. I miss all the stuff people complain about – getting up in the night if they've had a bad dream, making their lunches, sorting out uniforms, chasing around. So, if there's a cat that needs lots of time and attention, well, that's the cat for me.' He blushed, hoping he didn't sound like a complete lunatic.

Laura tilted her head to one side again, clearly thinking. 'Mark, what about a kitten?'

'A kitten? I'd never really considered that . . .'

Laura sat up straight, a gleam in her eye.

'You might be just right for one. The thing is, most people come in convinced they want a kitten and, actually, they're a huge commitment. Non-stop, full of energy, needing pretty much constant care and attention. And as you're around at home a lot of the day, you can give that.'

Mark grinned, feeling a spark of excitement light up. 'Sounds ideal.'

'I had a feeling you might say that,' Laura said with a smile. 'Now, it's not the usual season for kittens, but we have had one little one in recently. She's called Amber. As you'll have the kids living with you, at least some of the time, they'd need to come and meet her at some point to check everyone gets on, but she won't be ready for a home until a week or so anyway, so we've got a little bit of time.

You could meet her today, and take her home next week, perhaps?'

Mark felt his heart begin to pound. He suddenly wanted this so, so much. The thought of another little heartbeat in the flat – Sammia had been right after all. It wasn't good for him, being alone so much.

He nodded, and Laura explained he would meet Amber on the second floor.

An hour later, and Mark walked out of Battersea's gates, his head held high. It had been love at first sight when he was introduced to Amber, a tiny, fuzzy, ginger kitten. She'd mewed as soon as she saw him, and made her way over to him, with a purr so loud it seemed impossible that it came from her little body. He'd laughed, and felt pure joy bubble up in his chest for the first time in a long while. He knew the kids would love her as well – her boundless energy was evident as she tried chasing down a mouse toy, twisting into the air and flopping over on her side, before springing back up.

He'd taken a few pictures of her, and he sent those to Jess.

'Considering a new addition – what do you think? Kids would need to meet her first. She's at Battersea Dogs and Cats Home.'

Jess texted back almost instantly.

'Mark, brilliant idea! She's gorgeous. I can bring the kids to Battersea this Saturday? Be nice for us all to have an outing together.'

Mark smiled as he texted back to confirm the plan. He had a good feeling about this. And, en route back to his flat, he had a sudden realisation. If all went well, Amber would be in the flat in time for Christmas. Her very first Christmas. And if that wasn't worth making a fuss about, he didn't know what was. He didn't want to tempt fate, but, instantly, he found himself planning Amber's first Christmas morning. She would need a new bed, a festive bowl, some presents to open – although he suspected she'd be more into the wrapping paper. Yes, it was silly but, suddenly, he found himself counting down the days to Christmas with excitement, not dread, once more.

Chapter 5

'How was your morning?' said Jasmine, as Laura flopped down next to her in one of the office chairs. 'Hey, watch it, you're sitting on the carol concert posters!'

'Whoops,' said Laura, getting up and retrieving a stack of posters from underneath her. 'These look great!' The Battersea Christmas Carol Concert was one of the highlights of the festive season, and only a few weeks away. Mulled wine, mince pies and goody bags – all in aid of the dogs and cats Battersea helped. Laura couldn't wait. She knew Jasmine was keen to get her out afterwards as well, and she quite fancied letting her hair down for once.

Once she'd put the posters carefully aside, Laura told Jasmine about Mark and Amber, before asking how her morning had gone. Jasmine had been on intake. It was a role Laura wasn't sure she could handle. Sixty per cent of their cats were given up for adoption by their owners, with 35 per cent found as strays. And 5 per cent were those random cases no one could predict – such as the poor cats found outside Battersea's gates on occasion.

'It was a tough one,' replied Jasmine, wearily rubbing her hand over her face. 'Had an intake appointment with a guy giving up his cat. He was heartbroken about it. His girlfriend died a few months ago, and he has to move to another council property. Needless to say, the new one doesn't allow pets.'

'That's awful,' said Laura, a lump rising in her throat at the thought of this poor man separated from a beloved pet and at such a difficult time, just before Christmas too.

Jasmine nodded. 'Yeah, he was gutted. Lovely little cat as well, Missy's her name.'

Laura shook her head. Landlords not allowing pets was one of the main reasons cats were brought in for adoption. Changing the rules to be more flexible was one of Battersea's key campaigns, and one Laura believed in fervently. So many people could benefit from owning a pet, and could provide good and loving homes were it not for arbitrary rules.

'I'll keep an eye out for Missy once she's assessed,' promised Laura. Straight after an intake appointment, a cat was taken to one of Battersea's veterinary staff for an assessment, then to a pod on the third or second floor. These were closed to public access, and were a space for new cats to adjust, or for cats awaiting adoption who might be stressed by the hustle and bustle of the first floor.

'That would be great,' said Jasmine. 'If you can weave a bit of your magic for her photo and description, I'd love it. I promised the man we'd give him an update as to how Missy's getting on.'

Thanks to her advertising agency background, Laura was fast getting a reputation for being a dab hand at writing the online profile for each of the cats. When she'd started as a PA, she'd entertained thoughts of becoming a copywriter, but had quickly given up on that, given the cut-throat nature of it all. But she still loved writing, and this was a part of the role she really enjoyed – telling the story of each animal so the perfect match could be found. In fact, that was what she had planned to do after lunch. There had been a couple of assessed cats who were now ready to go online, and she wanted to write their profiles. And, while she was at it, maybe she'd look again at Felicia's.

A couple of hours later, Laura stretched in her chair. The afternoon had flown by, and she'd somehow managed to spend a little time with each new cat before writing their profiles. This was an important part of the rehomer role. They didn't care for the animals in the way welfare did, but they needed to be sure they knew each one as well as possible – both through chatting to the welfare team and slipping into a cat pod for a quick snuggle (one of the best parts of the job). She was pleased with her handiwork, and had given her pieces a little festive rhyme. The beneficiaries of a quick online makeover were:

Notch – a pretty tabby cat, aged nine years old, who'd had a traumatic past. Older cats were a little bit more difficult to home. People always wanted kittens, or younger cats, but the benefits of an older cat were huge. They were often calmer and more amenable to snuggling up peacefully for hours on end.

Along with some pictures, Laura had written:

'Twas the month before Christmas, and all through the house,
Cats were looking for homes, more so than a mouse.
Our shy lady Notch is looking for her fresh start –
Could you give her a place by your hearth?
She'll need love, care and lots of understanding,
From calm owners who aren't too demanding –
Notch needs plenty of time and plenty of space,
To start a new life at her own quiet pace.

*

Then she'd turned her attentions to Skittle, a very cute one-and-a-half-year-old cat, who was always up for a game. She'd been inspired by hearing 'Rudolph, the Red-Nosed Reindeer' on the radio, and had written:

> Skittle, the pink-nosed feline,
> Has some very active paws,
> And if you ever saw him,
> You would swear he never paused.
>
> Then one foggy Christmas time
> A family came to say,
> 'Skittle, our naughty festive sprite,
> Won't you come home with us tonight?'
>
> Then all the family loved him,
> And they shouted out with glee,
> Skittle, the playful feline,
> You're part of our history!

Laura craned her neck round the door. She could just about see Skittle batting his favourite knitted pink mouse around – she'd thoroughly enjoyed a frenzied game with the young cat not long before. The mouse would have been knitted by one of her favourite parts of the Battersea community: the monthly Knitting Kittens meeting. A group of knitters of all ages gathered in reception to knit blankets and toys for the feline residents. When they went to their new home, each cat took their own blanket and toy with them.

Finally, Laura had done a new profile for a Siamese cat named Teddy. He was typical of the breed: highly intelligent, vocal and very, very inquisitive. She'd livened up his requirements – he'd need lots of stimulation and attention – with a little festive jingle.

Sleigh bells ring,
Teddy's listening!
In Battersea,
He's mewing,
For a home of his own,
A garden to roam,
Walking in a winter wonderland!

Laura pulled up Felicia's profile and studied it. Did the photo do her justice? To Laura, she was the most gorgeous cat ever – a classic 'tuxedo' black and white pattern, with a splodge of black on her chin, as if dabbed there by an avant-garde painter. But black, and black and white cats, often proved the least popular at Battersea. Laura didn't know quite why – maybe some people thought they were bad luck, but she preferred to think the opposite about black cats. To her, they were completely stunning – a pair of green eyes set off by black velvet fur. What could be more quintessentially cat?

The phones were quiet now, and Laura went to Felicia's pod. She'd worked hard on the other profiles and was out of creative energy – it wasn't the time to attempt a revamp. The cat was snoozing in her bed at the back, one paw outstretched. She pricked up her ears and opened her eyes, offering up a loud rumble of a purr when she recognised Laura.

'Hello, girl,' murmured Laura. 'Busy day at the office, eh?'

Felicia stretched out fully, flipping onto her back and squirming. Laura laughed and gently tickled under Felicia's chin. How different this was to the timid, shy cat who delivered the occasional nip beforehand. Laura felt the stresses of the day melt away as Felicia purred. What she loved about cats was how they made you sink into the present moment – forget meditation, she just needed five minutes with a purring feline. Who could resist twitching a string about to snatch a cat's attention – they made you playful and silly, in a way modern life didn't often allow for.

Her mind turned over to what she'd do for the first date night with Rob. He was so stressed and serious these days. When was the last time he was playful and silly? She couldn't remember. Now, it was all late nights at the office and catching up on sleep at weekends. Then a brainwave hit her.

Chapter 6

'You've got to keep the blindfold *on*,' Laura said, tying a paw-printed scarf around Rob's eyes as soon as he got into the hallway. 'And no peeking!'

'All right, all right!' he said. 'Are you kidnapping me? Is this how we're livening things up?'

Laura giggled. 'Not quite. Come on, shuffle forward . . . That's it . . .'

'Just be careful of the walls,' said Rob, and Laura rolled her eyes. Rob's stress levels could be measured by how pernickety he got about the flat, and when he was that concerned about a few fingerprints on the Farrow & Ball paintwork, it was a sign he was pretty frazzled. It had taken a bit of persuading to get Rob to leave work on time that Thursday, and Laura had taken the afternoon off to get everything prepared at the flat. Now, as she guided Rob through the corridor to the open-plan kitchen and living room, she felt her excitement build. This was exactly why they needed these date nights!

'Now stop,' she said, bringing Rob to a halt just inside the door. 'Ready? One, two, three . . .' She untied the blindfold and let Rob see the date-night surprise.

'Oh my God, Laura, this is amazing!' He picked her up and spun her in his arms, kissing her, his fussing completely gone. 'Look at this! I can't believe you did all this!'

Laura had transformed the living room with bunting and balloons. She'd remembered Rob talking about how his birthday parties when he was a kid were the most fun he'd ever had, so she thought she'd try to recreate that simple joy.

'It's your Very Merry Unbirthday,' she said to him, beaming.

'Laura, it's incredible.' He made his way over to the table. 'All my favourite junk foods from when I was a kid!' There were potato faces, spaghetti hoops, cut-up bits of pizza, crisps and lots of pick 'n' mix. A stack of games awaited them too – pin the whiskers on the cat (Laura's preferred variation on tail on the donkey), Twister, and some classic 1980s board games.

Rob was grinning from ear to ear as he took it all in.

'And this isn't strictly kids' party territory – I think we deserve some real fizzy pop,' said Laura, going to the fridge and popping open a bottle of cava. Some spurted onto the granite worktop – she wiped it up quickly in case it stressed Rob out, but he didn't even notice. He'd gone straight in for some pizza slices and was looking about ten years younger, a cheeky grin on his face.

'Right then, what's first?' he said, through a mouthful. 'I think a round of Hungry Hungry Hippos is in order.'

*

A couple of hours later, after Mr Tomlinson next door had called round to see if everything was okay due to the noise, Rob and Laura lay on the floor, trying to laugh as quietly as possible. Several rounds of Hungry Hippos had been followed by more fizz to prepare them for Twister. With neither of them being particularly flexible, they'd soon been in hysterics, falling in every direction and landing with some pretty impressive thuds on the floorboards.

'You look like a geriatric crab!' Laura had giggled, as Rob tried to reach his right foot to a red spot.

'I'll have you know, I was quite the gymnast in my youth,' Rob had panted back, before a button from his shirt flew off, causing them both to collapse in laughter. 'I reckon I could still do a forward roll if I hadn't eaten my body weight in pick 'n' mix.'

Laura had said 'uh huh' sarcastically, and Rob had pinned her to the ground and tickled her into hysterics, before kissing her in a way he hadn't for, well, ages.

For the sake of Mr Tomlinson, they'd decided to declare Twister a draw, although Laura was convinced she'd only been getting warmed up and would have nailed the next round, especially after another handful of sweets. Her ribs hurt from laughing so much – she'd forgotten just how funny Rob could be. And how much she fancied him when he was like this.

He sat up, reached over and fed her a fizzy cola bottle. 'There you go, my gymnastic champion.'

'It's also important to rehydrate after sports,' said Laura, waggling her glass in his direction.

Rob poured the last of the cava into it, before kissing her on the lips. 'Thank you so much for doing this. I really needed it.'

'*We* really needed it,' said Laura.

'Agreed.'

They lay together in a joyful silence, Rob stroking Laura's hair. She shut her eyes, enjoying the sensation. They were good together. She'd always known it. She just needed to be reminded of it.

'Can't wait to see what your date night will be,' she murmured.

Rob smiled. 'Oh, I'll be sure to spoil you rotten, don't worry.'

A few more moments passed.

'Do you ever think about . . . the future?' Laura said, her slight tipsiness making the words spill over. Whoops. That wasn't meant to be what tonight was about. It was more about having fun and living in the moment.

Rob propped himself up on his elbow. 'How do you mean, Laur?'

'I suppose . . . just so many friends getting engaged. Having kids.' Laura's Instagram feed was now swamped with pictures of diamond rings and adorable toddlers, and she and Rob had attended about six lavish weddings over the summer. It seemed once people hit thirty, it was a race to get married and settle down as soon as possible. Were they ready for that? Could she imagine what her life would be like with Rob, in ten years' time, twenty, fifty? So many of her friends were now busy with family lives of their own and many had moved out of London. She sometimes felt like her life had shrunk these past few years. What about her uni friends, Rachel and Carys? How long had it been since she'd seen them? She realised with a lurch it had been at least a year. Rachel had moved out of London with her boyfriend, and Carys had had her second child. They kept in touch via their WhatsApp group but that wasn't the same as actually spending time together. Her social life was very much bound up with friends of Rob's, who were always organising things, apart from Jasmine, who dragged her out when she threatened to become too boring.

'Well, I don't know, Laur,' said Rob. 'I'm very happy with things as they are. And I see my future with you in it. Of that I'm sure.'

That was good enough for her. She smiled, and felt herself relax from the whirlwind of thoughts. The rest would work itself out in good time – she wasn't even sure she wanted marriage and kids anyway.

'I love you, Rob. Even if you're rubbish at Twister.'

He poked her in the ribs. 'Oi!'

Another silence, comfortable and happy. No mobiles. No emails. Just each other.

Rob got up.

'Where are you going?' said Laura, with a yawn.

'I'm making us a fort out of the sofa cushions and getting the duvet. Let's finish off date night number one in style.'

Chapter 7

Casey Lane counted down the seconds until her phone alarm clock went off. It didn't even get through one buzz before she'd turned it off, and seen that there were numerous WhatsApp messages from the one person who she never wanted to hear from again. Or that's what she told herself. Her silly heart said otherwise.

Anger coursed through her veins. She'd lain awake most of the night, thoughts spiralling around her head, rage mingling with sadness, crying into her pillow, getting up to make a hot milky drink, trying to keep calm and count her breaths. None of it had worked. Being in bed, lying in the dark with only her clashing thoughts for company, had felt like torture. And yet now that morning had arrived, she was gripped by a terrible grey feeling, as if some force was pressing her down and not letting her get out of bed.

Anxiety rose up in her chest. She couldn't possibly go to work. She was exhausted – how was she meant to cope for a whole day working in a school? She might have been in the front office as opposed to teaching, but she still had to cope with an endless stream of demands from teachers, pupils and parents. She thought of her inbox mounting up with correspondence to be filed. She worried about the phone ringing incessantly. She imagined the deafening sound of the bell and the kids laughing and shoving through the corridors as they moved from class to class. It would be even worse as the end of term drew nearer – the kids boisterous and sensing holidays, the admin of dealing with the Christmas play and staff party and all the rest of it. She curled tighter into a ball.

The next time she glanced at her phone, somehow half an hour had passed. *Shit.* She'd be late, unless she got up right away and hurried to get ready.

So, go on then, get yourself up, said the voice in her head.

But somehow her body didn't respond.

Instead, she thought of how she'd have to get her lunch in the canteen. How she'd have to fend off small talk from colleagues about what she was doing for Christmas. The thought of it made her heart pound.

She reached for the phone and opened WhatsApp. Maybe, just maybe, the messages would be him begging to have her back, explaining it all away. Could it have been a mistake? Some kind of terrible dream?

'Casey, I need to get my stuff.'

Great.

'I didn't mean to hurt you. You know that.

'It's just, I never felt like this about anyone before. I didn't mean for it to happen.'

As if that made it okay!

'Giving me the silent treatment isn't going to help either of us move on. Let me know when I can come round and pick up my things.'

Casey twitched her curtain aside. Rain was battering down, matching the anxious patter of her heart. She glanced around the room, full of half-packed boxes. She'd be moving back in with her mum soon. There was no way she could afford this rent on her own. She supposed she was lucky to even have that option, but it was hardly the future she'd imagined for herself.

Casey knew she shouldn't, but somehow she couldn't help herself – she loaded up the Instagram of Fern Redmond and tortured herself with images. Fern beaming, smiling, living her perfect life. Rosy-cheeked in the Winter Wonderland in Hyde Park. Decorating a Christmas tree. At least she'd had the decency not to include Adam in any of the shots, but Casey knew he'd taken them, and his flurry of heart emojis under them all was like a knife to the heart.

And worse than that was what only she knew. What wasn't Instagram ready, not quite yet. That Fern was pregnant.

She texted her boss. 'Sorry, still ill. Won't make it today.'

Janet texted back:

'Casey, I hope you feel better soon. But you've been off for more time than you've been in these past three weeks. Please let me know if there's anything we can do to help – I've been covering so far but soon we'll need something official, a doctor's note for example. Let me know if you want to talk.'

That was the last thing Casey wanted to do. Talking made it all real. Talking meant questions, pitying stares, being gossiped about.

Only four weeks ago, she'd been blissfully happy. She and Adam had been together since school and were finally planning their wedding, set for June of the following year. And then they were going to try for a baby. It was all Casey had ever wanted.

They'd said they would do a modest Christmas as they were saving for the big day, but she hadn't been able to resist splurging on a beautiful cashmere jumper for him – bought much earlier in a flash autumn sale. She'd wrapped it already, and she knew it lay hidden in the bottom of the wardrobe. He'd never unwrap it. What on earth was she meant to do with it? It wasn't refundable now.

The night that everything came crashing down had been a drizzly November one – too early to get excited about Christmas, but she'd been buoyed along by wedding fever. She was the one doing most of the planning, but she didn't mind that – she loved design, and it probably wasn't entirely reasonable to expect Adam to be as excited as she was about colour schemes. Looking back now, she realised how stupid she'd been to interpret his lack of interest as him being some kind of typical bloke.

She'd been looking up some possible honeymoon options online, when her laptop had died. She got up and looked for the charger, before realising she'd left it in her bag at work. But Adam's work laptop was on the living-room table. Casey had picked it up and turned it on, just intending to use the internet to look at scuba diving in Bali.

What she hadn't realised was that Adam's work iPhone messages were also linked to his work laptop. One popped up.

'When are you going to tell her? I need you here with me.'

She'd frowned. Tell who what? Her heart beating suddenly, she'd scrolled down the messages, all of them, until she'd run to the toilet and thrown up from the shock of it all.

Fern had started on the firm's graduate scheme about four months previously. She'd been placed on Adam's team and at first their messages had been purely work-focused. Then they got flirtier, Adam telling her he liked that outfit, things like that, until a message from Adam that said:

'Last night shouldn't have happened.'

She remembered the date. He'd been away for a work conference.

'I know,' Fern had replied. 'But I'm glad it did.'

46

Then, worst of all, Adam's response: 'Me too.'

Casey had confronted him as soon as he'd got in the door. He'd sat down on the sofa and looked at her as if she was a stranger.

'Casey. The thing is . . . I'm in love with her. I've never felt this way before. I'm sorry, I didn't want you to find out like this.'

She'd fallen apart, crying, pleading with him to reconsider. In her head, she'd practised being angry, dignified – making him beg for her forgiveness. So much for that when it came to reality. Then there was worse to come.

'Look, I need to tell you this now. We're pregnant. It was a shock, a surprise, but it means I need to go and be with her now.'

Casey had been stunned into silence, watching as Adam packed a suitcase and left. So that was it, then. Together since they were fifteen. She'd thought they were great together. Maybe that was the worst of it. That she'd had no inkling anything was wrong. They'd still laughed together, still had fun, still fancied each other. How could she possibly trust her emotions, or anyone, ever again? Was she stupid? Was she the problem here?

That grey December morning, Casey lay in bed for hours, heart pounding, thoughts whirring. The doorbell buzzed. She ignored it. It buzzed again, and again.

Sighing, she forced herself up and wrapped herself in her dressing gown, heading to the door and opening it.

Her mum stood on the doorstep.

'Casey.' She stepped forward and wrapped her daughter in a huge hug. 'I'm coming in. No arguments.'

Once her mum was over the threshold, Casey saw the flat with fresh eyes. The congealed takeaway packets, the stacked washing-up. 'Been a bit lazy,' she mumbled.

'Janet texted me. Said you'd called in sick again. Wanted to know if everything was okay.'

Casey suppressed an eye-roll. This was the major disadvantage of working at the school where your mum had been a much-beloved, long-term teacher.

'I'm fine. Just a cold.'

Her mum gazed at her kindly. 'This doesn't look fine, Case. It's okay if you're not. You've been through a hell of a lot.'

Casey sighed heavily. 'I wish everyone would just stop fussing! And leave me alone!' She swallowed back tears. Was that even what she wanted? She didn't know any more. She just knew that everything seemed overwhelming. Everything had changed. Had she been stupid to trust Adam? What signs had she missed? What more could she have done? What was so wrong with her that he'd fallen in love with someone else?

'Get yourself in the shower, Case. Run a brush through that hair and get dressed.'

There was something in her mum's tone of voice that made Casey feel like she was about six years old again. That feeling that her mum knew best. She found herself walking to the bathroom.

When she came back out, looking slightly more human, Trish had done some of the washing-up. She turned around and looked at her daughter.

'That's better. Right, shoes on – we're going somewhere.'

'Mum. No. I can't. Please, I just want to stay here.' The panic was rising again.

'Sweetheart, you need to do this or you're going to get swallowed up by what's going on. I know it's hard, and it's going to be hard for a while, but you can't go under. I thought we'd go to Battersea, look at the cats. You always loved going there when you were little.'

Casey remembered – she'd loved their trips there, memories of watching the cats play and pounce, and a bubbly, bustling, happy atmosphere.

'It'll be quiet on a morning like this,' continued Trish. 'We'll just go, the two of us, and have a look round and a cuppa. Or we can go to the shops. But it has to be something.'

Casey nodded reluctantly. 'Okay, then. Let's go to Battersea. But not for long.'

*

Laura watched as two women made their way around the cattery. They had to be a mother and daughter – the resemblance was clear. The daughter looked sad, her face pale and drawn, clinging to her mum's arm. She must have been in her mid-twenties, but her body language was like that of a little girl, somehow. Her mum pointed out different cats to her, and made comments.

'What do you think to that little one?'

'I love the markings on this boy.'

Whenever she said anything, though, her daughter just stared or sometimes nodded.

It was a quiet morning, and Laura approached them. She was fairly certain that they just enjoyed having a look around, as did many visitors to Battersea, but there was no harm in being friendly – she still wanted to work on her confidence, and she loved a chance to tell people about the work of the cattery.

'Hello, I'm Laura, one of the rehomers here. Just let me know if you've got any questions or if I can help with anything at all.'

The mum flashed her a kind smile, and nodded.

'We want to talk about rehoming a cat,' said the daughter.

Laura was startled. It seemed as if the daughter was too; she was looking around and licking her lips nervously as if she wasn't sure who had spoken.

'Do we?' her mum said.

The woman nodded. 'Yeah.'

'Well, okay,' said Laura. 'Do you want to head to one of the interview rooms downstairs?'

Twenty minutes later, Laura was perplexed. She'd run through the application form and, from the basics of what Trish had told her, she and Casey could provide a good home for one of their cats.

But Casey, after she'd spoken out on the first floor, was almost mute again, apart from monosyllabic answers about her job. Laura knew people could be shy, or nervous, in these interviews, but she wasn't sure about this complete absence of emotion. Then Casey excused herself and went to the loo.

Trish turned to Laura. 'She's had a rough time of it lately. I know she's coming across as . . . well, not exactly enthused, but when she said she wanted to speak to you about rehoming – it's about the first full sentence I've heard her utter in weeks.'

Laura nodded. 'Okay. I understand.'

Casey came back into the room.

'Would you like to meet a few cats?' said Laura. She explained that the way Battersea worked was that a different rehomer would introduce Trish and Casey to their likely matches. Privately, she was keen to know a bit more about Casey. People often responded differently to a rehomer on the first floor, away from the more formal interview setting – and it was always good to have a second pair of eyes to ensure a good match. They worked very much as a team to ensure the perfect fit.

She popped upstairs, glad that Jasmine was working, and explained some of Trish and Casey's situation.

'Daughter's moving back in again with her mum, but I don't know why. I think they could provide a lovely home – the house looks great, with a garden, and they both seem calm, quiet types. But I'm not quite sure what's going on with Casey.'

Jasmine nodded. 'Understood. Any cats in particular you're thinking of?'

'Well, I did wonder about Felicia. She'd do well in a quiet home. Or maybe Notch? Then I was thinking about the complete opposite, maybe a sparky cat might be a good fit?' Laura shrugged. 'They both were clear they just wanted to give a cat a good home and that they'd trust our judgement.'

'Gotcha. Well, I'll introduce a few of them and we'll see how it all goes.'

'Look, they're coming up now.'

Jasmine looked over to the stairs. 'Oh, Laur. Poor Casey.'

'What? What can you see?'

Jasmine shook her head. 'She's completely heartbroken. Honestly, it's like looking at a picture of myself from a year ago.' Jasmine chuckled. 'Trust you, loved up on a date night, not to see it!'

'But how can you be so sure?' Laura asked.

Jasmine shrugged. 'Instinct. But you're right, I can't be certain. I'll natter on to her a bit, see if I can't get her to open up. Go and make yourself scarce for a minute – enjoy those loved-up vibes,' she finished with a wink.

*

Had this been a terrible mistake? wondered Casey. She already felt like she was at the limit of what she could cope with. She couldn't utter a word in the interview.

The interviewer, Laura, was clearly in a perfect relationship. Casey had caught a glimpse of her mobile phone background, a gorgeous man laughing, lying back on what looked like a Twister mat. She could have done without seeing that, it just made her think of Adam and Fern. She'd changed the screensaver on her phone to a cold, icy lake. That's how she wanted her heart to be. Frozen, feeling nothing.

Another woman came up to them. She was a little older than Laura, with tight curly hair and brown eyes.

'Hi, I'm Jasmine,' she said. 'Shall I introduce you to a couple of cats?'

'Yes please,' said Trish, and Casey trailed over behind her mum to one of the cat pods.

'This little guy is called Skittle, and he's an absolute ball of energy,' she said. A black and white cat with a pink nose had cantered up to the front of the pod and was gazing at them intently, tail twitching.

'We'll let Mum have a few games, shall we?' said Jas, after Trish had gone into the pod. 'So, you all sorted for Christmas then?'

Why did she have to ask that question? Casey shook her head, hoping that would be the last of it.

'Me neither. Not my favourite time of year, I have to tell you that.'

Why would Jasmine say that? Normally people couldn't shut up about blimming Christmas. She used to be one of them, only seeing it as a positive time, not understanding why it could be so hard. She'd taken pride in getting sorted early; she thought of the carefully wrapped jumper she had for Adam, and winced. Inside the pod, Trish was giggling as Skittle chased a toy all over the floor. He was an adorable cat, no doubt about that.

'Far too many expectations swirling around,' continued Jasmine. 'Everyone else happily coupled up, perfect families – can be hard for those of us who don't have that.'

Casey flicked her eyes to the side, making eye contact with Jasmine briefly.

'Right, do you fancy a game then?' said Trish, coming out of the pod. 'He's absolutely gorgeous. What a playful little thing! I think he'd be perfect to liven up the house a bit.'

'You go in and see how you get on,' said Jasmine.

Casey went inside the pod, and looked down at Skittle. She felt awkward. She crouched down, and kept her arms folded. What was she meant to do?

'Maybe give the string toy a go?' suggested Jas. Skittle was arched and ready to play.

Casey picked it up reluctantly, and Skittle pounced. He skittered over her legs, causing her to wince.

'Ouch! He's scratching me!'

'He's just playing, love,' said Trish, but it was no good. Casey stood up suddenly and Skittle scampered off.

'I can't even get that right,' muttered Casey as she came back out, her cheeks flushing. 'Not even a cat wants to stick around with me.'

'Well, not every cat is right for every person,' said Jasmine, placing a hand on her arm. 'Let's meet one more.'

Trish said she needed to get a glass of water, so she headed off to the café. Jasmine and Casey sat down on a sofa. There was no one else around.

'So, what are you doing for Christmas then?' asked Jas.

'I'll be back at Mum's then,' said Casey, her voice flat.

'Moving back in?'

Casey nodded. This was all getting too close for comfort. She forced herself to ask a question: 'Where are you spending it?'

'Oh, I'll be here,' said Jas, her voice wobbling. 'My husband left me this year. So it'll be my first Christmas without him. I'd rather spend it helping these lovely animals and keeping busy than wallowing about by myself.'

Casey looked up sharply and for the first time made direct eye contact with Jasmine. 'God, I'm so, so sorry.' Suddenly her heart went out to this woman. She'd been so wrapped up in her own troubles that she hadn't seen how brave other people were in carrying on with their lives.

Jasmine smiled wryly. 'Why do I get the feeling you might know exactly what I've been through?'

Casey tried to smile back, but tears were suddenly streaming down her face. Jasmine put an arm round her.

'That's it. Let it all out. I'm covered in cat hair anyway, so a few tears will help the cause.'

Casey looked up, her face glistening. 'It's just . . . just . . . I mean, how do you ever get over it? I don't know what happened with you and your man, but mine, he . . . he left me for someone else.' She dissolved in tears again and Jasmine gave her another enormous hug.

'Casey, it was the same for me. And I'm not going to lie to you. This year has been pretty much the hardest of my life. And it's still hard sometimes. I laugh a lot more now, but there are still those nights where I'm crying into my pillow. But what really helped me, funnily enough, was the cats. You see, some of them have come from horrible pasts, and they don't trust people at all. They're shy, they run away, they've been hurt before and they expect to be hurt again.'

Casey hiccupped. 'Poor little things.'

Jasmine nodded. 'Yeah, it's rough. But you watch them change. You watch them, with our love and care, start to trust again. Start to enjoy their lives again. And it takes time. And maybe they will always be a little bit formed by what happened – less ready to jump all over a stranger's legs like young Skittle there. But you see it time and time again. Healing. Trust. It can be built. It comes back. Second chances. Fresh starts. They happen all the time.'

Casey's sobbing stilled. She nodded. 'And you've seen that happen?'

'Yeah. Yeah, I have. It's not overnight. But it happens. Want to meet the proof?'

Casey nodded.

'Come on then.'

Jasmine walked her over to Notch's pod. It was covered with a sheet – something the staff did if cats got particularly stressed with the visitors on the first floor.

'So this girl was brought in to us by an animal-rescue charity. She'd been really badly neglected by her owners. Full of worms, thin, and ever so scared. They'd had dogs and had let them terrorise her.'

Casey's eyes filled with tears again.

'Our team worked with her, really slowly. We had her on the third floor for a good while. We weren't sure, to be honest, if she would ever be suitable for rehoming. But day by day, little by little, we got her used to people again. It just takes as long as it takes. She learnt that not everyone was like the people she'd already met. And now we're sure that she can find a happy home again. I've got a feeling you might understand each other. But, when you go into her pod, just give her space. Sit at the front quietly. She'll be snoozing in her bed, probably, and you don't want to startle her.'

Casey nodded. 'Of course.'

She slipped inside the pod and sat down.

'I'll leave you for a bit,' said Jasmine. 'I'll just be in the office till your mum gets back.'

Sat in the warm, cosy pod, Casey felt like she could stay in there for ever. She smiled to herself. The thought was ridiculous! She pulled up her knees and rested her chin on them. She wondered if Notch knew she was in there. She resolved to be extra quiet and give the cat all the space she needed.

As she waited, she felt a kind of peace creep over her that she hadn't felt for a long time. She tipped her head to one side and allowed her eyes to shut, hoping that the cattery would stay as quiet as it presently was and that nobody would come in and see a crazy girl dozing off in a pod. Because she *was* dozing off. Sleep, which had eluded her for weeks, was creeping up on her. She kept thinking of the phrase, 'As long as it takes.' She'd give this little cat as long as it took for her to settle and feel comfortable again. She'd give herself as long as it took to heal her broken heart.

Peace settled on her like the first Christmas snowflakes. She knew she'd have to open her eyes soon or risk fully falling asleep. She was already losing track of time, but that seemed like a good thing right now. Adam felt very far away.

After a few moments more, she forced her eyes open. There, sitting quietly, about a foot away from her, with her paws neatly folded, was the prettiest tabby cat Casey had ever seen. Waiting.

Casey's heart filled with gladness.

'Hello,' she whispered, very quietly, so as not to startle her. 'Don't worry. I understand. Second chances, fresh starts.'

Chapter 8

'How's work, then? Did you find a home for your special cat yet?'

'Felicia.'

'Yes, that's the one. Feline Felicia.'

Rob was cooking a pasta sauce and fresh pasta. This was one of his passions – he adored choosing a special recipe, shopping for the ingredients, cooking for hours until the taste was just right. His perfectionistic nature shone through when it came to finding just the right type of tomato and olive oil. It was something Laura loved about him, his commitment to getting the very best results, and she appreciated the effort he was going to, despite her rumbling stomach. He'd declared this not a date night – he was still planning that – but a warm-up.

'No, not yet. We came near the other day. But not quite right.' At the mention of Felicia, Laura's heart clenched.

Rob stayed quiet, chopping an onion into tiny, even pieces. 'Well, look. Maybe I've got a solution.'

Laura sat bolt upright from where she was slumped on the sofa.

'Jeez, Laura, you gave me a fright! Careful, I'm using the Sabatier knife – don't want to slip with this one.'

'Sorry. But can we have her?'

Rob chuckled. 'Sorry, love, that's not what I meant.'

A flash of annoyance went through her. 'I'm still not sure why you're so against us having a cat.'

Rob measured out some herbs on a high-tech set of scales. 'Laur, we've been through this. Look at how lovely it is in here.' He gestured round. 'I just don't want a cat messing up all the sofas and scratching everything. Some of these pieces are really valuable, you know. And the thing is, as well, I just don't really like them that much. They creep me out, the way they stare. And they don't need people all that much, do they? Just for food.'

Laura was indignant. 'No! That's a huge misconception about cats, they are really loving creatures. Just a bit more independent.'

'You know, I saw some article today about how researchers have found that cats do recognise their own names when they're called, they just choose to ignore them.'

Laura smiled. She'd seen the same one. She loved that about cats – their strong, independent personalities.

'Well, very sensible if you ask me. There's tons of research on how they lower your stress levels.'

'I doubt my stress levels are going to be lowered if I come home and find a cat clawing the Mexican wall hangings to pieces.'

He came over and fed her a teaspoon of tomato sauce.

'What do you think?'

'Tastes perfect to me.'

'I think it needs more time on the hob. Look, I don't want to argue with you about this. I'd be more inclined to think about getting a dog, to be honest. One of those cute ones.'

'A dog? Rob, it's completely impractical. What's it meant to do all day when we're at work?'

Laura didn't mind dogs at all – she loved all animals, truth be told – but Rob was living in a dream world if he thought they were any less of a responsibility. A dog would love chewing the legs of the vintage Danish coffee table.

'There are dog babysitters, that kind of thing.'

Laura shook her head. 'I don't think you've thought this through.'

'Well, maybe we can think more on it over Christmas. I know how much a pet would mean to you. Can you feed the fish?'

Laura sprinkled some flakes into the tank and wondered if the fish even knew who she was. She had nothing against fish, but you couldn't actually cuddle one, could you? She wondered if her Christmas present for Rob was a bit too on the nose. She'd found a beautiful vintage cat statue, which she was sure he'd love – it was from a fancy retro shop she'd stumbled upon, full of furniture that looked like theirs. Laura had been hoping that putting a statue of a cat in the house would subliminally help Rob get used to the idea of a real-life cat. But now she wasn't so sure.

Rob began rolling out the pasta dough. Disloyally, Laura thought about how much quicker it would be to use the packet pasta. It would be after ten by the time they finally ate, at this rate. Banishing the thought from her head, she asked Rob what his solution for Felicia was.

'Oh yeah! Well, we're working with a pretty big celebrity client at the agency at the moment, for the FruitySoap campaign.'

Laura nodded. Their bathroom was currently full of free samples from the brand, which she couldn't complain about. Jas kept teasing her that she could smell Laura before she saw her in the cattery. 'It's like working with an enormous strawberry wandering around the place,' she'd said the other day.

'Can't say who it is just yet, as it's not totally confirmed, but anyway – what matters is that we were chatting the other day, not about the campaign, just life stuff, and she mentioned how much she'd like to get a cat.'

'Right. Okay.'

'So I told her you worked at Battersea, rehoming the cats, and she loved it! And I was saying how there was this one cat that you can't find a home for, and she was really keen to know more.'

Somehow, Laura didn't have a good feeling about this, but she appreciated Rob's efforts to help. Maybe she was just in a hunger-induced grumpy mood. Despite a flurry of rehomings, no one had settled on Felicia. She needed to take all the help she could get if she was going to make her Christmas wish come true.

'Well, sure. I mean, she'd need to sign up and go through the registration process.'

Rob nodded. 'Yeah, I'm sure she'll want to be treated just like a normal person. But is there any photo of Felicia I can show her or anything?'

'There's her online profile.' She pulled it up on her phone and passed it to Rob.

'Aw, she *is* cute.' He read through the text. 'Want me to see if I can liven this up for you?'

Laura considered. It was a generous offer. Rob was extremely savvy when it came to advertising. Maybe he could sprinkle a little stardust on Felicia's profile and help her find that perfect home.

*

Rob emailed her the revised copy for Felicia the following day. It read:

Everybody loves an underdog – but could you love this under-cat? To us at Battersea, Felicia is something of a wonder-cat but there's no denying she's not had much luck.

Found as a stray, Felicia was shy and timid to begin with, but her purr-sonality now shines through. This fabulous feline only wants one thing for Christmas from Santa Paws – a home all of her own!

Laura couldn't deny it was snappy and fun – it was sure to grab people's notice. She decided it was worth a shot. She'd arrange an Instagram post to get Felicia as much attention as possible. That lunchtime, she snuck into Felicia's pod with some festive toys and snapped a few cute pictures of her. Maybe Rob's star treatment was just what she needed.

*

A few days later, Laura was taking advantage of a quiet moment to hang up some tinsel in the cattery, blue and white to go with Battersea's colour scheme, alongside extra posters advertising the carol concert. Jasmine was insisting that they dress up for it, and Laura was looking forward to it more and more. It had been a busy couple of days. Alongside the usual rehoming duties, there had been a flurry of interest following Felicia's revamped profile and the Instagram post. *Surely a perfect home could be found among this lot?* Laura thought to herself. The tricky part was distinguishing between the people who had genuinely thought about whether they could meet a cat's needs, and those who had responded impulsively having seen her story. But, as Rob had told her last night, 'all publicity is good publicity'. She supposed that anything that helped Felicia find her forever home was indeed a good thing. Rob was also hopeful that his celebrity candidate would be in touch soon – according to him, she'd 'gone wild' for Felicia.

Jasmine arrived by her side, looking up at the decorations.

'Looks amazing, Laur. And have I got a treat for you.'

'Is it biscuits?' Laura said hopefully, before she noticed a gleam in Jasmine's eyes.

Jasmine snorted. 'Better than biscuits! There's a witch looking for her cat, and she's waiting in reception!'

Laura shook her head, wondering if she'd heard right.

Jasmine nodded, grinning with mischief. 'Yep. I have a feeling you might enjoy this one.'

Laura made her way to reception, wondering if Jas had been winding her up – she wouldn't put it past her. Then she saw a tall, slender woman in her twenties waiting, her long hair dyed a light silver colour and shot through with pink. Laura smiled. This had to be Jasmine's witch. She loved the range of people they got through Battersea's doors – you never knew who you were going to meet next.

'Hello, I hear you'd like to adopt a cat?' said Laura, approaching.

The woman nodded vigorously. 'Yes, absolutely.'

Laura showed her through to an interview room, marvelling at the silver jewellery the woman wore. Once she was settled, with much jangling and arranging of her clothes, Laura began the interview by asking for her name and a few basic details.

'My name is Wanda and I'm a witch,' said the woman, straight-faced.

Laura couldn't help but smile. 'Really?'

Fortunately, Wanda smiled back, her face lighting up. 'Yes, really. But not like you see on the telly, or in *Harry Potter* or whatever. I help people channel good energy, so they can make changes in their lives. And I'm trained in a variety of ways.'

Laura was intrigued. 'So . . . like what?'

'Well, it depends what the person needs. I might do a tarot reading, or I might use crystals to help clear negative energy. I'm trained in acupuncture too, and I also teach yoga. It's just about getting the good energy flowing.'

Despite her cynicism, Laura couldn't help but feel positive energy radiating from Wanda. Her skin shone like it was lit from within.

'So . . . Where does a cat fit into all this?' asked Laura.

'Well, every witch needs a familiar to help cast their spells, right? And the last frog I had was pretty workshy.'

Laura wasn't quite sure what to say. Images of cauldrons bubbling sprang up in her mind.

Wanda laughed. 'I'm just teasing, don't worry. I work from home, and it would be nice to have a little friend around. Plus, cats are amazing healers!'

Laura agreed on that front. Who wouldn't feel better with a purring cat on their lap?

'Did you know,' Wanda continued, 'that a cat's purr has a frequency of 25–150 hertz? And that frequency has been scientifically proven to promote healing, in bones and in tissues.'

Laura was amazed. It wasn't often someone came up with a fact about cats that she didn't know. 'Really?'

'Yep, really. There's loads of research on it now. So they think that cats purr as a way to heal themselves, as well as to communicate. And if a human is lucky enough to be around, we can benefit as well.'

Laura made a mental note to look that up later. She asked Wanda about her living arrangements, and she explained she lived alone, in a small cottage in the countryside. She'd travelled to London specially to visit Battersea, as she was convinced she wanted a rescue cat.

'I've brought photos of the house and everything,' Wanda continued, getting out her phone and showing Laura a beautiful little cottage, the inside light and airy and filled with crystals and candles. There was a lovely garden too, where Wanda grew herbs and vegetables. 'I guess I'm a bit of a weirdo, really. Much more into this stuff than going out clubbing and all that, like everyone else my age.'

'And do you have any ideas about the kind of cat you'd like to adopt?'

'Well, I don't mind in terms of colour and that kind of thing. I like a cat with a bit of personality. I'm a free spirit, so I'll understand if they're the same. They can come and go as they please, but the odd cuddle wouldn't go amiss.'

Laura's mind turned over. Skittle wasn't the right match – he'd do better with a family, she felt. The strong personality characteristics of a Siamese might well suit Wanda. Or, of course, there was Felicia. Laura sensed that Wanda would understand the cat's need for her own space. It would depend on whether she was willing to take on an FIV cat with a complicated heart.

'What about cats who have a medical condition?' she asked.

Wanda shrugged. 'Depends a bit. I suppose my sense is that they should get a chance at a home as well. But I'd need to know more about the specific condition and what was involved.'

Laura nodded. She popped upstairs to have a brief chat with Jasmine, quickly summarising Wanda's circumstances and preferences.

'Is she going to put a spell on me?' giggled Jas.

Laura poked her in the ribs. 'I hope it's one to shut you up. She's absolutely lovely! And I love the idea of a witch finding her cat at Battersea.'

About forty minutes later, Laura saw Wanda leaving the cattery. She came over to see how it had gone.

'Well, I met two gorgeous cats. Teddy, the Siamese. Never thought I'd consider one of them, but I just adored that personality. And the yowling! He can definitely help with the spells and I'm guessing it's a good thing I don't have immediate neighbours as he does like to be heard, doesn't he? And the other was a cat called Felicia.'

'Oh, I love Felicia,' said Laura, crossing her fingers in her pockets. 'She's very special to me.'

'I loved her too,' said Wanda. 'She has a great energy, once she gets comfortable with you.'

Laura nodded. That was exactly Felicia.

'But Jasmine explained the heart murmur to me, and that she'd need an enclosed garden,' said Wanda. 'I just need to think if I can one hundred per cent support her with those conditions, given the worst-case scenarios. So, I'm going to take a night to sleep on it, and I'm sure the right decision will arrive. Hey – to say thank you for your help, how about I draw a tarot card for you?'

Laura hesitated. It wasn't really her thing, but it seemed rude to say no.

'Don't worry, I don't see it as predicting the future or anything like that. It's like a fun way to reflect on where you're at. You'd be surprised at what it shows you. Think of it like an early Christmas present.'

'Go on then,' said Laura, curious.

Wanda took out a pack of cards from her bag and got Laura to shuffle them, then draw one out.

'Oooh!' she said. 'The lovers!'

Laura immediately blushed furiously, causing Wanda to cackle.

'Don't worry, it's not necessarily rude,' she grinned. 'And it's a good card! Obviously, it represents love, and that can be romantic love, but also maybe platonic love. It might represent a close bond in a relationship, with all the confidence and strength that comes from that.'

Laura liked the sound of that. Wasn't that exactly what she and Rob were working on? She thought of him taking the time to rewrite Felicia's bio and her heart warmed.

'Or, it can represent a decision that needs to be made in the context of a relationship. A choice. Some say temptation, even.'

Could that apply to her? She thought again of all the wedding and baby pictures she kept seeing on Instagram. That felt like a choice that might be in the future for her and Rob. Temptation – well, unless it was the temptation to adopt a cat secretly, she wasn't sure how that applied.

Laura walked Wanda to Battersea's gates, keen for a bit of fresh air. As she bade the witch goodbye, she noticed a massive SUV pull up outside. A girl got out and instantly started taking selfies and posing in front of the entrance, fingers in a V for victory sign, tongue stuck out. Did she look vaguely familiar? Her hair was long and expensively highlighted, and she had a teeny pinched nose and full lips that Laura suspected weren't entirely natural.

The girl strutted over to the security desk, and tossed her hair back.

'I want to see Laura Summers, please.'

The receptionist looked nonplussed. 'Well, are you here to visit the cattery? Or the dogs?'

The girl threw back her head and laughed. 'Babes, I'm here to get *my* cat. I've been told to ask for Laura Summers and she can sort it out.'

Laura frowned. What on earth was this?

The receptionist was explaining how Battersea asked for a small donation from visitors, to help with their costs as they received no government support. It was £2 for adults to enter.

'Are you actually kidding?' said the girl, with another toss of her hair. 'I mean, the amount of publicity I could get this place!'

Oh God. Laura suddenly twigged, as a smell of artificial strawberry wafted towards her. This had to be the famous celebrity Rob had mentioned as a potential adopter for Felicia.

Chapter 9

'Can I just get a few selfies first?' Letitia Maddox asked, as Laura attempted to lead her to an interview room.

Laura bit back the temptation to say that Letitia – or Lettie, as she was known to her army of social media fans – had done nothing but take selfies since her arrival in Battersea. Laura wasn't sure she'd actually had a moment of eye contact with her, and Lettie's right arm was almost permanently extended in order to snap about a hundred photos every minute. She chattered away into her phone almost incessantly, making videos to upload to her 'Little Lettuces'.

'Hey, my Lettuce army, today we're at Battersea Dogs and Cats Home about to give a home to the tragic cats that find their way here, and hopefully lead them to a better life away from these terrible conditions . . .' Lettie babbled.

Laura bristled. 'Actually, our conditions are state of the art! Maybe if you saw the cat pods—'

Lettie zapped out the arm that wasn't holding the phone and actually tapped Laura on the mouth before returning to talk into the screen.

'Sorry about that! One of the mad cat ladies here getting a bit overexcited! I'm gonna take home one of the saddest little cats they've ever had, who's been stuck here for way too long, and give her an amazing new life, with her own YouTube channel! So, stay tuned to meet her, and to win your chance to rename her!'

Lettie shut off the video. 'Babes, you really nearly almost ruined that, in front of about half a million people.'

'Er, sorry?'

'Honestly, it's fine, just don't do it again. Yes, some of it is kind of authentic which is a really important element for my brand, but what you did just looks sloppy.'

Laura had no idea what she was talking about. 'So, um . . . maybe we could actually talk about you wanting to rehome a cat?'

'Totes. When can I meet the one Rob told me about? OMG WE LOVE ROB, don't we! Isn't he just the best?' Lettie couldn't get through a sentence without erratically shouting, and Laura's nerves were already on edge from it.

Laura nodded. 'He is indeed.' Though she couldn't help but feel he should have warned her about the exact nature of the celeb he had in mind.

'Even though he's old, he's still kind of cool, ya know? And when he told me all about the animals here, I was like, OMG, that is COMPLETELY PERFECT for me – I've been needing a new angle for Insta and animals go down so well. Everyone's got the pugs and those well-furry cats now, and there's Grumpy Cat – she's got like 2.5 MILLION followers, but I think it'd be kind of amazeballs to just make one of those normal cats like, completely famous, don't you? Like, you know, anyone can do it kind of thing! Rags to riches! Or like, rags to whiskers?! Does that work? Anyway whatever, it's inspiring!'

This had all been delivered at about five thousand miles an hour, and Laura's head was reeling. She cleared her throat and tried to sound assertive.

'Well, to be honest, it's more about making sure that you're a good match for the cat. That you can provide a good home. I mean, a cat isn't going to know how many followers it has on YouTube, is it?'

'Totes. I mean you can see how many followers you have, hun, look.'

With an air of long-standing patience, Lettie showed her phone to Laura and very slowly explained the concept of the internet to her.

'I have been on YouTube before,' said Laura, annoyed.

'OMG that's so great, well done you!' cooed Lettie.

'Right, so if you want to come this way, we'll go through some basic questions.'

'To be honest, I just really want to meet Fleecie.'

'Felicia. Her name is Felicia.'

Lettie pouted. 'Hmm. Fleecie is cuter. But I suppose it'll be up to the fans, we can do a quick vote!'

Somehow, Laura managed to get Lettie's basic details taken down in an interview, although it took twice as long as usual and several times she had to repeat questions so Lettie could capture it all on film. Lettie was an 'influencer', using her brief appearance on a TV dating show to catapult her to fame. Her fans, she explained, were her world. She shared everything with them, right from the moment she woke up until the moment she went to bed. Laura wasn't particularly comfortable with being filmed and photographed, but she was also aware of the importance of this girl to Rob's career, so she was trying to be polite. She'd texted him while Lettie was filming the entire array of cat toys in the shop.

'Could have warned me about Lettie . . .'

'Isn't she great!' Rob had texted back. 'I know she's a bit high-energy but her heart is in the right place!'

Laura wasn't entirely convinced about that. Lettie had given her some answers about how much she wanted a cat and how she'd always had them when she was growing up with her mum, and had shown her pictures of a beautiful ground-floor London flat, with access to a garden. Clearly, being an influencer was paying well.

'There's even a catflap already there!' she'd grinned.

Maybe you're just being a prejudiced old stuck-in-the-mud, Laura thought to herself. Yes, Lettie was pretty annoying, but that didn't mean she couldn't be a good, responsible cat owner. And she seemed to have her heart set on Felicia, saying she could absolutely cope with any medical issues – money and time were no problem.

Laura decided she would hover around upstairs to see how the meet and greets went, and also to provide any back-up should Lettie get opinionated. She'd seen some serious attitude exhibited towards the receptionist, and wasn't about to leave one of her colleagues alone with her.

Lettie took the steps up to the first-floor cattery three at a time. Was it natural to have that much energy? Laura wondered. She'd told Lettie to keep it quiet when she actually got to the floor and was pleased to see the girl had followed her advice.

Lettie was greeted by Simone, another rehomer. Simone was a real sweetie, but could be a little shy, so Laura hoped she'd be able to cope with the storm of energy that was Lettie.

Oh God, the phone was out again.

'Hi, Lettuces,' Lettie said, in a stage whisper with her finger held to her lips. 'So here we are with the cats. I have to be, like, really, really quiet so they can sleep – we all love a lie-in anyway, don't we! Let's meet some cuties, including the lucky lady I'm gonna take home with me. And in the meantime, I've set up a little vote for you guys in my stories. So, at the moment, she's called Felicia – urgh boring! – and I think Fleecie is SO. MUCH. CUTER. But lemme know what you think! Or if you have an amazing idea for her new name, put it in the comments! Love ya, bye!'

Simone looked baffled.

'Okay, sorry, hun, we can go and meet my fans – I mean, the cats! – now!'

Simone took her round to Skittle's pod – Laura had thought the cat's high energy might be a good match for Lettie. Simone explained to Lettie how to enter the pod and, after pulling her baseball cap down low over her eyes, as if to avoid being recognised by the cats, Lettie went inside.

'Hi, fella!' she said, as Skittle bowled forward for attention. The little cat didn't hesitate to start pawing at Lettie for a game, and the celebrity gave the first genuine smile and giggle Laura had seen. Maybe she had judged Lettie too harshly.

After a ferocious game with Skittle, including some inevitable mobile phone footage, Laura was convinced that Lettie would ask to rehome that little cat. She wished that she could shake off her prejudices about the girl – all the evidence that Laura had seen was that she would provide a good home for a cat. So why the niggling sense of doubt in the back of her mind?

'OMG SO CUTE!' she heard Lettie say breathlessly. 'But I still wanna meet Fleecie.'

Simone took her round to Felicia's pod, explaining that this cat was a little different to Skittle and should be left to approach in her own time.

'Absolutely, I get it,' said Lettie. 'She's a diva. Like me.'

To her credit, Lettie went in slowly. This was the calmest Laura had ever seen her. Felicia came down from her bed to see what was going on, and Lettie held out a hand to her, which Felicia sniffed with the attitude of a grand duchess receiving visitors.

Lettie reached out and tickled her ears. Then she got out her phone and began recording.

'So here she is, the little lady who we are going to take from rags to riches,' she whispered, moving the phone closer to Felicia's face.

Intrigued, the cat sniffed at the screen.

'So cool, huh!' continued Lettie. 'So, get ready to know this amazing cat a whole lot more. We're gonna be best pals, you and me!'

Lettie shuffled next to Felicia and brought the phone round to take a selfie of them. Laura noticed the cat's tail swish in what looked a lot like irritation. Maybe it was time to give Felicia some space. She could read Felicia's body language well, given how much time she'd spent with her.

She began to walk over to Felicia's pod, but not before Lettie had picked up Felicia by her tummy and held her face next to her own. Fortunately, the cat didn't swipe at Lettie, but wriggled away, evidently displeased.

'Sorry girl, didn't mean to crowd you,' said Lettie, stepping back.

Then Felicia played her masterstroke. She stepped over to her litter tray and flipped it right over, scattering litter everywhere, before stalking back up to her bed and curling up into a tight ball. Laura could have sworn Felicia winked at her. If that wasn't sure to put Lettie off, then she didn't know what was! The cat was a genius! Laura bit her lip to avoid laughing.

Lettie backed out of the pod, brushing litter from her trainers.

'So . . . any thoughts?' Simone said, nervously.

'I'll just pop to the loo, babes. These are box-fresh and limited edition so I need to wipe them down.'

Lettie went downstairs, the bounce gone from her step, and Laura made her way over to Simone.

'Well, that could have gone better,' said Simone, looking anxious.

'Yeah. But you handled it all so well. I'm guessing she won't want Felicia now – the litter-tray flip hardly fits in with the Instagram image!'

But then, a few minutes later, Lettie came bouncing back up the stairs, chattering into her phone.

'I *knew* you guys would love her! She's the one for us, right!! What a rebel!'

She dashed over to Laura. 'I want her! Fleecie is awesome! People are going nuts for the litter-box moment! Look.'

She held out her phone, and Laura saw a video of Felicia with comments and likes rolling in.

DON'T MESS WITH MISS KITTY!
Omg LURRRVVEEEE HER!
Little Lettuce Feline! She's perfect for us!

'Okay, so,' began Simone uncertainly, 'you'd like to adopt her, then?'

'Absolutely,' said Lettie. 'She's the only one for me.'

Laura's heart plunged. She just couldn't help her instinctive feeling that this wasn't the right home for Felicia.

'I'll just have a quick word with Simone,' said Laura. 'And you'll need to talk to one of our Battersea vets about her heart murmur.'

Tucked away in the cattery office, with Lettie chattering into her phone outside the closed door, Laura tried to explain her doubts to Simone. 'I don't know, it's just a feeling I have.'

'Do you think it's because she's a celeb? Is that what's bothering you?'

Laura considered this. 'I'm not sure. We've had lots of celebrity adopters before and they've given brilliant homes to our cats. I mean, I think this whole YouTuber video thing is a load of nonsense, but plenty of people don't. And going by everything she's said, her home is more than suitable.'

'And she did try with Felicia,' added Simone. 'She was patient and I'm sure we can give her a bit of support to help her settle Felicia in?'

Laura wished that Jasmine was still there to chat to. She trusted her friend's instincts almost more than her own, and she was second-guessing herself terribly. It was so hard working out whether she was being prejudiced about the YouTube star, or if there was something genuinely not right. But this was the first home Felicia had been offered that seemed suitable. Yes, there was still the possibility that Wanda might take her, but she hadn't asked for Felicia to be formally reserved, and Laura wondered if after a night's sleep she might go for the Siamese. Plus, Rob knew Lettie from work and seemed to think her heart was in the right place. He wouldn't send someone along who wasn't right, and he'd worked his advertising magic to get Felicia a new home. She should be thankful.

'Well, she'll need to speak to a vet first, at any rate,' said Laura. That would also buy Laura a bit of time to calm down and see things more clearly. She knew that she had a deep emotional attachment to Felicia, and that saying goodbye was always going to be hard. Was that it too? She called Jill, one of Battersea's vets. Once Jill had arrived, Lettie entered to join Simone in the office, and the three of them began their chat.

Laura decided to leave them to it and headed off for a cup of tea. As the kettle boiled, she opened up Lettie's Instagram page. At least she wouldn't have to worry about not having updates on how Felicia was getting along, she thought wryly. There'd be new photos and videos almost hourly.

She watched the video of Felicia, or Fleecie as she now seemed to be known, staring intently into the screen and then flipping over the litter tray. Now there were even more views and comments, thousands of them. Laura sighed, and looked at the other photos on Lettie's account. Loads of selfies: Lettie wrapped up in a cute scarf and hat, pouting; posing against a backdrop of Christmas lights; setting up an extravagant tree in her penthouse apartment. Wait – penthouse apartment?

Heart beating, Laura scrolled on. She found an image called 'Home Sweet Home' with Lettie in the bay window of a top-floor flat, overlooking a view of the Thames. A flat that was completely different to the ground-floor flat Lettie had shown her pictures of. And a top-floor, penthouse flat that most definitely did not have a garden.

Laura was furious. It was one of Battersea's chief principles that they only housed cats to homes with access to outdoor space, allowing them to exhibit their natural behaviours. And Lettie had flat-out lied to her!

Fuming, she stormed back up to the first floor and barged into the room where Jill and Lettie were talking.

'What the hell is this?' said Laura, brandishing her phone. She knew she was being rude, but she didn't care. This was no time to be timid.

'What? My flat?' said Lettie.

'Yes, exactly, a *flat* that's very different to the one you claimed you lived in!'

Lettie blushed deeply. 'Well. Yeah. But I mean, how much difference does it make?'

'It makes *all the difference*. We rely on giving our cats good homes, and people telling us the truth in order to make that happen.'

Lettie scowled. 'Honestly, you should be grateful. Giving that unwanted little moggy a home in a penthouse apartment! What more do you want? They're a bunch of rejects here.'

'That's not how Battersea works. And that certainly isn't how we see our cats. I'm sorry, Lettie, but you're clearly not suitable as a rehomer.'

'Whatever! I'm taking that little cat with me – the fans have seen her now, they'll want to follow her story, and I've already registered her an Instagram account. She'll be verified in no time. So, pack her up and let's get going.' This was delivered with a double click of the fingers.

Laura couldn't believe it. 'Lettie. I said no.'

'Do you really want that bad publicity? I do one story and say you were horrible to me, and that's it.' Lettie's eyes were blazing with fury.

Laura didn't know what to say. She'd never been in this kind of situation before. Her heart pounded; confrontation of any kind always stressed her out.

'My Lettuce army will be so mad,' Lettie continued gleefully.

There was no way Laura was going to let Felicia go to this woman. She dug deep and made sure her voice was steady when she spoke. 'Lettie, I'm sorry, but it's a no. And you also need to consider how it would look in terms of your, err, personal brand, if your fans knew you'd lied. To an *animal charity*. That's not going to go down well.'

Lettie paused then, before shoving her chair back and getting up abruptly. 'Fine then. I've changed my mind. Who wants one of these sad cats anyway? I'm gonna get a pedigree one, they're really pretty.'

'I hope you'll think about what's best for a cat and not just for yourself,' said Laura. She felt sure Lettie would probably buy some beautiful pedigree cat and then discover it wasn't so easy living with a wilful creature and maintaining an

Instagram-perfect flat. And who knew, that poor cat might end up in Battersea after all. She felt sad at the thought of it. But she knew she was right to stand firm.

She stood up as Lettie darted out of the office, and down the stairs. After the girl had gone, Laura realised she was shaking. She hated conflict at the best of times, and Lettie had been particularly difficult. She was also worried she'd make Rob's job hell – he was stressed enough as it was – but she could also have killed him for sending that particular hurricane in her direction. What if Lettie did say something bad about Battersea? She felt sick at the thought.

Suddenly, Laura found herself bursting into tears with the stress and adrenaline. And the thought that Felicia could nearly have gone to a home like that! She didn't want to bother the cat again, but she longed for a cuddle.

'Are you okay?' came a man's voice from behind her.

She turned around and looked into the warmest brown eyes she'd ever seen.

'Oh God, yes, sorry, just a stressful moment,' Laura said, pasting on a smile and sniffing heavily.

'Here, have a tissue,' said the man. Laura reckoned he must be about her age. There were just the faintest beginnings of some salt and pepper at his temples, and a few laughter lines at the sides of his brown eyes.

Laura took it gratefully and blew her nose loudly. She had to recover some degree of professionalism.

'How can I help you?' she said, pulling herself together.

'Give yourself a minute,' he said. 'Look, you're shaking. Are you sure you're okay?' He placed a hand gently on her arm.

'We just had a very tricky customer in,' said Laura. And despite the fact that this man was a stranger, and she knew that she was being indiscreet, she found herself telling him all about it. Of course, she left out the specifics of who Lettie actually was to avoid any gossip.

'It sounds awful,' said the man, sincerely. 'To be honest, I don't get this influencer thing at all. Does that make me very uncool, that I'm not very interested in watching someone tie their shoelaces?'

Laura laughed. 'Not in my book. I mean, I don't get it either. Every decision to be shared with an audience of thousands?'

'Do you want a cup of tea?'

'Yes, exactly, that kind of thing! And then you ask all your fans what they think!'

He laughed. 'I mean, do *you* want a cup of tea? Or shall we do an online poll first?'

'Oh! Sorry. Gosh, well, I'm aware that you must have come in for a reason – just to look around? Or were you interested in rehoming?'

'Well, actually, in rehoming a cat for my nana, but it's quite late in the day now.'

He glanced at his watch, and Laura saw that it was already past four.

'I'm sorry, with all that drama I've taken up way too much of your time,' she said.

'Don't worry. I can easily come back another day.'

'Shall I walk you around and show you a few of our residents?'

'That'd be lovely. Look, I'm going to run and get you a tea, and dump a few sugars in it for good measure. You sit down for a moment.'

Laura took a seat on one of the sofas, and tried to calm herself down. Her stomach was full of butterflies – it must be the adrenaline from the Lettie confrontation.

In a few minutes, the man was back, clutching two teas. Now that she'd calmed down, Laura noticed how good-looking he was. His hair was wavy and messy, and fell frequently into his face. He had a tiny chip out of one of his front teeth, but that only seemed to make him more attractive – without it, his smile might have been a bit too perfect. Laura told herself to stop this running commentary, and explained the history of Battersea to him as they walked around looking at the cats in their pods.

'And you, what about your work here?' the man asked.

'Well, I'm pretty new to rehoming, but I was in the welfare department before, caring for the animals day to day.' She told him how she'd worked in advertising before, but was happy to have made the move over to Battersea.

'And, from what you've told me about your visitor today, it seems the cats might be better behaved than some of the clients you'd have found yourself dealing with at an agency,' he grinned.

God, *Rob*. She thought of him suddenly and blushed. She should have texted him to warn him that it had gone badly with Lettie. She realised she'd been so absorbed in talking to this man that all her stress had melted away – he'd certainly made her forget all about the drama.

'Do you need to get back?' he asked.

'No, no,' she said. She'd actually meant to say 'Yes', but talking to this man was really calming her down. And, to be honest, she was enjoying herself.

'I have a question then. Do you have a favourite cat, or is that an unfair question?'

Laura laughed. 'Well, you can't but help have your particular favourites. Here's mine. She's called Felicia.'

The man crouched down by the pod and craned his neck, trying to see her.

'She's probably snoozing off her brush with fame,' said Laura.

'Ah. This is the one who was bound for the high life?'

Laura nodded. At that moment, Felicia woke up and decided to wander down and see them.

'What a beauty,' said the man. 'Look, I love that little splodge she has on her chin.'

'Me too,' said Laura. 'It's so individual.'

'Mr Binks had some very unusual markings as well,' said the man, before going bright red.

'Who's Mr Binks?'

'He was my cat – and Nana's – when I was growing up.'

Laura smiled. 'How lovely.'

'Yes, he was a real character. An adventurous eater, given half the chance. The amount of times I thought he was coming for a snuggle and it was actually to shove his face in my dinner. I've never met a cat as keen on mashed potato.'

The two of them laughed together.

'He also loved digging up my plants,' said the man. 'I used to plant runner beans and sweet peas when I was little. Thankfully, Mr Binks didn't manage to put me off with his trails of destruction, although my heart was always in my mouth when I went outside after school to see what he'd done.'

'Oh, you're into gardening?'

He nodded. 'Yeah. I am the crazy plants-man equivalent of crazy cat ladies.'

Laura giggled. 'Really? Is your place full of Venus flytraps and weird stuff like that?'

'Oh, absolutely. *Jumanji* has nothing on me.'

Laura couldn't stop smiling. She locked eyes with the man and felt her heart jump into her throat. The two of them were suddenly quiet, the silence charged and awkward.

She cleared her throat, hoping she wasn't blushing too much. 'Well, I should get back to work. But do come again. What was your name?'

'Aaron,' he said.

'And I'm Laura.'

'Do you want me to take your cup?' said Aaron, at the exact moment Laura offered the same thing. They both demurred, and then reached their hands out at the same time, their fingers brushing briefly, causing her stomach to swirl around.

Good God, what was wrong with her. A dose of festive madness. It was just that he'd been kind to her after Lettie.

She pulled her shoulders back and said determinedly, 'I'll deal with the cups. Have a lovely evening and we hope to see you soon.'

Behind her, Felicia let out an enormous, happy miaow.

Chapter 10

Carlos Davies Gonzales kicked off his school shoes and dumped his bag down, hoping to slink off upstairs before his mum heard he was back.

'*Hola, cariño,*' she called from the kitchen. It was a relief to hear Spanish after a day of struggling through lessons in English. 'How was school?'

'It was fine,' he told her, and hoped she'd leave it at that. How could he explain what it was really like? How tough he found it fitting in, how most of the other kids had already formed friendship groups. He'd started in Year 8, in September, as the new kid, and the children in his classes had all been at the school a year already. He was far from the only child who was from another country, but he hadn't met anyone from Spain yet. It was so hard finding his feet. He spoke good English, but got teased for his accent and pronunciation, and that made him reluctant to talk in groups. Danny Taylor was the worst of them, always shrieking in a fake Spanish accent, and shouting 'Mamma mia' even though that was Italian. Carlos also had no idea about all the TV shows the other kids spent so long talking about. 'Don't they have the internet in Spain?' Danny had laughed, that lunchtime.

'What did you learn?'

He shrugged. 'About cells in biology.' Fortunately, Carlos already knew a lot about biology and so this lesson wasn't too difficult for him to cope with.

'I'm proud of you! Will you be a scientist like your mum and dad, then?'

Both Carlos's parents worked in scientific research. His mum was from Barcelona, and his dad from London, and they'd met in the Spanish city when they were studying there. Carlos had been born there, and so had his brother and sister, and everything had been going swimmingly as far as he was concerned, until his parents – Maria and Paul – had decided to move to the UK for work. The worst part was that his brother and sister, twins, and seven years older than Carlos, had gone to university in Barcelona instead of coming to London with the rest of the family. They were going to live in a flat all of their own. Carlos had been gutted at the decision.

'Can't I stay with them?' he'd begged.

'You're too young, *cariño*,' he'd been told. 'You need to be with us. It won't be for ever that we're in London, but this is too big an opportunity for your mother to turn down.'

He knew his parents felt bad about the upheaval, and he didn't want to make them feel any worse. But it was hard for him how homesick he felt. He talked to his friends from Barcelona almost every evening, and it was terrible hearing about all their new in-jokes and things that had happened at school. He missed the blue skies, their light and airy flat with the little roof terrace, living near the sea. And that was without even getting started on the food. His parents had reassured him he would settle into London, but so far it seemed grey and miserable and big and lonely.

He shook his head in response to his mum's question. 'No, mama. I'm going to be a vet. You know that.'

She smiled. 'Well, you will need to get your head down and study the sciences hard, then.'

Carlos knew he could do it. He loved science – loved learning all the facts about how things worked, especially living creatures. And ever since he had been able to crawl, he'd loved animals. His mum used to joke that he'd learnt to walk only to follow his grandma's elderly dog around; and, if they wondered where he'd gone, he'd generally be found curled up in the dog's bed or quietly watching the birds feed on the seeds he'd put out. He couldn't think of anything better than helping animals as a job.

He opened the door on his advent calendar to uncover a picture of a little kitten, peeking out of a stocking. He checked the date. That meant only fourteen days until Antonio and Isabella arrived. He couldn't wait to see them.

Carlos worshipped his big brother and sister. To him, they were the coolest people ever to have walked the planet. He always wished he was older so that he could be a part of their social life – it was so hard when he saw them go out to enjoy Barcelona's nightlife while he stayed at home, the baby. Sometimes they let him hang around with their friends, but he generally had to go to bed at the point when they left the house. And now they were off at university; Antonio was studying mathematics and Isabella linguistics. Carlos heard all about the fun they were having, from their regular phone calls.

'Only fourteen days until I see you!' he texted Isabella.

She replied, 'Oh, is that all? I have so much to do here! It's been so busy, lots of parties and studying – I don't know where the time is going! How's London?'

In contrast, the days crawled past for Carlos.

'London is good,' he typed. He couldn't bear to tell her how it really was. He didn't want her thinking he was the loser kid brother.

'How's school?'

'It's okay.'

'Making any new friends?'

'Some . . .'

'You'll get there, don't worry. We're all proud of you for how you're coping.'

'It will be nice to see you and Antonio. I miss home.'

'We can't wait to see you too. You have to show us all the cool things you've discovered in London!'

What on earth was he going to show them?

'Mama,' he said, wandering back through to the kitchen. 'Isabella says I have to show her what I've discovered in London.'

Maria was making a tortilla. She turned around to see the worried little frown on her son's face, and gave him a tight hug.

'Well, that's meant to be a nice thing! I'm sure there are lots of places you can show her. What about Hampstead Heath, the Christmas lights?'

Carlos shook his head. 'Not cool places like she'll know in Barcelona. She and Antonio will just want to go out to the bars and clubs. They won't want to spend time here with me.' He felt like he was being a baby, but he was close to tears. His friends in Barcelona were chatting on WhatsApp about their festive plans, and he wished they were going back there.

'Now, you know that's not true. It's our first Christmas in England! So we have lots of new traditions to explore, the ones Dad is always telling you about.'

Paul arrived home at that point. 'What's wrong, Carlos?'

The boy bit his lip, and checked his emotions. He didn't want his parents worrying. 'I just miss home a bit, is all.' He went up to his room and began doing his science home-work, telling himself that one day he'd be grateful for all this time studying.

There came a knock on the door. Paul and Maria peered round.

'Can we come in?'

He nodded.

They came and sat on the edge of his bed.

'Look, we know that this change hasn't been easy for you,' began Maria. 'And we were thinking, to help you feel at home here, what about we give a home to someone else?'

Carlos shook his head. 'I don't understand.'

'Your dad was telling me a few weeks ago, and we've been talking about it since, that there's an animal charity nearby, where they have cats in search of a new home.'

Carlos sat up, heart pounding. 'We can have a cat?' He'd always dreamed of a pet, but his parents had been adamant that it wouldn't have been fair to keep a cat or a dog in their city apartment on the fourth floor.

Maria laughed. 'Well, I think we should go and look. But yes. We have the right space for it now, with our little garden. And I think you would do an excellent job of helping us take care of a cat.'

Carlos hugged his parents tightly, and immediately pushed his homework aside to google Battersea Dogs and Cats Home.

*

A few days later, and Carlos bounded up the steps to the first floor of the cattery. He'd barely slept the night before, full of excitement about the cat he'd be bringing home – if all went well. He and his parents had been interviewed and approved, to his great relief, and now they were finally going to meet some cats. He couldn't wait! Why were his parents being so slow?

A lady called Laura met them at the top of the stairs and said she'd introduce them to a cat called Skittle. Carlos had seen him on the website, and thought he would be a perfect match. He imagined showing Skittle to Antonio and Isabella when they came to visit, and his heart swelled. School wouldn't be so bad either, not with a cat waiting for him when he got back home. Danny Taylor could mock him all he wanted.

'We'd normally like the whole family to meet a cat, but Skittle is what we call pretty bomb-proof – he doesn't seem fazed by people at all,' Laura was explaining to his mum.

Indeed, the black and white cat had run forward and was standing on his hind legs, paws pressed to the glass. Carlos was in love, and the feeling only deepened when he went into the pod and Skittle leapt onto his lap for cuddles, bumping his head against Carlos's chin and bringing his pink knitted toy mouse forward to play with.

'I think that might be a match,' smiled Maria to Laura. And Laura agreed. Often, they'd encourage people to meet another cat to compare, but Skittle seemed perfect for this family – and, with frequent family visitors on the horizon, it was important to match them with a cat who would be able to cope with that.

Eventually, Carlos emerged and Maria and Paul took it in turns to go in for a cuddle. Both decided quickly that Skittle would be the ideal addition to their family, and went to fill in the paperwork while Carlos stayed by the pod, as if to guard Skittle from anyone else who might want to take him home.

On the pod next door, a sign said that the cat was due for an operation. Carlos wondered what that was for. Then, a lady in a white coat arrived, alongside one of the carers, and stood by the pod.

'Excuse me,' said Carlos, speaking out before he could stop himself, 'but are you a *vet*?'

The lady smiled. 'I am.'

'Oh! I'm going to be a vet when I'm older!'

'Are you now?'

Carlos nodded. 'Yes. I'm studying hard.'

'That's good. And are you going to adopt a cat from here?'

'Yes! Skittle. I think he can come home with us today,' he beamed up at Jill.

'Ah yes, little Skittle! Well, that's wonderful news for both of you. I'd better get busy as this cat is having an operation on her teeth today. Who knows, maybe one day we'll see you back at Battersea again – as a vet!'

Carlos looked around, and imagined himself in the cosy, busy atmosphere, making sure the animals were fit and well. Maybe London wasn't *all* bad, after all.

His parents came over to him, and said they would need to buy a cat carrier from the Battersea shop.

'Don't worry,' said Laura, sensing Carlos's reluctance to leave Skittle, 'he's officially yours now! Why don't you go and choose a nice carrier for him?'

Carlos agreed and went downstairs.

'Hey! Don't I know you?' came a girl's voice.

He turned around and saw a girl with red hair looking at him. He recognised her from school and his heart sank. Was she going to tease him? Had she witnessed Danny's bullying?

'Oh y-y-yeah,' he stammered. 'I think we go to the same school.'

'Me too. I'm Tilly. What form are you in?'

'Miss Hitchen's.'

'I've got her for English. I'm in Mr Khan's form. What's your name?'

'Carlos.'

They both looked at the ground, awkwardly. Carlos scuffed his toe against the floor.

'So how come you're here?' he asked.

Her face lit up. 'We're picking up my dad's kitten! Amber!'

Carlos grinned. 'That's so cool! We're getting a cat too! He's called Skittle and he's black and white.'

With that, the two kids were off chattering about their new cats, and Carlos plucked up the courage to ask Tilly for her help in choosing a carrier. They were deliberating between a purple and a pink one, to go with Skittle's mouse, when Maria came up and asked who Carlos's friend was.

'Tilly! We go to the same school,' said Carlos, smiling.

At that moment, Tilly's dad came to find her, along with her brother Ben, and everyone introduced themselves.

'Do you want to see Skittle?' said Carlos, and Tilly nodded.

'I'll show you Amber as well!'

They darted off back to the cattery, and introduced each other to their new cats, before Jasmine and Laura prepared to pop Skittle and Amber in their respective carriers.

'They each get to bring their special knitted blanket with them,' said Tilly, proud of her knowledge.

'Cool! That's a bit like me – I brought the blanket my grandma made for me back in Barcelona when I came to London.' Carlos cringed. He'd said that without thinking, and hoped she didn't think he was a baby for it. Danny Taylor would love that kind of ammunition.

Tilly regarded him for a moment before speaking. 'That must have been hard, coming from Spain all the way here. We went on holiday there once, and I thought it was much nicer than here.'

Carlos laughed. 'Well, yeah, I miss it. It'll be my first Christmas here.'

'What's Christmas like in Spain?'

'Well, the twenty-fourth is our big day of celebrations.'

Her eyes widened. 'A day early!'

'I suppose it is, yeah.'

'That's cool. And do you get your presents then?'

'We get some. But presents mainly come on Three Kings' Day.' He told her more about how they celebrated Christmas in Catalonia, appreciating her wide-eyed interest. It made him feel less alone, somehow, to be sharing these things with someone else.

Eventually, Tilly's dad came to get her and said they had to go.

'Dad,' said Tilly, 'can Carlos come round and see Amber in the Christmas holidays?'

'Well,' said her dad, 'of course he can. If he'd like to.'

Tilly turned to Carlos, her eyes shining hopefully.

'Yeah,' he said, 'yeah, I'd like that.' And he truly meant it.

She grinned. 'And I'll see you at school on Monday!'

Chapter 11

'Laura, do you think you could leave the biscuits alone now? There won't be any left for Mum and Dad by the time we get there.'

Laura grumpily removed her hand from the packet. 'I did bring extra, don't worry. They'll have their posh biscuits. The world will keep turning.'

She and Rob were driving down to his parents' place for their annual Christmas tree party, and the atmosphere in the car was frostier than the fields outside. Letitia had made Rob's life hell after the 'Fleecie' debacle, threatening to pull out of the campaign altogether. And, while Laura didn't envy him having to deal with her, she knew she'd done the right thing in refusing her request to rehome Felicia.

'What was I meant to do, just give her the cat after she'd lied?' Laura had hissed in the kitchen the other night, stressed out. They'd been meant to be decorating the Christmas tree, but the atmosphere had quickly soured. The date-night fuzzies had well and truly worn off.

'Well, it would have bloody well helped everyone out, since no one else seems to be clamouring to give her a home!' Rob had yelled back. That had stung, especially as Wanda had made her decision and was taking the Siamese cat, leaving Felicia back at square one. Rob had later apologised to Laura, saying he knew she'd done the right thing, and Laura had accepted his apology, but things between them still felt raw. Laura had banned all the FruitySoap samples from the bathroom as the smell was triggering for both of them. She'd also seen a very photogenic pedigree kitten popping up on Lettie's feed – clearly, she was visiting breeders. Laura only hoped she would consider the decision more responsibly than she had at Battersea.

In the driver's seat now, Rob sighed. 'Laura, I was only asking you not to eat all the biscuits before we get to Mum and Dad's. I didn't realise we had another packet, okay.'

Laura had bought a gift and a bottle of fizz to take to Rob's parents, even staying up late to bake some homemade mince pies while he'd been working late, in addition to the biscuits. Truth be told, she dreaded the trips to Malcolm and Izzy's. She just didn't naturally click with Rob's parents – she felt shy and awkward around them – and she and Rob were staying over after the buffet so it would be ages until she was off their territory and safely back at home. She always managed to do something that made her feel out of place – use the wrong knife, knock over a crystal glass, mispronounce the name of some painter. But she'd put a brave face on it. She had a pang of missing her own parents. They'd chatted briefly the other day, and they were full of tales about their time in a cookery school in Thailand. Laura wondered if she'd ever have a family of her own in the way that she imagined – bustling around for Christmas, making jokes, but kind jokes, and with space for everyone to just be themselves.

She placed a hand on Rob's knee and gave it a squeeze. He turned to face her briefly and smiled, changing the radio station to KISS FM so she could listen to her Christmas favourites. She appreciated the conciliatory gesture.

An hour or so later, they waited on the doorstep. There came the clicking of heels from within, and Izzy opened the door, in a waft of expensive perfume.

'Rob! Darling!' she said, throwing her arms round Rob and kissing him loudly on both cheeks.

'And here's lovely little Laura,' she added, patting Laura on the arm. Laura couldn't help but feel Izzy was always disappointed to see her, and that she wasn't more like Rob's ex-girlfriend, now a prominent performance artist who still kept up a friendship with Izzy.

'Hi, Izzy,' said Laura, giving her a hug. 'We brought some supplies.'

'Ooh, gorgeous!' said Izzy, taking the biscuits (from Harrods) and the Tupperware of mince pies (from Laura's fair hand). 'We'll get these set up on the dessert table, just head on in and help yourself.'

Trailing behind Rob, Laura braced herself for the rapturous reception he would receive upon entering the living room. It was as if a minor – make that major – celebrity had somehow appeared in the midst of the family and friends assembled, and everyone clustered round, cooing about how wonderful Rob looked, how well he was doing in London, and asking what campaigns he was working on.

'And who are you, dear?' said an elderly woman, dressed in purple, and peering at Laura through a pair of ginormous spectacles.

Laura knew this woman to be Batty Aunt Betty, and tried not to take offence that she hadn't remembered her, despite having met her several times before at family events.

'I'm Laura,' she smiled. 'Rob's girlfriend.'

Betty looked shocked, but recovered quickly. 'Well, well done you, dear!'

Laura forced a smile before excusing herself and heading to the buffet table, noting that the Harrods biscuits were prominently displayed out front, with her mince pies shoved behind a giant candle mounted in festive greenery. She pulled them forwards.

'I don't know why I bother,' she muttered to herself, loading up her plate. If in doubt, cheese. She hovered by the side of the room, smiling nervously, watching as Rob circulated effortlessly, a glass of champagne in his hand. Occasionally he'd look over and give her a thumbs-up, and she'd smile back. Why did she find this so difficult? She should just go and join him. Everyone else just seemed so sure of themselves and with so much to say. She felt her confidence draining away and grasped the last of it to walk over to where Rob was standing, near a gigantic Christmas tree exquisitely decorated in a colour scheme of white and gold. She preferred colourful, messy Christmas trees, but she couldn't deny the effect was stunning.

'Laura, this is Mary-Lou,' Rob said, introducing her to a very thin, very glamorous woman. She was quite difficult to age as her hair was pulled tightly back in a bun, removing all signs of life from her skin. She was dressed entirely in black, a bold slash of lipstick the only concession to the festive season.

'Nice to meet you,' said Laura, holding out her hand. Mary-Lou took it briefly, before dropping it as a cat might a dead bird.

'And so how do you know Rob's family?' said Laura, trying not to wither under Mary-Lou's glare.

'I'm Seline's mother.'

Oh God. Seline. The ex. *The* ex. Laura had made the mistake of Facebook stalking her once, to be met with a multitude of impossibly glamorous black and white photos. Seline was a dancer and performance artist, which in practical terms meant she was able to put her foot behind her head, while wearing a lace bodysuit, and keep pouting while doing it.

'PUT THE LAPTOP DOWN!' Jasmine had texted her forcefully when Laura had shared the photos – and her insecurities. 'No good can come of this, Laura! You've nothing to worry about anyway, you're gorgeous AND a wonderful person.'

Laura tried to remember those words now, as she choked out, 'Oh, lovely. I've heard so much about her. How is Seline?'

'She's quite wonderful. She would have been here today, of course – she's so marvellously close to Izzy still! – but she's in New York on a dance residency.'

Laura nodded and took some large gulps of champagne. Rob looked awkward.

'Well, good for her,' he said. 'Do send my regards.'

'Oh, Rob, I absolutely will, she'll be so thrilled to hear from you,' purred Mary-Lou. 'Now, tell me, what do you do, Lauren?'

'Laura,' Rob said, cringing.

'Yes, Laura.' Laura gave a little wave of her hand and instantly regretted it. Why did Mary-Lou forgetting *her* name make her feel like she had some making up to do? She obviously wasn't very memorable. 'I work at Battersea Dogs and Cats Home.'

Normally, talking about her job made Laura swell with pride, but the look of judgement on Mary-Lou's face was poisonous.

'I see. With all the little unwanted doggies and catties?'

'Well, we don't see it quite like that. Actually, they're amazing. There's one cat in particular I—'

At that moment came the tinkling sound of a knife being tapped against a champagne flute.

'Maybe now's not quite the time to talk about Felicia,' Rob whispered in her ear, laying a hand on her arm. Laura shook it off, feeling like an idiot. But why shouldn't she talk about Felicia? Rob didn't hesitate to launch into the details of his latest campaigns.

His mum took to the middle of the room. 'Ladies and gentlemen, thank you so much for coming to our little party! Please, eat, drink and be very merry. It just remains for the star to be put on top of the Christmas tree – and who better than our very own shining star, our darling son, Rob.'

The room cooed as Rob stepped forward and up onto a small ladder, fastening the star to the top of the tree and taking a theatrical bow, which was met by laughter and applause. Laura wished she could be as confident as he was. She found it so difficult at these kinds of events, seeing the way Rob circulated so effortlessly, and she just felt more and more out of place. She didn't want to be his needy girlfriend clinging to his arm – she just wanted to find a voice of her own.

She watched as he was absorbed by yet another cluster of Izzy and Malcolm's friends, and poured herself a further generous glass of champagne.

What would a cat do? thought Laura. Cats didn't hesitate to come and go as they pleased. With that, she snuck upstairs to the spare bedroom where they'd be staying, just for a few moments of respite. It was a beautiful room, with exposed beams and a view out over the country fields. She sank onto the patchwork quilt and kicked off her smart heels, wondering if anyone would notice if she put on her trainers and preparing to shut her eyes just for five minutes of complete calm.

'I don't mean to give you a fright,' came a voice from the side of the bed, doing exactly that.

Laura leapt bolt upright, heart pounding. She looked over to where the voice had come from. A middle-aged man in a bright-blue shirt and red tie was sitting on the floor between the window and a tall bedside cabinet, knees pulled up to his chin, a bottle of champagne open beside him.

'I'm sorry,' he said. 'I just needed a few moments away from the hustle and bustle. Didn't realise anyone was staying in here.'

He started to get up.

'I know how you feel,' said Laura. 'Stay put, don't move on my account.'

'Not enjoying the glitz and the glamour either?'

Laura shook her head. 'It just gets a bit much. Needed a few moments of peace and quiet.'

The man stretched out his hand to shake hers. 'Rufus.'

'I'm Laura.'

'And how do you know Izzy and Malcolm?'

'I'm Rob's girlfriend,' Laura said with a sigh.

'Gosh, the golden boy!'

'Indeed.'

'Is that interminable tree-topping ceremony over yet?' Rufus delivered this in a stage whisper, one eyebrow raised, a twinkle in his eyes.

Laura giggled disloyally. 'Yes, don't worry.'

'I'm sorry, I'm not that mean really. I've been watching Rob put the star on the tree since he was in some very stinky nappies. I went to art school with Izzy. Been good pals ever since.'

'Ah, you're Uncle Rufus!'

'The very same. Glad to see my reputation precedes me.'

Laura had heard many stories about Rufus and his husband Alan – what a wild, fun couple they were. Somehow, this didn't fit with the man hiding himself away from a party.

'I've heard a lot about you – wasn't there that Christmas when you actually tried to climb down the chimney?'

He smiled ruefully. 'Yup. Didn't get very far, but some delicious firemen appeared, so it was all worth it. I'm sorry to disappoint you. Just not really feeling myself this year – I'm just not up to being the life and soul. It's hard to cope with all those confident social butterflies downstairs.'

'I know exactly what you mean,' said Laura. 'I always feel like that, really. Like I'm too shy to speak up, and no one notices me.' Maybe it was the champagne making her so candid, but she found Rufus really easy to talk to. He had a kind, open face, with plenty of laughter lines around his eyes.

'We all have those moments,' said Rufus. 'Some people are just better at covering them up than others.' He proffered her some champagne. 'Fancy hiding out here a little bit longer? I can offer you a toothbrush mug of this fine vintage.'

Laura gladly accepted. Rufus asked her what she did, and she began to talk about Battersea.

His eyes lit up. 'That wonderful place!'

And then, to her surprise, he began to cry. 'Gosh, I'm sorry, Laura. We just lost our little cat, we got her from there. Alan's so upset he couldn't even face today. It's going to be a miserable Christmas.'

Rufus went on to explain how they'd adopted Evie seventeen years ago, as a kitten, shortly after they'd moved in together.

'Here she is,' he said, pulling out his phone. He showed Laura a range of pictures of an evidently much-adored cat – she was black and white, with long hair, and a mischievous expression. 'Her hair! She was such a diva, we were always combing it and giving it a trim. Alan's a hairdresser so Evie was the most stylish cat going, and she loved the attention. I know it sounds silly, but she was our family. She made that first little house of ours into a home.'

'It doesn't, not at all,' said Laura. 'How wonderful that she had such a long and happy life with you.'

Rufus nodded. 'We're so grateful for that, and the joy she brought us. But, my, we are going to miss her. How do you cope with that at the job? The emotion of it all – surely you must miss the cats you're close to?'

'It's hard,' said Laura. 'I think we're always happy when a cat finds a new home. But there are those ones that you bond with, and it's so bittersweet when they go. For example, there's this cat at the moment – Felicia.' In return, she got out her phone and showed Rufus a few photos of her. 'And I just adore her. I was really involved with her care, right from when she came in as a stray. It was such an honour to help her recover and build her trust in people again. But she's not had much luck yet – she's been with us a lot longer than average. I don't know why some cats just can't catch a break. She takes a little while to get to know you, but then she's the soppiest, most loving cat you could ever wish for.'

Rufus nodded, and looked at her thoughtfully. 'You know, Laura, when you speak about Felicia, you're so confident. You speak up for people – animals – and that's where you find your voice.'

Laura blushed, moved by Rufus's words. 'Gosh, thank you. I mean, I don't know, it's really just my job.'

He laughed. 'And there you go, when the spotlight is on you, you don't like it. But the world would be a better place if there were more people like you in it. Those cats are lucky to have you speaking up for them, and don't forget it. Come on, we'd better get downstairs and show our faces before they send out a search party.'

*

Taking a deep breath and re-entering the bustling living room, Laura sought out Rob.

'Sorry to be gone for so long,' she said, catching his elbow.

'Were you?' he said. 'Don't worry, pea, I didn't notice.'

'I was talking to your uncle Rufus,' she said.

'Oh! Where is the old scoundrel?'

They looked around, but Rufus had gone. Laura wondered if he'd been unable to face the chattering room when he was so upset about Evie. But his words stuck with her. That she'd found her voice when she was speaking up for Felicia. So maybe that was what she needed to do – there had to be loads of brilliant potential homes in among this lot, and probably with amazing gardens to boot. She'd tried Rob's snazzy advertising approach and look where that had got them. She was going to try something a bit more old-fashioned – making new connections with people, in real life. And when she surveyed the room again, there were plenty of people standing a bit nervously around the edges, unsure of themselves. Not everyone had Rob's confidence. Laura took a deep breath, and plucked up the courage to go up to a shy-looking woman in her fifties and start a conversation.

Later that night, Laura and Rob prepared for bed, shattered and a little tipsy after all the socialising.

'Did you have a good time?' asked Rob, doing his teeth.

Laura considered this. 'Yes. Yes, I suppose I did. At first it was a bit weird, with you being the star of the show and all that.'

He groaned. 'Sorry, Laur, it's always like that. I just get caught up in talking to everyone. But you were all right, weren't you?'

'No, it's fine. Then actually I ended up talking to some nice people. I decided there must be a home for Felicia in among that crowd.'

He laughed. 'You're amazing, always working for that little moggy. Any luck?'

'Maybe. There was a nice couple, missing their daughter now she's gone away to university. They could be a match.'

She and Rob got into bed, and fell asleep almost instantly, wiped out by the day.

*

Laura woke up with a start. Her mobile said 3 a.m.

Was it a dream, or had she just heard a cat's miaowing? She poked Rob awake.

'Rob. *Rob*. I think I can hear a cat,' she whispered.

'Laura, you are *obsessed*, go back to sleep,' he moaned, turning over.

She listened again. Yes, definitely a miaowing. Faint, but definitely there. She got up and put on her trainers, pulling a blanket over her pyjamas, and went down to the living room. The remains of the party were scattered all around – glasses on the buffet table, scraps of food, shiny cracker remains.

The miaowing had stopped when she turned on the light. *Had* she been hearing things? She'd been working awfully hard recently; maybe it was time for a Christmas break.

She turned around and went to head back upstairs, leaving the room in darkness. Then she heard a scuffling sound. She turned the light on again, and listened.

'Puss puss!' she called, softly, in her special cat voice. 'Here puss puss!'

She heard a soft chirruping miaow from further inside the room. Laura crept forward slowly, making encouraging sounds.

But despite a continual patter of miaows, she couldn't see where the cat actually was. Then she stopped, and looked at the fireplace. The fire from the afternoon had gone out several hours ago, so the grate would be cool. Laura crouched down and peered up into the chimney.

A pair of yellow-green eyes stared back down at her, accompanied by a rumbling purr.

'Hello there,' Laura murmured. 'Are you practising for Christmas Eve?'

There was a ginger and white cat perched on the smoke shelf, looking down at her.

Laura thought that temptation would be the best option to coax the cat down. She opened the fridge and got out some chicken leftovers, checking for bones first.

She came back through and let the cat sniff it, before bringing it a distance away from the chimney and waiting. Sure enough, the cat dropped down and came across for the food.

Hungry, then, thought Laura, noting how thin the cat was. She suspected the cat had been a pet – it wasn't scared of humans – but could have gone missing, or been abandoned, for a few weeks now.

Rob walked into the living room, and the cat scuttled away back up the chimney.

Not scared of humans, but a bit wary, Laura added to her assessment.

'I take it all back, Laur, it's not a ghost cat after all,' said Rob, coming to crouch down beside her. 'And it's gone up the chimney?'

Laura nodded. 'Yeah. Coaxed her down with a bit of chicken, but she's popped back up there pretty quick.'

Rob yawned. 'We could just leave her there until morning? Put a bit of food out? Bunty won't be back until then anyway.'

Laura had forgotten about Bunty, Malcolm and Izzy's ageing and quite flatulent Labrador. He got stressed out by so many people in the house, so stayed with a neighbour whenever they had a big party.

'Yeah. The only thing is if the cat goes by then. Looks pretty skinny. Wouldn't surprise me if it'd been stuck somewhere for a while.' There were tons of farm buildings and sheds in the countryside near Rob's parents – easy places for a cat to sneak into and accidentally get locked in. They'd have to ring around any immediate neighbours to see if they could locate the cat's owners.

Laura continued, 'I think we should try to get this kitty down and we could put her in the downstairs bathroom overnight, with a little bed. And maybe we can find a makeshift litter tray.'

Rob groaned as Laura got to work. She set up the bathroom, which was quite warm and cosy, plus would be easy to clean if the cat had an accident. She piled up old blankets to make a cosy bed, along with a cardboard box for hiding purposes, and improvised a litter tray using some sawdust and an old plant tray she found at the back door. Finally, she put down some fresh water and a bit more chicken. She used another piece to tempt the cat down again from the chimney, and encourage it to the bathroom, noting that the cat lapped thirstily at the clean water. She left the hall light on and went back to bed, barely able to sleep at the excitement of having a cat in the vicinity.

*

'What on earth is that!' came a cry from downstairs, just a few hours later.

Laura's eyes flew open. She'd meant to set her alarm clock to wake up early, but had clearly snoozed right through it due to her exhaustion. Damn! That meant Izzy had discovered the Christmas cat.

She scampered downstairs. 'Izzy! I'm sorry, I meant to get up early and wake you. We found this cat up the chimney last night.'

Izzy was standing outside the bathroom, the door firmly shut. 'Well, he or she is still in there. Snoozing in some of my artisanal hand-woven blankets!' Laura cringed. Well, it wouldn't be a visit to Rob's parents without her committing some terrible faux pas, and plonking a cat on Izzy's posh blankets – they didn't *look* posh, with all the bits hanging off them – was clearly her crime this time.

'Sorry, Izzy. I thought she must be a stray and I didn't want her to wander off before we got her help.'

Izzy tutted loudly. 'Well, she'll need to be gone soon. Bunty is going to be delivered back shortly and he will not be happy with a cat around the place.'

Laura nodded. 'Could we ring around any neighbours and see if they're missing a cat?'

Izzy looked annoyed. 'Well, really, there're only a few of us around here so I think I would have heard. I suppose I can ring one or two.'

She stalked off and Laura heard her making some calls before she returned.

'As I thought, no one has heard of her. She'll have to be out of here, Laura, Bunty will go nuclear.'

Scratch the idea of Rob's parents offering the Christmas cat a home, then. Laura would take her to Battersea, where they could check her over medically and see if there was any way of tracing her owners.

Laura told Izzy they'd be off and take the Christmas cat with them, but Izzy reminded her – eyebrows raised, expression frosty – that they'd made reservations at a local pub for lunch.

Leaving the cat safely in the bathroom for the time being, Laura went to talk to a groggy Rob.

'Can't we just leave the cat in the bathroom until later?' he said, rolling himself back up in the duvet and screwing his eyes shut.

'Not for too long,' said Laura. 'I want to get her to Battersea before 4 p.m. so they can get her in the system. And your mum is adamant she goes before Bunty gets back. The cat probably won't appreciate being barked at either.'

'But we've got lunch with the Pinkington-Smythes. Mum will go ballistic if I miss it.' Rob stared at her with an agonised expression. Laura wondered how he could be such a powerful, dynamic account director and yet so utterly terrified of his own mother.

'Rob, I could really use your help here. Tell her we'll come down next weekend for lunch.'

Rob nodded. 'Okay.'

He got up and went to speak to Izzy. Laura showered and got dressed quickly, wondering if they could borrow a cat carrier for the trip home. Back downstairs, and helping herself to tea and toast, she heard Rob talking to Izzy and hoped it was all fine. She didn't want to make trouble with Rob and his family, but she had to look after this little cat. And she'd done her duty yesterday, hadn't she?

'All sorted,' Rob said, coming back through with a smile on his face.

'Really?'

'Yes, absolutely,' said Izzy, grinning like a Cheshire cat. 'Rob will drop you at the station, with the cat, and then come for lunch with us while you get the train up to London. Look, I've even found a carrier you can use.' She held up an enormous pet carrier, the size of a small crate – it must have been used for Bunty, once upon a time.

No wonder Izzy was grinning, thought Laura. She'd managed to get rid of both the cat *and* Laura, and ensure she'd have Rob to herself the whole lunch – no doubt giving her the opportunity to suggest he get back in touch with blimming Seline. Meanwhile, Laura would struggle up to London with a frightened cat in a container the size of a small spacecraft. She gritted her teeth.

Rob looked a bit more nervous. 'Laur? All okay? We thought it was for the best. That way you get up to Battersea in time and I can go for lunch with the family. I'll bring your stuff up later.'

Was she being unreasonable? She supposed in a way she was, and yet she couldn't help but wish Rob was more on her team sometimes.

'No, no, that's fine,' she said brightly. 'I'll just put her in the carrier and then we'll be off, eh?'

'Well, you don't have to go right away,' said Rob. 'Stay for breakfast, at least?'

'To be honest, darling, we really do need that creature out of the bathroom sooner rather than later. And Bunty's coming back over very shortly – we don't want a terrible hullaballoo.'

Laura wondered why Bunty couldn't stay with the neighbours for just half an hour more and let her finish her tea, but she found herself bundling the cat into the carrier and taking her to the car. She decided to take one of the 'artisanal blankets' with her to drape over the top and hopefully keep the cat warm and calm. Rob started up the engine and they drove the twenty minutes or so to the station.

'Thanks for understanding,' he said, reaching over and giving her a kiss. 'I checked and there's a train in about ten minutes.'

'That's fine,' she said, stiffly. 'See you when you get home.'

She got the cat out of the boot, bought her ticket and went to wait on the platform, shivering in the chill wind. The cat was still and quiet inside the carrier. Laura hoped she wasn't too stressed. Ten minutes passed, and no train came. She went back down to the ticket office and asked when it would arrive.

'Sunday trains and engineering works, love,' came the reply. 'It'll be another half-hour and then you'll have to change.'

Laura shut her eyes momentarily, before picking up the cat and going to wait in the waiting room, where she hoped it would be a fraction warmer. 'Come on then, Santa Paws. It's just me and you now.'

*

Several hours later, Laura arrived at Battersea, freezing, her arms aching, and her shins bruised from where the enormous carrier had bumped against them. She'd texted Jas on the way to say she'd be bringing in a cat.

'Jeez, Laura, you're meant to be rehoming them, not making my life harder!' said Jasmine, meeting her in reception with a big hug.

'Don't, Jas, I've had the most terrible day,' said Laura, very much not in a joking mood.

'Get yourself a tea and I'll start processing this little one.'

Laura did as she was told, adding in a slice of lemon drizzle cake and warming her hands around the mug of tea, before joining Jasmine back downstairs and filling her in on the story.

'So you actually found her in the chimney? That's brilliant!'

Laura nodded, smiling.

'So it has to be Santa Paws, bless her.'

The team at Battersea were fond of giving their cats names with a seasonal twist. They already had a Holly and an Ivy waiting for a new home, and Laura suspected two new cats named Brandy and Pie might have had something to do with a hungry Jasmine on intake duty that day.

After entering the cat on the system, they took her for a quick medical inspection by one of the veterinary nurses, who also took a blood sample. Santa Paws would have a fuller examination when a vet was free. The girls then took her to one of the holding pens, where the cat would be kept briefly before her examination, after which she'd be taken up to the third floor to settle in before an assessment.

'So, let me get this right. Rob just chucked you out at a train station, left you on a freezing-cold platform, clutching a stray cat, to face down a nightmare journey here, while he swans off for his Sunday roast?' Jas said, with a frown.

Laura cringed. 'No! I mean, it wasn't like that.'

'Uh huh.' Jasmine didn't look convinced. 'Well, sounds a bit of a nightmare to me, Laur.'

'It was, but his mum is just really tricky and demanding. He honestly had to stay.'

Jasmine raised her eyebrows. 'Well. If you say so. By the way, a man came in asking for you yesterday. By the name of Aaron?'

Laura's heart gave a leap. 'Oh?' she said, trying to be casual.

'No idea why you're blushing like that, Laur. Anyhow, he was keen on talking to you about Felicia, for his nana. I said that she'd have to meet the cat first, and he said she's having a lot of problems leaving the house at the moment. I said I'd drop by for a home visit, but I thought you might like to do it. Especially as it's Felicia they're interested in – I know how much she means to you.'

Laura nodded fervently. Yes, it was absolutely right that she should be the one to make the home visit on Felicia's behalf. Felicia was what mattered most here. And, if it so happened that there was the opportunity to say hello to Aaron, this time without being a snotty disaster, well, that was just a pleasant bonus.

Chapter 12

Laura went into work that Monday absolutely knackered. With the stress of the visit to Rob's parents and the unexpected mission to Battersea the day before, she felt like she hadn't had a weekend at all. Rob had arrived back late, and she'd already gone to bed early, feeling like she was getting a cold after her chilly wait on the station platform. She didn't feel very festive at all, and had to remind herself of all there was to look forward to – in particular, the Battersea Christmas Carol Concert. Jasmine had ominously said she had a surprise accessory for them to wear, and Laura could only imagine what she had in mind. But the thought of carols, mince pies and mulled wine on the near horizon was enough to give her back a bit of festive glow.

After an enormous coffee, she spent some time with Brandy and Pie, chatted to the welfare team about them, and went to write up their bios. Brandy was quite shy and timid at first; she'd need time to settle in with a new owner and let her playful side emerge. Pie was the opposite – a very chilled-out cat who took everything in his stride. Laura put her best creative hat on, and came up with some rhymes.

> Our beautiful Brandy
> Is looking for a home fine and dandy,
> Her Christmas desire?
> That she will acquire

A calm place of her own,
An understanding home,
With time to unwind,
Then her owner will find,
A most loving girl,
Who'll make you the centre of her world.

And for Pie, she'd written:

There once was a cat called Pie,
Independent, but with a loving side,
He longed for a home,
His own garden to roam,
With a cosy spot waiting inside!

After writing the bios, Laura spent some time answering emails, and made follow-up calls to see how a few of their recent rehomings were getting on. The Battersea team was always on hand to help with any teething issues as cats and owners settled into life together.

She would be on rehoming duty that afternoon, but expected a quiet day of it. After the bustle of the weekends, Mondays were usually spent assessing which other cats might be ready for adoption, taking care of admin arising from the weekend, and preparing for an increased volume of adoptions later in the week. At lunch, she also went to see how Santa Paws was getting on. After being examined by a vet, who had declared that she was a little underweight but had no serious health issues, she was transferred to the third floor of the cattery. Once she'd settled into a pod there and was comfortable with her surroundings, she would be assessed to see what type of home might suit her. Laura paused outside the door. Santa Paws was curled up sleeping, but raised her head when she realised Laura was there. She didn't come over, but Laura was pleased to see that she didn't appear too stressed by her environment. Fingers crossed she would find a new home as soon as possible. She also popped in to give Felicia some love, telling her all about the drama of the weekend and trying to decipher the look in the cat's eyes when she told her about Rob staying down for the lunch. If only Felicia could tell her what she really thought.

As expected, the afternoon was really quiet. Only a few people came in to look around, which meant Laura had time to spend getting to know the cats on the floor – Battersea was quick at rehoming, so it was crucial for rehomers to know the candidates as well and as quickly as possible.

Cuddling Pie, who really was a remarkably chilled cat, Laura heard a familiar voice coming up the stairs. It was Rufus in a colourful tartan scarf, hand in hand with another man, who Laura presumed must be Alan.

Rufus waved cheerily at her, and she let herself out of the pod, delighted to see him.

'Hello, Laura! So sorry to leave without saying goodbye the other day – couldn't quite face the maelstrom again after our cosy chat. This is Alan – I told him all about you.'

'Thanks for looking after him at the party,' said Alan, with a smile. He was slim and dark, with a neat moustache and beard, and seemed a bit more reserved than Rufus.

'Not at all, I think it was entirely mutual,' said Laura.

'Ah yes, it can't be easy being Rob's other half at events like that,' said Alan. 'I should know – this one's generally something of a show-off when it comes to parties,' he said with a smile and a gentle poke of Rufus's ribs.

'Oi!' said Rufus back, but Laura could tell the teasing was good-natured.

'And have you just come for a look around?'

The two men glanced at each other. 'Well, actually,' said Rufus, 'I couldn't stop thinking about the cat you spoke so beautifully about. Felicia. As you know, we've just lost our darling Evie. But we have a wonderful home to give to another cat in need.'

Alan nodded in agreement, his lips pressed together with emotion.

Laura felt joy rush through her. This *had* to be Felicia's home. She just felt it in her bones. And if Felicia went to Rufus and Alan, she could see her again – trips to Rob's parents might suddenly become tolerable if it meant a way to keep Felicia in her life.

'Well, that's fantastic,' she beamed. 'Look, Felicia's right here.'

She took Alan and Rufus round to her pod, where Felicia was snoozing in one of her classic positions – on her side, fluffy belly out, front paws tucked up.

'Oh, she's a darling,' said Rufus. 'That tummy!'

'She is,' said Laura, smiling fondly at the cat. 'Listen, I'll get you set up with an interview, and then perhaps you can meet her?'

Alan and Rufus went downstairs to chat to one of the other rehomers, who quickly approved them. They had showered Evie with loving care for her whole life, including through several health issues, and, living in the countryside, had a beautiful garden with ample space for a cat. They were certain that enclosing the garden due to Felicia's FIV status wouldn't be a problem either.

As Simone brought them back upstairs and showed Laura photos of their home, Laura's excitement went up a level. This would be the perfect home for Felicia! This was the silver lining to a crappy weekend! She could almost feel warm towards Izzy, Rob's mum, for leading her to Rufus.

Rufus was beaming. 'We're approved! Shall we go and meet our girl?'

Laura brought them back round to Felicia's pod. This time, the cat was awake and even trotted down to the front of the pod to greet her visitors. This was a good sign!

Rufus went inside first, and Felicia greeted him warmly, bumping her head against his hand for strokes, and even settling on his knee, purring.

'The best feeling in the world,' said Laura, and Alan nodded beside her.

'Your turn, my dear,' said Rufus, coming out of the pod and switching places.

Alan sat on the floor and waited for Felicia to come over to him. If anything, she was even more affectionate with Alan – and Laura felt this was her way of saying, 'Yes please' to going home with this new family. As she sat purring on his lap, Alan kissed her on the head, right between the ears, and Felicia looked up, blinking her golden eyes in joy.

'What do you think?' said Rufus, when Alan emerged.

'She's just wonderful,' said Alan.

'Well, shall we take her? Shall we get the paperwork sorted? Laura says we need to speak to a vet to be clear on her little heart problem, so maybe we do that first? And do we need to know anything else about this FIV business? I think I've got a handle on it, but maybe there're other things we need to consider?' Rufus had a hundred and one questions.

Then, suddenly, tears were rolling down Alan's face. 'She's just wonderful,' he repeated. 'And that's the problem.'

'What do you mean, dear?' said Rufus, his arm around his husband's shoulders in an instant.

'Doesn't . . .' sniffed Alan, choking the words out. 'Doesn't she remind you too much of our Evie?'

'Yes, she does,' said Rufus softly. 'They even look the same. Somehow it feels like they could have been sisters, or something. But that's why I thought she'd be perfect for us.'

Alan shook his head. 'Rufus, she is . . . But I just can't do it so soon. I feel like we're replacing our Evie. It was only a few weeks ago that we lost her.'

Laura stood back respectfully to give them some space. She couldn't bear to look at Felicia, sitting eagerly at the front of the pod, staring up at Alan and Rufus with a hopeful look in her golden eyes.

'It's okay, girl, it's okay,' murmured Laura, telling herself that Alan and Rufus would make the right decision. Her heart felt fit to burst. She could see how much they'd adored Evie – the depth of their grief at losing her was testament to that. And it was that love that would make them such wonderful owners for Felicia. She ducked into the office and took some deep breaths, before going back out.

'Laura, I'm sorry to be so indecisive,' said Alan, stepping forward. 'I'm going to have a cup of tea and sort myself out, and think about what to do.'

Laura nodded. 'Of course, Alan. Take all the time you need.'

'Will I come with you?' said Rufus.

Alan shook his head. 'I think I just need a moment or two alone.' He headed downstairs and out to the café.

Rufus groaned softly. 'He's a wonderful, sensitive soul, my husband. I should have thought it through more clearly, but I was so fired up after talking to you. You see, we got Evie after we moved in together, but it was also when his mum was very, very ill. She had breast cancer, she was in the final stages. We were in and out of the hospice all the time, of course. And Evie was a real ray of light in that time. She used to make Alan smile when nothing else could, including me. She was just a kitten, really, and she used to try to climb up his leg as soon as he got in the door, purring for his attention. A real daddy's girl, we used to joke about her! We even took her to see Alan's mum once, in the hospice. We were a bit worried as she could be boisterous, but Rose insisted she wanted to meet her. And she was good as gold. She sat purring, right by Rose's neck. We've got a photo of it, actually. And she said to Evie, "You be sure to look after my boy, won't you?", and she really did.'

Rufus sighed and passed his hand over his face. 'Sorry, you don't need the whole story. But I think, when Evie died, it was like losing Alan's last connection with his mum. It's brought a lot of stuff up.'

'I understand completely,' said Laura.

'And she really does look an awful lot like Evie, right down to that splodge on her chin. A sister from another mister.'

He smiled wryly. Not for the first time, Laura marvelled at how animals triggered such deep feelings in human beings.

After a few moments of silence contemplating Felicia, Rufus turned to Laura and, with an effort to look cheerful, asked her how the rest of the party had been.

'Well, it wasn't as fun as our champagne retreat in the spare bedroom,' smiled Laura. 'But we did have an unexpected visitor during the night!'

She told him about finding Santa Paws in the chimney, and Rufus guffawed, especially when she got to the bit about using Izzy's posh blankets to make the cat a nest in the downstairs bathroom.

'Oh Lord, bet Izzy just loved that – I mean, don't tell her this but I do agree with you actually. I was there when she bought them, and I thought they were *awful* but she wouldn't be told. They cost an absolute fortune as well.'

Laura giggled too.

'What's all this merriment?' said Alan, coming back upstairs. His eyes were pink, but he had a smile, even if it was a bit wobbly.

'Laura found a cat at Izzy and Malcolm's party – she was stuck in the chimney.'

'Isn't that your party trick, darling?' said Alan.

'Indeed. I suspect the cat was somewhat easier to get out, although no one tried tempting me down with chicken, as far as I can remember,' said Rufus.

Laura's heart was beating fast. She couldn't wait any longer to hear their decision. 'So, what do you think?' she said to Alan.

He looked at them both, and the smile dropped from his face. He shook his head gently from side to side. Rufus pressed his mouth into a line and took Alan's hand.

'Of course. Maybe it was stupid of me to bring you. I'm sorry.'

'No, no,' said Alan. 'I've more to say. I do want another cat. They bring us such joy. And I realised, coming back here all these years later, that Evie would want another cat to have the second chance that she did. But, this little one . . . she's just too similar . . . it feels like . . . we're just replacing her, especially so soon. I am sorry, I'm so, so sorry.'

Laura swallowed hard. She understood, of course she did. She just couldn't help but be bitterly disappointed. She simply nodded, unable to speak.

'What happened to the cat in the chimney?' said Rufus, to break the awkwardness.

'Oh, she's here,' said Laura. 'We have to wait seven days for someone to claim her, which seems unlikely, then she'll be up for adoption. Once she's had a chance to settle here, and be assessed, of course.'

Alan glanced at Rufus. 'So . . . a bit longer, then. What colour is she?'

Laura pulled out her phone to show them. She'd taken a few snaps of Santa Paws during their long journey, and a couple more this morning once she was settled in the pod.

'Ginger and white!' exclaimed Alan.

'What are you thinking?' said Rufus.

'I'm thinking that, with a little more time to prepare, to get used to Evie not being around, maybe this cat could be the one for us. She was replicating your most famous stunt, after all. It's like she was giving you a sign.'

Rufus laughed. 'Are you sure you're not just saying this? Don't feel under pressure.'

Alan shook his head. 'I'm not. Why don't we just see? If Laura could let us know once she's ready to receive visitors, then we can come again.'

'Of course I will,' said Laura.

'Happy Christmas, if we don't see you beforehand,' said Rufus, while Alan invited her and Rob to their New Year's drinks party, and they all hugged goodbye.

Before they left, Alan crouched down by Felicia's pod and pressed his fingers to the glass.

'Goodbye, sweetheart. I'm sorry I couldn't be what you needed.' He straightened up, and headed out with Rufus.

Laura went into Felicia's pod, slumped down, and promptly burst into tears. She felt ill, a little feverish, and she'd so wanted Felicia to go home with Alan and Rufus. The cat came up to her and put a paw on her arm, making a little chirruping miaow, as if to ask where Alan and Rufus had gone.

Laura shook her head, slowly. 'I'm sorry, Felicia. They're not the ones for you after all. But I'll keep looking, don't you worry about that.'

Chapter 13

'She's not replied to my text, even though she's clearly read it,' Alison Thompson called out to her husband.

John came through from the kitchen, and put a cup of tea down next to where Alison was positioned on the sofa. The room was absolutely pristine. Alison had cleaned and polished everything that morning, adjusting the Christmas decorations until they were perfect.

'Well, it's probably a good thing, love. Means she's out having fun with her new friends. Maybe even studying.'

Alison knew John was putting a brave face on it. He missed Fiona just as much as she did.

'I know. I just can't help but worry about her.'

She knew that was a little bit of a lie. Yes, of course she worried about her, but it was also that she really, really missed their only daughter. She'd gone off to university in late September and, after an initial flurry of nerves and anxious phone calls, had clearly settled in and begun enjoying herself thoroughly, especially if her Instagram posts were anything to go by.

Alison sighed. Of course she was glad Fiona was enjoying herself. But the house seemed so empty without her. They'd put the tree up in preparation for her arrival, and asked her for a Christmas list, to which the reply had been, 'MONEY PLEASE!!!' It didn't seem five minutes ago that Fiona had been toddling around, more interested in the wrapping paper than the present, or then, as a teenager, moodily unwrapping her presents and either beaming with delight or stropping off as a result.

And yes, they spoilt her a bit, but things hadn't been easy. It had started before Fiona was born. Alison and John had had trouble conceiving, and then a series of miscarriages. After a gruelling round of IVF, Fiona was their miracle baby. Alison had hoped desperately for another but it hadn't happened, and so she contented herself with pouring all her love and energy into Fiona. Her early childhood had been fantastic. A whirlwind of parties and outings and holidays in the sun. Alison had made sure that Fiona had lots of contact with other children, was always the one to host playdates and sleepovers. Alison also made sure that she stayed in touch with her own friends – rarely a week went by that she didn't head out to a wine bar, or to a book club, or even to have a boogie with some of her party pals.

But when Fiona was twelve, she'd been diagnosed with leukaemia. Even the word made Alison shudder. It sounded like some Disney villain, only this one was horrifyingly real. The terrible disease had almost caused Fiona to fade from life. Alison would spend nights awake, telling herself that she, Fiona's mother, would beat this disease. She would fight even when her little girl wasn't strong enough to do so. She would love Fiona hard enough, do every little thing for her, to make it impossible for her to leave this life. Alison knew she had to be tough. She would beat this. She couldn't let a chink of uncertainty in.

Fiona's adolescence was years of being in and out of hospital, appointments with specialists, the dreaded rounds of chemotherapy, missed school, friends and normal life dropping by the wayside. Alison couldn't help but feel that they simply didn't understand. It was easier to keep themselves tucked away. Fiona hated missing out on what her schoolfriends were doing – the school trips, the first kisses, the messing around in class. A few friends did keep calling round after school, but it was more painful for Fiona to hear their stories and gossip. Alison stopped returning calls and invites. All her energy needed to be for Fiona – she couldn't bear the thought of spending time doing something normal, whatever that meant now. What if her girl needed her? She and the other mothers at the hospital would nod to each other, sombre-faced, their faces lined with fatigue. Allies across the battlefield, Alison always thought. The strain between her and John was considerable. Alison had given up work in order to better manage Fiona's condition. She'd been studying part-time to become a veterinary nurse, and that fell by the wayside as well. Sometimes she'd resented that John could escape to his job on a building site. Her life was Fiona now.

Then, Fiona underwent the gruelling procedure of a bone-marrow transplant, followed by more months in hospital, plus careful monitoring and follow-ups for the year after. But then, hope. Suddenly, the c-word didn't mean cancer, but cure. They could see it almost daily – Fiona's strength returning, her confidence growing. She was on her phone more and more, arranging to see people, gossiping, staying out past her curfew, enjoying the ordinary teenage rebellions she'd been denied for so long.

Alison's heart swelled with joy when she thought of that time. How wonderful it had been to see Fiona blossom, finally. But when she looked in the mirror, she felt like the opposite had happened to her. Who was this careworn woman, with grey roots and frown lines? She used to be fun, many, many years ago, before life ground her down. John said he'd fallen in love with her mischievous smile.

She'd been independent, with a huge gang of friends, always up for adventure. She'd been the one who wasn't sure she wanted to settle down – it had taken a special man like John to persuade her.

When Fiona went out with her friends, Alison realised she had no one to call. She just sat at home, waiting for John to get back from work. Even hospital appointments didn't structure her routine any more – Fiona insisted she would go to check-ups on her own, kissing her mum and saying she'd done so much for her, now it was her time to relax and get back to doing what she enjoyed.

But Alison didn't have a clue what she enjoyed any more.

If anything, she felt increasingly nervous about heading out on her own and having to talk to people. What did she have to talk about? Why would anyone be interested in what she had to say? She used to be the life and soul of the party, unimaginable as it was now. These days she preferred to go unnoticed, dressing unobtrusively and sticking as near to John as possible.

She checked Fiona's Instagram for any updates. There was a new picture! Fiona posing in fancy dress, laughing her head off outside a bar in Bristol, where she was at uni. She might be a year or two older than her course-mates, thanks to all the disruption to her education, but that didn't seem to be holding her back. She looked at the faces of the people she was with. They all seemed so young and happy – a pretty, confident girl with long dark hair, her arm around Fiona's waist, and a handsome boy, tall and gangly.

Alison smiled and typed a message: 'They look wonderful, Fi-Fi! I'm so happy you're having fun, me and Daddy miss you xxxx.'

Her phone beeped almost instantly.

'MUM. You do realise that people can see your comments?'

Oh God.

'No, I'm sorry!'

Her phone buzzed with an Instagram notification.

Someone called Pete had typed: 'We are very wonderful, Fiona's mum!! We think the same about you!!', with a laughing emoji and some hearts. It felt quite nice to be included in the teasing.

There were more messages from Fiona. 'God, Mum, please don't do it again!'

'Okay, I won't. Sorry, darling. But how are you? Is everything okay? Are you eating enough?'

'I'm fine, having a good time! Love you and Dad xxxx,' came back the answer.

'And how's the course? Is your winter coat warm enough?'

A reply didn't come. Alison put the phone to one side, sipping her tea and feeling lost. The house was already decorated for Christmas; it was spick and span. She'd bought their presents and made a stocking for Fiona. She glanced around. What more was there to be done?

Nothing.

She felt afraid suddenly, and stretched out her legs over John's lap for reassurance.

'What are we doing this weekend?' asked Alison.

'Absolutely nothing if I have my way,' said John. 'I'm completely knackered. The amount of people who want impossible jobs finished before Christmas!'

'Couldn't we, I don't know, go to a museum or something? Or to the shops together? The cinema? Dinner?'

'All in the same afternoon?' he smiled. 'Maybe something on the Sunday, love, but I need to rest up. Why don't you ask one of your friends? Julie?'

Alison squirmed. Julie had been one of her closest friends. She used to invite Alison to things, all through Fiona's illness, and had offered her genuine support, but Alison had kept her distance. Somehow it had seemed easier to just block everything out and keep going. Julie's invites had fizzled out these past few years. Alison supposed that she wouldn't keep inviting a friend to things either, if she just got constantly rejected. She knew she should reach out to Julie, but it seemed daunting. What did she have to offer? Julie would have been up to lots of interesting stuff.

'Maybe,' she answered.

John looked at her. 'Everything okay, love?'

'I don't know.'

'What do you mean? It's all good, isn't it? We've got our lovely, healthy daughter away at university, our own place, bit of spare cash for the first time in for ever – each other.'

'I know all those things, John, but that just makes me feel worse – especially when a lot of people don't have anything. But it's me. I just don't know what to do with myself.'

John turned off the TV. 'Oh, love. You've given so much to Fiona. You were a rock, to all of us. I used to marvel at how strong you were, when I felt like I was going to pieces.'

Alison felt tears spring up in her eyes. She remembered the dark days. Days when John would drink a bit too much, days when he'd stay longer at the worksite, and she knew it was because he didn't want to come home. He couldn't bear that he couldn't do more to alleviate Fiona's suffering, he told her once, through a whisky haze. He felt like he was letting her down.

But Alison had never wavered. She'd discovered a strength she'd never thought she had. She'd been there, by Fiona's side, always. Whenever she woke up, whenever she was in pain – no matter how bad, Alison had kept strong. She didn't think she'd even cried, once. That had come later, when Fiona had finally grown stronger. It was stupid, but she often cried herself to sleep now, lying awake and worrying about what might happen to her little daughter now that she couldn't be by her side.

'So why am I not strong now?' she said, her voice wavering. 'What do I do with myself?'

'You give yourself a break,' said John, firmly, 'after everything we went through. It's no wonder you miss Fiona – any mum would, and it's a hard adjustment. Then you get yourself a project. You use all that strength and energy and put it towards something. You've always been a doer, Allie.'

Alison knew what John said made sense. She needed to build herself back up, slowly. There was no point just wishing that the fun, confident woman she'd once been would magically reappear. She thought back to the party they'd gone to at the weekend, that couple, Malcolm and Izzy. Malcolm was an architect and John had worked on a few of his projects that year. They'd not known anyone there, and Alison had been reluctant to go, but John had said it would be good for his work.

She'd stayed around the edge of the room, nibbling on some tasty homemade mince pies, before a kind girl had come and said hello to her. What was her name? Laura. She'd been so animated and confident, chattering away about her job as a rehomer at Battersea, all the amazing people she got to meet through it.

An idea popped into Alison's head.

Maybe that was something she could do for herself. Go to Battersea, have a nice look around and maybe another natter with Laura. And see if she might be able to put herself to good use there.

*

Alison stood outside the gates of Battersea and shivered, pulling her coat round her. She felt nervous, for some silly reason. John had offered to come with her, but she'd said no – this was something she needed to do for herself.

She paid her entry fee and wandered up into the cattery, feeling very unsure what to do next. Laura was nowhere to be seen. She looked at some cats, some of whom were meeting potential new owners. It was heart-warming to see the kids – and adults – get so excited about a possible new addition to the family.

'Can I help you?' asked a woman.

'Oh, no, thank you,' Alison stammered. 'I'm just . . . just having a look, really. Don't mind me.'

'I'll leave you to it,' said the woman. 'But just let me know if I can help.'

Alison nodded, dropping eye contact.

It was hardly the engaging conversational opener she'd imagined. She'd wanted to say how she'd been training as a veterinary nurse, once upon a time, and that she was good with animals, but she'd been silly to think she could help much here. Alison turned to go, and almost bumped into Laura coming up the stairs.

'Hello!' said Laura, with a smile.

She looked tired, Alison thought. She looked like she needed a bit of looking after.

'Hello, Laura,' said Alison. 'I just thought I'd come and see you, and Battersea, after all you told me.'

'Wonderful!' said Laura. 'Are you here to rehome a cat, then?'

'Actually,' said Alison, 'I wondered if I might volunteer here.' She swallowed nervously. 'Laura, could I buy you a cuppa? I just . . . I just need to do this for myself.'

She knew she sounded silly, but Laura's gaze was so kind and understanding, she felt she could talk to her about anything.

'Of course,' said Laura. 'I can take a break about now, actually, so let's go to the café.'

They walked across the chilly courtyard, listening to the trains clanking into the nearby station.

Once they were sat down with two steaming cups of tea, Alison began to try to explain herself, forcing herself to get the words out. It was now or never. 'You see, my daughter was really ill, for years and years. And I looked after her every day – we barely took a holiday, in all that time. Then, miraculously, she got better. She's able to have a normal life. She's even away at university. And, believe me, I wouldn't have it any other way, but suddenly I don't know what to do with myself. I need something of my own. Some way to be independent, to be useful.'

She blushed furiously after this speech. It was the most she'd spoken to a stranger in years. But Laura was nodding.

'I understand, Alison. We have loads of volunteer roles here – they're always popular, so you might have to wait for the right one, but it sounds like you have a lot to give.'

Alison smiled in relief. 'I do, I'm sure of it!'

'And as long as you don't mind mucking in and getting dirty? I was on welfare before this job, and I have to warn you, there's an awful lot of poop.'

Alison laughed. 'I'm not fazed by a bit of poop. Actually, I was studying to be a veterinary nurse before Fi got so ill.'

'Oh, you'll be well used to the nitty-gritty then!'

The two women smiled warmly at each other.

'Sure you don't fancy another look around the cattery?' said Laura.

'Oh, go on then,' said Alison, feeling more chatty and confident than she had in ages. Her phone beeped. A message from Fiona.

'Hi Mum! Sorry about yesterday. Around now if you want to chat for a minute? xxx.'

Alison paused. She *did* want to chat to Fiona, desperately, but she also knew she needed to start building her own life.

She typed back: 'Can't now darling, but later?'

'What! What are you up to?' came the reply.

'I'm at Battersea, seeing about volunteering here!'

'That's so cool! Mum! I'm so proud of you! Talk later and you can tell me all about it xxx.'

'My daughter,' said Alison by way of explanation, feeling proud that Fiona was impressed by what she was doing. It would be nice to have something to tell her for a change, as opposed to just asking questions.

Laura grinned. 'Wish my mum was always on hand like you are.'

'Oh?' said Alison. 'Are you not close, then?'

'No, no, we get on – she and my dad are just always away on their travels. They retired a few years ago, then Dad had a bit of a health scare – he's fine now – but they resolved to make the most of it. I think they're in Thailand this Christmas.'

Alison couldn't imagine ever being so far away from Fiona, but she supposed it was inspiring.

'Come on, I'll show you a few of our current guests,' said Laura, getting up.

*

Twenty minutes later, and Alison was in love. Laura had shown her the cutest little cat, named Brandy, who she'd said would need a patient new home in order to help her settle in. Alison just knew she could do it. She looked at Brandy, perched at the bottom of the ramp leading up to her bed, her paws neatly together. Wanting to come forward and engage, unsure of herself. Well, Alison could relate pretty much exactly to that.

'Laura, I think this is the one,' she said, her cheeks flushed, eyes sparkling in excitement. She was completely transformed from the shy woman who had come in – her body language was different, her shoulders straighter, even her voice sounded different.

Laura grinned at her, the fatigue melting from her face. Alison's enthusiasm was infectious.

'Well, let's take it one step at a time. I'll have to set you up with a rehoming interview, and your husband would need to be here as well.'

'I'll call him right away,' said Alison, a woman on a mission. She dialled home.

'Hello, love, ready to come home?' said John. 'Shall I pick you up from the station?'

'No, darling, I want you to come down here!' God, it was years since she'd called him darling.

He laughed. 'Wow, Allie, I've not heard you like this in ages! What's happened?'

'I've met a little cat, she's called Brandy. And when I was here, it just fell into place. I want to volunteer here, but we could also give a home to a little one.'

John paused. 'Alison, it sounds like a good idea. Let me get there and we'll see what Battersea think. No promises, though.'

Alison nodded. 'Yes, that's true. I can't let excitement run away with me. Come down here, and we'll see how the interview goes. I love you.'

'Love you too,' said John, his voice bright. 'See you in a bit.'

Alison hung up and turned to Laura. 'He's on his way.'

'Brilliant,' smiled Laura. 'I'll put you down for an interview with one of our rehoming team. I'm heading off soon, but you will keep me posted, won't you?'

'Absolutely, Laura. And listen, I'd have just walked out if I hadn't bumped into you. I'm not the most confident person. Thank you for taking care of me.'

'It was a pleasure, Alison. Any time.'

Alison hesitated. She was wary of speaking out of turn, but having found her voice, she wasn't about to lose it again. And she'd noticed something at the party – she might be quiet, but she was observant. She'd seen how often Laura glanced over to check that the family's son – Rob, was it? – was okay, looking to catch his eye, to share a smile. Sometimes she'd crossed over and asked if he wanted another drink, or brought him something from the buffet table to try. And he'd rarely done the same for her. When she'd approached him, he'd taken whatever she brought gladly, and with a flashy smile, but then he'd often turned back to the group of people he was with, doing little to draw Laura in.

She chose her words carefully, not wanting to be seen as interfering. 'Laura, I do hope you've got someone to take care of you as well. Just make sure you do, because you absolutely deserve it.'

Chapter 14

Aaron Sanderson stared doubtfully at the green sludge he'd just prepared in a costly blender. How on earth was he going to get his nana to drink this? Converting it into a cocktail seemed the only plausible option, yet, given that it was 8 a.m. and he was trying to get Enid to lose some weight, as per doctor's orders, he could hardly take that course of action.

He put some avocado on toasted sourdough bread and set it on a little tray. What was he playing at, trying to turn his 75-year-old grandma into some kind of hipster? He suppressed a smile at the thought. She'd surely qualify, given the outlandishness of some of her outfits – although more and more recently, she'd given up her long-standing habit of wearing outrageous kaftans paired with huge glasses, and was increasingly tending to stay in bed. His groovy granny, that's what she'd called herself.

And she really was. Aaron had been raised by his grandmother – his own mum had had him as a teenager, to some man who hadn't wanted to know, and then promptly fled off to a kibbutz in Israel. Aaron was in touch with her, sporadically, whenever she turned up unannounced in a whirlwind of tie-dye clothes and stank the house out with incense and various other fumes, but he could hardly see her as a mother figure. It was Enid who had provided that. Don't be fooled by the zany dress sense, he often thought to himself. She had provided love and stability in abundance, as well as a firm set of rules, and he shuddered to think where he would be without her in his life.

He reminded himself of that as he went to take her tray in. He needed to be patient with her.

'Morning, Nana,' he said, setting it down gently on her bedside table. She stirred. She looked so old, he thought to himself. Her skin papery, her hair still dyed defiantly red.

Enid opened her eyes, which were as bright as ever, and peered at the breakfast tray. 'What's that?'

'It's a delicious smoothie.'

Enid looked none the wiser, so Aaron tried again. 'Lots of nice fruit and vegetables. Blended up, so it's easy for you to drink.'

'Puree!' she cackled. 'You're trying to feed me puree for breakfast, just like I did for you when you were a baby.' She waggled a finger at him.

Still sharp as a tack, thought Aaron, smiling. 'Well, they're called smoothies now and they're in fashion. Come on, let's get you upright.'

He helped Enid wriggle up to a seated position, and propped cushions around her.

She glanced at the tray, now in full view. 'Aaron! This is all sludge! I want my bacon and eggs!'

'Just try this, Nana,' said Aaron. 'You know what the doctor said about diet. You need to, erm, drop a few pounds.'

Enid glared at him and folded her arms.

'Please, Nana. It's with spinach and apple.'

She tutted and took a sip, shuddering theatrically.

Aaron counted to ten and reminded himself to be patient. Nana was more and more grumpy these days. She'd been hit hard a year ago by the death of one of her oldest friends, Reenie.

'They're all dying,' she'd said to Aaron, mournfully. 'I don't want to go, but this is like being the last one left at the party.'

Aaron missed Reenie too. She had been Enid's partner in crime – a regular fixture when he'd got home from school, finding the two of them sat at the kitchen table, cackling away together, wreathed in cigarette smoke, playing cards, and making him egg and chips for tea. At least Nana had stopped her smoking habit, although he suspected that was what had led to the weight gain. That, and not getting out and about like before. Reenie had been behind that as well, always coming up with some plan to visit a gallery, or to stroll around one of the neighbourhoods and comment on how much it had changed 'since our day', this leading to a shower of reminiscing.

'What about some lovely toast, eh, Nana?' said Aaron, brandishing the avocado toast. Was he about to pretend it was an aeroplane to get Enid to take a bite? More and more, the lines between them were getting blurred. It was the way of the world, he knew, that first you were taken care of and then it was your turn to take care. But it was tough sometimes. He also knew that Nana could be a lot more independent than she currently was. The problem was motivation. Her sparkle had gone.

Nana took the toast from him and bit into it. 'Ugh, slime!' she said.

'It's healthy avocado,' said Aaron, taking a bite himself. To be fair, it didn't taste amazing. He wasn't the best cook in the world.

'At least pop a bit of salt on it, darling,' said Nana.

He nodded. 'Will do. And don't forget, we've got the lady from Battersea coming round to pay you a visit today.'

Enid groaned. 'Aaron! This scheme of yours. You know I don't want visitors. I'm not even sure I want a cat in this place,' she said defiantly.

'Well, she's coming now anyway, and you need to get up and about, Nana.' He turned and went downstairs. He sprinkled salt on the avocado plus a layer of cheese for good measure – surely that would tempt Nana. He was putting a lot on this scheme to get a cat, he knew that. She'd had them before, but since the death of Mr Binks, five years ago, had said she didn't want another. He wasn't so sure about that. She'd always stopped to coo over cats on her walks with Reenie, and on the rare occasions he got her out of the house nowadays, she was no different.

He was convinced that Enid was depressed after the loss of Reenie. She relied on him heavily. He lived just a few streets across, but popped round several times a day to check in on her. He'd started staying the night a few times as well. The doctor had said that Nana was physically well, more or less, and she should keep moving as much as possible. Her blood pressure was a bit too high, as was her cholesterol, and they were slightly concerned about her heart. She was on medication, but she needed to change her lifestyle as much as possible too.

Aaron sighed. Of course he would care for her, but he wanted his own life too. He was studying to be a landscape gardener, and hoped to set up his business once he was qualified, which he knew would take significant time and energy. He was also thinking, more and more, how nice it would be to settle down with someone. He'd had a few relationships over the years, with a couple of them longer term, but nothing had quite worked out. He'd tried meeting people through dating apps but had found the whole experience quite baffling – he'd met up with one girl, called Seline, who was some kind of dancer. They'd gone to some incredibly trendy bar where he'd struggled to hear anything she'd said at all, and he'd got the feeling she was staring disapprovingly at his trainers for most of the night. She'd monologued for a long time about the stresses of being an artist, and when he'd tried to talk to her a little bit about his favourite plants, she'd said, 'Oh, so is that why your fingernails are so dirty?' He'd cringed and hidden them under the table for the rest of the night – he'd been potting seedlings all day and clearly hadn't scrubbed all the soil away.

He'd messaged her the next day to say 'thanks for a nice night, all the best with your dance', and she'd replied saying she was going to New York that very night and couldn't see him again for at least a month, but he could contact her in February, remind her who he was, and she'd see what her situation was. Breathtaking! He'd only been trying to do the polite thing and wrap things up between them – he didn't fancy a second date with Seline, thanks all the same. He'd deleted the apps after that.

He took a bite of the toast, which had now gone cold. It wasn't very appetising. He may as well make Nana some fresh.

He called up to her. 'Are you getting up? If you are, I'll make you tea and toast.'

'With butter?' came the reply.

'With a little bit of butter,' he conceded, smiling as he heard two feet land on the floor upstairs and the sounds of Nana moving about. She was a lot more mobile than she appeared. She'd been positively sprightly when Reenie was around, proud of her fitness and the fact she could touch her toes, and that was only a year ago. It was just the motivation she lacked.

Right, what time was the visit? Noon, wasn't it? He'd tidy up a little bit here, and then pop home, shower and change his clothes. And do his hair. He couldn't be scruffy when Jasmine came by; he wanted to make the right impression about the home they could provide. It was a shame Laura wasn't coming round. When he'd gone back to Battersea, he'd hoped she might be there, but he'd been greeted by Jasmine instead. She'd been more than helpful, but he was disappointed not to have seen Laura. She'd been so lovely, even when she was upset about the terrible Lettie Maddox and her nose was pink from crying – which strangely set off her big green eyes. He'd liked how open she was with him about what had happened, how easily she'd talked to him. He'd wanted to wrap her up in a big hug, as that was what it looked like she really needed. Well, maybe if this home visit with Jasmine went well, he might see Laura again when they went to choose a cat.

*

Shortly before 10 a.m., Laura walked up the steps to Enid Sanderson's house, noticing the pretty alpine shrubs someone had planted in large tubs by the front door. They added a touch of life, even in the midst of winter. She could do with that, if she was honest. Alison's comment about having someone to take care of her had resonated later that night, when she got back to the empty, beautiful house and heated up another ready meal. Rob had endless client dinners in December – she knew it wasn't his fault, and he was exhausted, but she kept thinking how nice it would be to have someone there to chat her day through with, cook with, have a cup of tea with. When Alison's husband John had turned up, rushing as he was so happy to see his wife animated again, she'd been struck by what a team they were. They'd been approved as rehomers, and John had fallen similarly in love with Brandy. All being well, they would pick her up this week – Alison had wanted to get the house ready, moving anything out of the way that might be dangerous to a feline arrival. Christmas was a surprisingly hazardous time for cats. They liked to scramble into a Christmas tree, play with ornaments and even chew on tinsel. Not to mention the fact that lots of festive leftovers were potentially harmful to hungry felines. It was a great sign that Alison was going to give the house the once-over, before introducing Brandy. Laura had been so touched to see John help Alison carry out a new bed and litter tray, keeping one arm free to sling around his wife. She tried not to think of her arduous journey with the cat carrier and Santa Paws.

Laura had felt her heart give a leap when she saw she was down to visit Aaron and his nana at home that morning. She'd put on a freshly laundered Battersea jumper, determined to make a better impression than last time – and had added a slick of the lipstick Lucie had given her, before deciding it was too much and rubbing it off. And then putting it on again, just a bit, with some lip balm over the top. It didn't hurt to look nice, did it?

She buzzed, and footsteps echoed down the hallway. The door opened, and there he was, Aaron. Looking flustered, his hair sticking up, dressed in jogging bottoms and a T-shirt that said 'I'm Sexy and I Mow It' with a picture of a lawnmower on it. He was even more gorgeous than she remembered. Laura loved this scruffy look, and wondered if he'd just got out of bed. The thought of Aaron in bed made her blush as red as her lipstick. What was she playing at? She had a boyfriend, the man of her dreams, and she needed to stop this.

And, anyway, Aaron looked anything but pleased to see her.

'What are you doing here?' he exclaimed, running his fingers through his hair, a worried frown on his face. 'Is it not Jasmine who's coming? At noon?'

Ah. Laura's heart fell. It was Jasmine he liked. Jasmine he was after. Made sense. Who wouldn't prefer Jasmine, with her easy laugh and smile that lit up any room? Well, that made things easier. She just had to be professional and do her job, and try to ignore how dismayed Aaron presently looked to see her.

'Good morning, Mr Sanderson,' she said, sticking out her hand and acting like she was in a 1940s film.

'Yes, yes, good morning,' replied Aaron, taking her hand and dropping it as soon as he could. 'I suppose you'd better come in then.' He looked agonised for a moment, before leaning back to allow her to pass.

He brought her through into a cosy kitchen, the walls lined with old postcards from exhibitions, travels and random black and white photos of London. It was a small room with a hatch through to the living room, and Laura could see a pair of double doors that opened onto the garden.

'I'll make you a cuppa, Nana's just getting up,' said Aaron. The kettle boiled and they both stared at it for what felt like a lifetime.

'Sorry, would you mind moving?' he said, gesturing for Laura to get out of the way. She moved, and he reached above her, taking down some mugs and teabags. She got a whiff of a delicious musty smell coming from him. *Stop it, brain*, she told herself firmly

Once he'd got the mugs, Aaron moved even further away from her and stared out of the window in complete silence. She shouldn't even be indulging thoughts of whether he was attracted to her, or wanting to talk to him more, or thinking about how nice it would be to be wrapped up in those arms. She was committed to her relationship with Rob, and she'd clearly built Aaron up to be some kind of fantasy figure – based on what? Him being kind to her when she'd been crying her eyes out? He was probably just being polite. What on earth had she been expecting? Certainly not this awkward, frosty reception.

She excused herself to the living room and tried to regain her composure. This would be a lovely home for a cat, she could see that. The living room, like the kitchen, was homely and comfy, and the back garden was a good size. It had been beautifully tended to. Red- and mustard-coloured grasses provided a splash of colour even in the midst of winter.

She pretended to look through the homing questionnaire as Aaron came through with two mugs of tea.

'Lovely garden,' Laura remarked.

'Yes, Laura, look—' but Aaron was cut off by Enid's entry into the room. She had wrapped herself in an enormous kaftan, and put on a pair of horn-rimmed glasses.

'Now you listen to me, I've decided I don't want a cat after all,' Enid said, her voice wobbly and yet determined.

Aaron groaned. 'Nana. We talked about this. You said you did and that's why Laura is here. To talk about the possibility.'

Enid eyed Laura. 'Listen to me, young lady. Sit down, in fact.'

Laura didn't dare disobey, and sat herself on a well-worn couch.

Enid settled into a rocking chair with the air of a queen, drawing a colourful rug around her.

'Now then, dear, I don't want to waste your time. I don't want a cat, and that's that.'

Well, that was easy, thought Laura. She could be back at Battersea and catching up on her admin within half an hour. She started to pack away the forms, then suddenly she caught a look between Aaron and Enid. She couldn't read it, exactly, but it contained so much hope, so much love, so much fear, so much frustration, that it made her pause. Laura glanced around the room again, wondering what to do, then her eyes lit on a photo frame, perched among others on the sideboard.

'Who's that, then?' she said, pointing to the photograph.

Enid turned to look and her face lit up with joy. 'That's my darling Mr Binks.' She took down the photo frame and passed it over. Laura gazed down at an enormous ginger cat, with a smiling expression on his face. Rob always made fun of her for thinking that cats had smiles, but they absolutely did.

'He's gorgeous,' said Laura.

'Light of my life, after Aaron. Master thief. Terror of the neighbourhood. Expert psychologist.'

'Psychologist?'

Enid nodded. 'Yes. When Aaron was a teenager, I knew there were things he wouldn't tell me. And if I was ever worried about him, I used to send Mr Binks into his room, and Aaron would soon be chattering away to him, in that special cat voice he uses – do your special cat voice for her, love?'

Aaron shook his head. 'I've no idea what you're talking about,' he said, firmly.

Enid rolled her eyes. 'Anyway, I knew he at least had Mr Binks as a listening ear. And Mr Binks gave *excellent* advice.'

Laura liked Enid an awful lot. A shame she'd decided so adamantly she didn't want a cat.

Enid passed her another photo. 'Here's Mr Binks on his birthday.'

Mr Binks sat proudly in front of some kind of birthday dinner, a single candle in his bowl and a bow tie on his collar.

Enid was getting into her stride now. She passed Laura another photo frame.

'And here's Aaron, dressed up as Mr Binks for his school fancy dress day!'

'Nana, please,' said Aaron desperately, but it was too late. Laura had the frame in her hands and was stifling an enormous laugh at the sight of a young Aaron dressed in a cat suit, his face painted to match Mr Binks, his gloved hands up at his face like paws, and his mouth open in a miaow.

'I like your whiskers,' Laura said, before she could help herself.

'Thanks,' Aaron muttered, staring at the ceiling.

'So, what happened to Mr Binks?' asked Laura, deciding she wouldn't torment Aaron any more and handing the frame back to Enid.

Enid's face fell. 'He was put down, poor darling. A few years back now. He'd had a mighty good innings, the vet said, especially as he had that feline immunowotsit, the last few years of his life. He just got too poorly to enjoy his life any more. And when that happened, straightaway I thought enough's enough. It would have been cruel, selfish, of me to keep him alive when he was suffering, just because I knew it would break my heart to let him go.'

Laura nodded. From the sound of things, it seemed like Enid had been a wonderful cat owner.

'And there's just not room for another in your life?' she asked.

There was a silence. Enid gazed out of the window and Laura wondered if the old lady had heard her.

Aaron cleared his throat. 'So, how's Felicia doing?'

Enid looked at him. 'Who's Felicia?'

'One of Laura's special cats at Battersea,' he answered.

'Oh, well, she's fine,' said Laura. 'We thought we'd found a home for her recently, but no luck. She's been putting on a bit of weight, so we're trying to keep her active and watch her diet a bit.'

'Hmph!' said Enid, loudly, looking at Aaron.

'How are you doing that?' said Aaron, studiously ignoring his grandma.

'Just lots of games. She does like to snooze, being in her senior years, but she can still be sprightly when she chooses to.'

'She needs the right motivation?'

'Exactly.'

'Remind me what she looks like?'

Laura loaded up her phone and passed it to Aaron. She could sense Enid twitching to ask, and she suddenly clocked what Aaron was doing.

'I think she's ever so cute,' said Laura. 'Black and white, with a unique splodge on her chin.'

'Agreed!' said Aaron.

'It's a shame she's not had much luck,' continued Laura. 'She was ever so scared and nervous when she came to us. When she comes out of her shell now, you'll have a friend for life – you just need to give her a bit of time. But I do feel sorry for her. I want her to have a home so much – it's hard when a perfect match comes in, and then they choose another cat.'

'A bit like being the last one left at the party,' said Enid, wistfully.

'Yes,' said Laura, 'I suppose it is a bit like that. The other thing too is that she has a heart murmur.'

'Just like me!' said Enid.

Laura smiled. 'Yes, and I hope you take good care of yourself. Chances are, with the right care, Felicia will live a good while yet, but some people are reluctant to take on a cat who might have additional health costs. And she has a type of virus, called FIV.'

Enid harrumphed. 'Well, when you love someone, you love them just as they are! Didn't stop me loving Mr Binks, because he had that little virus too. And I've plenty squirrelled away for a rainy day.'

Laura caught Aaron's eye. 'Well, I guess I should be off, if you've decided against it. It was lovely to meet you, though.'

Enid's tone was wavering now. 'I mean, I suppose it couldn't hurt just to take a look at her if you've got those photos on your phone?'

Laura shrugged. 'Sure.'

She passed her phone over to Enid.

'You're going to have to come and help me, love. I'm no good with technology.'

Aaron and Laura both moved over to Enid's side at the same time, and Laura walked straight into his chest. *FIRM*, screamed her brain, before she told it to shut up. They each moved to either side of the rocking chair, but she was still aware of how close he was.

Laura swiped through a few photos of Felicia staring into the camera with those gorgeous eyes, playing with her mouse, rolling on her back. She'd taken a few videos of Felicia, and she played those too. The cat was even more charming – purring wildly and doing little hops and headbutts against the phone screen.

'Oh, my pet!' cried Enid. 'What a darling she is!'

Aaron grinned and touched his hand to Laura's arm briefly, before snatching it away.

'She really is,' said Laura. 'I just know she'll find the right home eventually.'

'Well,' said Enid, 'I don't suppose it would do any harm just to take a look at her? Be nice to get out and about, wouldn't it, Aaron? We never go out these days! A trip to Battersea, and maybe a hot chocolate after.'

Aaron beamed at her. 'Great idea, Nana.'

'In fact, I'll just get myself dressed and put my shoes on now, and then we'll be off!' Enid scrambled up out of her chair, moving about three times as fast as when she'd come in.

Aaron laughed. 'Nana, hold on just a second. You've got the doctor this afternoon, remember, and I have to go to work in the meantime.'

Enid's face fell.

'But soon – this week?' said Aaron.

Enid nodded vigorously. 'And we'll see you there, Laura! Give Felicia a big cuddle and tell her she'll be home soon.'

Laura smiled in delight. Could this be it, finally? She'd hold her breath until they actually met.

Aaron saw her out of the front door and, for the first time, she felt the awkwardness between them drop away.

'Laura, thanks so much for sticking with us,' he said. 'It means the world. I want to get Nana loving life again, and I think Felicia could be the key.'

With that, he gave her an impulsive hug, gathering her in his arms and holding her tightly for a moment. She inhaled the scent of him.

'God, I'm so sorry,' he said, aghast, pulling back so rapidly that Laura staggered for a second. 'The moment running away with me. Sorry. I do apologise. Completely uncalled for.'

Well, the awkwardness was back.

'Well, I'll see you both soon,' Laura said, backing away too. 'Bye! Don't forget to wear your whiskers!' She cringed as soon as she'd said it, noticing Aaron's obvious embarrassment.

*

Idiot! Aaron told himself, as he watched Laura disappear down the path and out of the gate. He should have said something funny and smart back when she made her cute whiskers remark. What a disaster the whole thing had been. He'd been expecting Jasmine in two hours' time, so when the doorbell went and it was Laura, looking absolutely gorgeous and completely together, he'd got the shock of his life. And he was a mess. He hadn't showered, his hair was all over the place, and he was wearing that ridiculous slogan T-shirt Enid had bought him. Then his nana had got out that awful photos of him and started going on about his cat voice, which he would *never* use in front of anyone but her.

What else, oh yes – his Mr Darcy act, when he'd been staring at the garden for several minutes, trying to think of something, anything, to say to Laura, and failing miserably. She'd seemed cold with him too. Thank goodness he'd had the presence of mind to get her to move out of the way in the kitchen, so she wouldn't pass out from his smelly T-shirt. Only to completely undo it when he'd taken leave of his senses and hugged her at the end, happy and relieved that Nana had responded to their tactics to get her interested. He'd actually heard Laura take a deep sniff when she was in his arms, probably in complete disgust, and of course then he'd had to shove her away as quickly as possible, although he'd wanted to keep her in his arms for ever. Oh well. Maybe, just maybe, he could redeem himself if he saw her again at Battersea.

Chapter 15

Laura's guilt about crushing on Aaron cranked up a notch when she got home that night to find Rob already home from work and making her a Thai red curry, his absolute speciality.

'And Laur, I wanted to ask what you're doing on Thursday,' he said. 'I'm hoping you might agree to a date night with me? I've got something special up my sleeve.'

He looked so hopeful standing there by the stove, Laura's heart melted.

'Of course I'm free,' she said.

'Great,' said Rob. 'I promise you, you're going to love this!'

Laura loved a surprise, and her mind already kicked into gear, imagining what they could possibly be doing.

It was only the next day when Jasmine came to find her that she remembered what she was meant to be doing on Thursday. The Battersea Christmas Carol Concert.

'Don't tell me you've forgotten,' said Jasmine, rolling her eyes. 'I've ordered us cat ears to wear and everything.'

Laura groaned. 'I'm so sorry, Jas. But I've said yes to Rob now, and he's arranged everything for that night.'

'Ah,' said Jasmine. 'Of course. He wouldn't fancy popping into the carols first?'

Laura shook her head. 'There's not time. He said he'd pick me up here at 6 p.m., sharp.' She was so disappointed by the clash. She loved the carol concert, and it was a festive social occasion that really felt like *hers*. But she could hardly back out of whatever Rob had organised now.

'Well, enjoy it,' said Jasmine. 'There'll be other years. I'm sure Mr Perfect has something wonderful planned for you and you won't even give it a second thought when you're out and about having fun.'

Laura hoped so. Aaron and Enid were meant to be popping in on Thursday afternoon and, if all went well, Felicia would be off to a new home. Laura gulped. She knew she would find it a very emotional moment, and an evening with Rob would be just what she needed to cheer her up.

*

As Laura prepared to leave the house on Thursday morning, Rob got up and staggered through to meet her.

'Morning, pea,' he said, kissing her blearily. 'Now, no peeking, but I bought you something new to wear tonight.' With a flourish, he reached up to behind the living-room door and brought down a zipped clothing case.

Laura clapped her hands. 'Really! Can't I just take a look? Are we going somewhere fancy?'

He laughed. 'Well, you might want to look a bit glam.'

She couldn't remember the last time she'd been glam. She went back to the wardrobe and rummaged around, looking for her heels. Thankfully, the nude colour tended to go with everything, and she shoved them in her rucksack for later.

She tumbled out of the front door, giving Rob a peck on the lips.

'Remember, be ready by six!'

Laura spent the morning wondering where he was taking her, and wanting to take a peek at the dress, but she'd promised Rob, and this was part of the surprise. *His* surprise.

Her heart warmed. In the mirror in the loos, she stared doubtfully at her hair. She'd washed it that morning, but left it to dry naturally and it had gone flat. Was it worth getting it done for the night?

She decided yes. She'd take a tiny bit longer in her lunch hour, and treat herself.

She messaged Alan, who'd taken her number to invite her to New Year's drinks and to stay in touch about Santa Paws. Hadn't Rufus mentioned he was a hairdresser, always trimming Evie's long fur? Yes, that was right. She asked if he could recommend any salons in London that were nearby, explaining about her date night with Rob.

'How THRILLING!' he texted back. 'Maybe the opera! Maybe the London Eye at night – what if he proposes?!!!'

Laura's heart jolted. God, what if Rob *did* propose? She'd say yes, of course, but she suddenly felt anxious. She hoped it wasn't one of those big dramatic proposals with loads of people watching, that wasn't her at all. Before her imagination could run away with her, Alan had messaged her again with the name of a stylist.

She went over at lunchtime, to be met by a smiling woman called Carly, who shampooed her hair, trimmed it and gave her the biggest, bounciest blow-dry of her life, finished off with lashings of spray so it would last the afternoon.

'I love it!' said Laura, gazing at herself in the mirror and tossing her mane about. 'What do I owe you?'

Carly shook her head. 'No charge. Alan's already paid. Said he wanted to treat you after all you'd done for him.'

Laura was touched. She took a selfie of her hair and sent it to Alan, thanking him profusely.

He texted back almost immediately. 'Beautiful, Laura! He's lucky to have you. We'll see you soon, and maybe with Santa Paws as well!'

As Laura headed back into Battersea, she saw a familiar face browsing the Christmas gifts in the shop.

'Lucie?' said Laura, walking over to her.

The girl from the make-up counter turned. She looked pale, drawn, but smiled hugely to see Laura.

'Your hair!' Lucie said. 'You should wear it down more often!'

She thanked Lucie, and asked how her granny was doing.

Lucie's face fell a little. 'She's not good, Laura. We're hoping she can make one last Christmas, without being in too much pain. Mum's coming over as well. I'm here stocking up on goodies for Bumpkin – we're all determined to make it a good one. But, hey, what are you doing tonight – I hope something special with hair like that!'

'My boyfriend's taking me somewhere where I have to look glamorous,' Laura said. 'To be honest I'm getting increasingly nervous as the day goes on!'

Instantly, Lucie was a woman on a mission. 'Nails?'

'I have them?'

Lucie inspected Laura's short nails. 'Disaster. I would say varnish, but let's not draw attention to these. And I'm guessing falsies wouldn't last a minute with you working here.'

Laura bit back a laugh. Now she knew Lucie's soft side, she could take this kind of thing with a pinch of salt.

'Now, make-up? You've got the lipstick?'

'I've got my make-up bag with me.'

'So, what's your look going to be?'

'Well, just some mascara, maybe?'

'Oh my God Laura, have I taught you *nothing*? Right. Get into the loos. I'm going to spruce you up a bit.'

Fifteen minutes later, Lucie had done what she called 'a basic face', with foundation, blusher, eyebrow pencil, eyeshadow, eyeliner, mascara, bronzer and powder.

'Then you just have to slick on your lipstick and go,' said Lucie encouragingly. 'That's all. Very easy.'

Laura stared at herself in the mirror. She liked this look better than the one Lucie had done previously, though she didn't feel very much like herself. But even she had to acknowledge she looked glamorous. She hugged Lucie goodbye, and made her promise to stay in touch with updates about Bumpkin's first Christmas.

'Who are you and what have you done with Laura Summers?' said Jasmine upstairs, goggling at her. 'We're going to have to put you on email and phone duty. Can't possibly have you messing up this look before your big night! If I know you, you'll have your face buried in a cat's fur before too long and smudge the whole thing off.'

Just how scruffy did she look the rest of the time, Laura was beginning to wonder, as her colleagues boggled at the transformation. She was glad to pass most of the afternoon in the office. Truth be told, she felt more and more nervous, almost light-headed. She was desperately hoping Aaron and Enid would take Felicia, while being terrified of the moment that she had to say goodbye. She was also suddenly anxious about the date night with Rob – what exactly did he have planned? She'd texted him hoping for a clue, but had received no reply.

'What's this hanging on the door?' asked Jas, wandering in later.

'It's a dress Rob got for me to wear tonight,' Laura said, her voice tight.

'What's it like?' said Jas eagerly.

'I haven't looked yet.'

'What!'

'Rob said it had to be a surprise!'

Jasmine looked at the clock.

'Oh, come on, it's three-thirty – you've held out this long! I'm dying to have a peek.'

Maybe it would make her feel less nervous if she knew what she would be wearing. Laura unzipped the bag to reveal a stunning gold sequin dress.

Jasmine gasped. 'That's gorgeous! Go and try it on immediately, Laura! No arguments!'

Laura nipped into an empty office, locking the door behind her, and got changed into the dress. It was a tight fit, and quite short too. And quite plunging. And there wasn't much of a back either. There wasn't that much to it at all. She wasn't sure how she felt in it, turning this way and that in front of her reflection in the window. But it was bound to feel weird wearing such a glamorous dress in the cattery, she told herself. She'd enjoy looking the part later on.

Grabbing her jumper to quickly cover up with in case anyone came, she emerged from the office. Thankfully, the cattery seemed quiet and she hoped she could show Jasmine the dress without anyone else seeing.

She dashed across, in her bare feet, to where Jasmine waited for her in the office.

'Bloody hell!' said Jasmine. 'You look like the fairy on top of the Christmas tree!'

'You don't think it's too much?'

'No! It looks amazing! Stop clutching that tatty old jumper to you, for God's sake, and give us a twirl.' Jasmine took the offending item from Laura's hands.

Laura sighed and made a twirl.

'Laura! Like you mean it!' said Jasmine. 'Come on, there's no one around, you might as well go for it. Try the "Dance of the Sugar Plum Fairy", or something!'

Laura giggled. Jasmine always knew how to bring her out of herself. And she was right, she might as well loosen up and enjoy herself.

'Oh God, this is such a tune,' said Jasmine, as Mariah Carey's 'All I Want for Christmas Is You' came on the radio.

Laura loved that song too. She backed out of the office and began to sing along, giving it her best diva attitude. Taking advantage of the empty floor, she pranced in front of the cat pods, singing the lyrics and pointing at each cat in turn, saving an extra-special wiggle and finger-point for Felicia as she attempted to hit the high note, twirling round and bumping straight into –

Aaron.

'Don't let us stop you, girl!' called Enid, clapping her hands together as she came up the stairs just a little way behind. 'I'm about to join in myself!'

Aaron's mouth was open in shock. Laura couldn't blame him, especially if he'd heard her high-note attempt, which had sent some of the cats scurrying off to the back of their pods. Oh my God, she was mortified. She couldn't even look at him. This was even worse than the home visit.

'Er, hello,' he muttered, staring at his feet.

'Right, yes, hello,' said Laura, as Jasmine came up behind her.

'What a stunning dress!' said Enid, as Laura folded her arms and hunched over, desperate to avoid attention. 'Oh, come on, dear, stand up straight and let's have a look at you! Oh, Aaron, doesn't she look a dream?'

Aaron was staring straight ahead, apparently incredibly interested in a poster about cat flu.

'I suppose,' he said stiffly.

Suppose, thought Laura indignantly. *Well, fine!* Jasmine handed her the jumper and she quickly shoved it back on, only to find that she was trying to get her head through an armhole and couldn't find her way back out. Laura heard Jasmine snort with laughter beside her.

'Come here, Laura, right, there you go. There's where your head goes,' said Jas, helping her navigate the jumper.

Laura wished she could stay inside the safe cocoon of the jumper instead of having to look at Aaron's appalled face one moment longer. But that wasn't really an option, and she emerged, finally, from its confines.

'I will leave you in Jasmine's capable hands,' she said, her voice squeaking, stalking off with her head held high, before realising the jumper was actually on the wrong way round. Well, that was that. Any ideas of Aaron having a crush on her were well and truly out of the window. She remembered his disappointment that it had been her, and not Jasmine, coming to do the home visit, his coldness, the way he'd pulled back from hugging her.

She returned, dressed in her jumper and jeans, to find Jasmine leading Aaron and Enid to Felicia's pod. She hung back, not wanting to intrude, waiting with bated breath.

'Here's our ladyship!' cried Enid joyfully, her face aglow.

Enid went in first. Felicia was in her bed, and she pricked up her ears and gave a little chirruping miaow as Enid approached. Enid reached out a hand, and Felicia stood up, stretched and sniffed it, before butting her head against Enid's fingers.

'That's a girl, that's a girl,' Enid murmured. After a few moments, she gently picked Felicia up in her arms. The cat was calm and happy, blinking and purring and glancing up at Enid as if recognising a kindred spirit. And in that moment, Laura knew Felicia was home.

Aaron went in afterwards, leaving Enid with Jasmine. Laura walked over to them.

'I love her, I love her!' beamed Enid, doing a little hop from foot to foot. 'Can she come with us today?'

'I think she can,' said Jasmine. 'I'll just have you talk to our vet first, make sure everything is explained about the heart murmur.'

Laura's attention was focused on Aaron's meeting with Felicia. He'd crouched down on the floor and she was sure she could hear him muttering to the cat. Was this the famous cat voice that Enid had teased him about? She wished she could hear.

Felicia pricked up her ears and trotted over to meet him, rubbing her cheek along his hand. He picked her up, and she looked quite frankly delighted to be cuddled in his arms. *Well, who wouldn't be?* Laura thought. Did Felicia make eye contact and wink?

Her phone buzzed in her pocket. A message from Rob.

'Laur, I'm so sorry but I have to stay in a meeting till six. I'm sending a car for you, early – and it'll drop you off for a bit of pampering before to make up for it. Can you be ready in a half-hour or so?'

'Yes, sure,' Laura typed back. Her nerves were rising again. This was stupid – it was a date with her boyfriend, not a job interview.

She let Jasmine handle the rest of the paperwork for Felicia's adoption, and let herself into the pod with Felicia to spend as much time with her as possible before saying goodbye.

She snuggled the cat on her lap, burying her face in her fur before remembering the make-up. Oh well. She breathed in and listened to Felicia purr, feeling her nerves calm.

'I'm scared, Felicia,' she said, but she didn't know quite why. The cat simply stayed still in her arms, rubbing her head against Laura's chin.

'I'll miss you,' whispered Laura, tears springing up in her eyes. 'Thank you for being my friend. Thank you for always listening. Thank you for teaching me so much. I hope you have a wonderful first Christmas in your new home.'

Felicia purred even more loudly.

Then, before she knew it, Aaron and Enid were standing in front of the pod, a cat carrier by their feet.

'You take as long as you need to,' said Enid, but Laura was worried that if she dragged this goodbye out much longer, her make-up would be cried all down her face.

'Do you want to put her in, Laur?' said Jasmine, and Laura nodded. She prepared the cat carrier with Felicia's blankets and favourite toy mouse, and encouraged the cat to walk in. Felicia trotted in happily, as if she couldn't wait to start her new life.

'Goodbye, Felicia,' whispered Laura, trying not to have a total meltdown. 'Now be good, and be happy in your new home.' She pushed her fingers through the mesh at the front, and Felicia bumped against them, before giving a little miaow as if to say, 'Be brave!'

And, with that, Laura opened the pod door and passed the carrier to Aaron. Her phone beeped – the driver was almost near Battersea to pick her up.

'Let me know how she's getting on,' said Laura, trying to keep the tremble from her voice. 'Let me know how her first Christmas is.'

Enid nodded. 'We will, dear, don't you worry. She's going to live life like the queen she is.'

Laura said goodbye before she burst into tears completely, quickly crossing back to the office and getting changed into her fancy dress and heels. She'd forgotten a bag, so she had to bring along her rucksack, filled to bursting with her jeans and fleece, which hardly went with the look.

She inhaled deeply a few times and told herself to get it together. This was what she had dreamed of, wasn't it? A home for Felicia in time for Christmas, and a wonderful date night with Rob. She pulled her shoulders back, held her head high, and went down the stairs.

*

Aaron had just finished loading up his battered car with Felicia's new bed, litter tray, food and all the extra goodies that Enid had decided were essentials. Enid was sitting in the back with Felicia in the carrier beside her, the two of them getting along famously already. She looked years younger – she had a grin on her face the likes of which he'd not seen for ages.

But Aaron couldn't shake the image of Laura hugging Felicia goodbye, the way she'd hurried away with tears streaking down her face. He couldn't shake the image of her full stop – he'd thought about her constantly ever since she'd paid them the home visit. He wasn't so sure about the sequin dress and glamorous get-up, and, judging by how keen Laura had been to get back into her Battersea uniform, neither was she. But when he'd seen her prancing about and laughing today, his heart had skipped a beat. He was kicking himself for how awkward he'd been when she was at Enid's house. What must she have thought? The moments when they'd relaxed and worked together to convince Enid to visit Felicia; the moment he'd touched her arm and felt a spark that he was certain must have been visible from space; the moment he'd dared to gather her up into an enormous hug. He couldn't shake how alive he'd felt. He had been nagging at Enid to start living her life again – wasn't it time he did the same?

He took a deep breath. He'd seen a sign advertising the Battersea Christmas Carol Concert, that evening. He could go in, ask Laura if she wanted to go – casually, playing it cool – and, if she said yes, drop Nana and Felicia off and leave them to settle in, before making it to the service.

Right. No time like the present.

He marched back round to Battersea's gates – only to see Laura, wearing her stunning short dress and a pair of heels, strutting over to a posh car, and looking like a movie star. All the awkwardness had gone. Now she looked glamorous, poised, completely in control. The driver got out and opened the door for her. Laura got in and he shut it behind her, with a definitive clunk.

So much for that plan. He swallowed down his disappointment.

'Not fair, is it?' came a voice nearby. Jasmine.

'What?'

'Laura, swanning off in posh cars while the rest of us lump it!' she said, jokingly.

'Where's she off to?'

'Her boyfriend's whisking her away for some posh secret surprise evening. Got her that fancy dress and everything.'

Boyfriend. Of course. The kind of guy who spoilt her rotten, who sent private cars for her, who was probably going to propose with a ginormous diamond to delight her just in time for Christmas. Why did he think someone like her would have been single? And, even if she was, why would she be interested in a man like him, with soil under his fingernails and a rust-bucket Vauxhall Astra?

Chapter 16

Laura sipped on a glass of champagne, glancing around the opulent room. She was waiting for Rob in the bar of one of London's best hotels, where the walls were painted in coral and chandeliers dripped from the ceiling. It was like being in a film. She'd been whisked to the hotel's spa beforehand, where an attentive therapist had done her nails (Lucie would approve, even if Laura did find her new talons a bit weird – she could probably make good use of a scratching post with them) and spruced up her make-up. Afterwards, she'd been led through to the bar to find a glass of champagne waiting for her, and a text message from Rob saying he'd be ten minutes more. A waiter came up to her and asked if he could get madam anything more, and she said, 'No thank you', stuttering out her reply.

Then Rob was there, making his way towards her with a big smile, wearing a charcoal suit and a white shirt, open at the neck. Laura was glad to see him, he looked so at home here, and she felt herself relax a little. She'd been silly to get that nervous. This was Rob, who she woke up next to and went to sleep next to every day. Who she loved, she reminded herself.

'You look completely gorgeous,' he said, kissing her on the lips and then regarding her again. 'Wow, Laura! Just look at you!'

She felt suddenly shy. 'Thanks. So do you. And thanks for the posh treatments, it was really nice.'

'You deserve a bit of pampering, Laur. Was your manicurist good? The girls in the office say she's the best.'

'Well, I don't have much experience to compare her with, but I think my new claws are pretty impressive.'

She moved her red nails up to her mouth and made a little 'miaow' sound.

Rob laughed, and then put his hands over hers to gently halt the cat impression. He glanced at his watch. 'Better drink this fizz quickly, sweetheart. We need to be out of here in about ten. How was your day, anyway?'

Laura gulped at the glass. 'To be honest, it was a bit weird. Remember Felicia? The cat?'

'How could I forget,' said Rob, drily. 'The cat who almost cost us a multimillion-pound campaign.'

Laura chose to ignore that.

'She found a new home. She went off just before I got picked up.' Laura felt upset again. Maybe she was coming down with something. She imagined Felicia settling into her new surroundings, spending the night in her new home, and hoped everything was going well. She pictured Aaron helping her settle in, and was glad that he was there. He might be awkward with her, but she knew how kind he was.

'Aw, but that's good news, isn't it? You've been wanting that for ages! Congratulations, Laura!'

Rob clinked his glass against hers. She supposed it was good news. She put a bright smile on and pushed down the hollow feeling. She was tired, that was all. The Christmas break was badly needed.

'How about your day? Winding down at all for Christmas?'

He groaned. 'I wish. It's non-stop. Near-constant disaster on the FruitySoap campaign, but I'll spare you the details – we should get going.'

Rob waved the barman across and paid the bill with a flourish, slipping down from his seat and holding out his arm to Laura. As they moved across to the entrance, Laura noticed people glancing at them – at the young, glamorous, successful couple they were. She collected her coat from the cloakroom and Rob helped her into it, shouldering the bulging rucksack himself.

'I think I've just worked out your Christmas present,' he said, smiling. 'This coat is getting pretty tatty.'

Laura supposed it was. That would be nice, she told herself, a glam new coat from Rob. She wasn't renowned for looking after her things, she had to admit. Jasmine was always rolling her eyes at the number of holes, cake crumbs, cat hairs and tea spills that appeared on Laura's clothes. She should try harder. Be more of a grown-up. She and Rob made their way out into the glittering drizzle of December in London, and walked down the street for about five minutes.

'Here we are,' said Rob, drawing her towards a small entrance way, roped off and guarded by a ferociously trendy-looking woman.

'Name?' she asked, blinking her enormous lashes. *Could they be real?* Laura wondered.

'Rob Henderson. We're with Andre and Rebecca.'

'Of course,' said the woman, instantly snapping back the rope. 'Rob and guest. Welcome.'

'Who are we with?' asked Laura, as they made their way down the stairs. 'I thought it'd be just us?'

But maybe Rob didn't hear her and she had to concentrate on not tripping up. Soon, the staircase opened out into a spectacular space, a high, arched ceiling, which was decorated with thousands of dangling stalactites, lit up with tiny fairy lights. The floor was rocky and uneven, interspersed with ornamental pools of water and weird sculptural fountains. Laura had to admit the effect was breathtaking. It was like a cathedral, almost, or a very cool Santa's grotto. She glanced around at the diners, seated at tables and chairs carved from stone, lit with candles. They were a trendy bunch, all black-framed glasses and no smiling.

Laura slipped her hand into Rob's. He gave it a squeeze and then they arrived at a large marble booth, where two people were seated.

They rose to their feet. The woman was impossibly tall, with high cheekbones and those perfectly groomed eyebrows, like you only saw on movie stars, and dressed in a long, form-fitting silver dress. In contrast, the man was short and quite round, stuffed into a black polo neck that he didn't quite have enough neck for. What on earth was going on? How were they part of the date night? Rob greeted them.

'Rebecca, you look stunning,' he said, kissing her on both cheeks, and shaking the man's hand.

'And this must be your girlfriend?' said Rebecca, in perfect cut-glass tones. 'My dear, you look charming! So nice to see our creations being worn by real people!'

What did she mean?

'Hi, I'm Laura,' she said, clutching her hands together. Should she attempt to kiss Rebecca, like Rob had done? She wasn't sure she could reach that high.

'*Enchanté*,' said the man, in a French accent. 'Andre.'

They sat down, and Laura stared at what she supposed was the menu. The place appeared to be called 'Cave' and each dish was named after a precious gem or mineral. She had very little idea what each dish was – everything seemed to be deconstructed or some kind of variation, and the descriptions by each one didn't help much. They tended to be something like, 'Trust us on this journey into darkness

162

– smoky, oily, forbidden', and a list of ingredients she'd never heard of.

'We can't thank you enough for getting us in here,' said Rob, sounding like a radio show host. 'The hottest restaurant in London! Can you believe it, Laura?'

'No,' said Laura, which was an honest response, especially given that she was very chilly in her dress. She cast about for something to say. 'The Cave,' she read from the menu. 'What's it all about, then?'

Rebecca laughed. 'You're so funny! Le Cave' – she pronounced it like 'kaaav' and Laura remembered Rob doing something similar when they visited a wine cellar in France – 'is an immersive dining experience, fusing cuisine from all around the world with the sheer raw brutality of nature.'

Laura nodded.

'The chef is only twenty-two,' added Andre. 'She's quite the sensation.'

'I've read so much about her,' said Rob. 'Didn't she spend her adolescence in Japan?'

'Yes, that's where she learnt her knife skills.'

When had Rob been reading about this chef? And who *were* these people?

'So, how do you know Rob?' she asked Rebecca.

'We're clients,' said Rebecca. 'We just signed up with the agency for their help in building our brand – we're fashion designers, and looking to break out into the mainstream a bit more. Still high-end, of course,' she finished with a little laugh.

Laura's blood ran cold. Rob had brought her on a *client dinner* as their date night?

'And my dress?' she asked, her heart thudding.

'One of our creations! We left a couple of samples with the agency, of course, and it's just splendid to see it worn by a real woman, not our usual supermodels.'

Laura forced herself to smile. So much for her Cinderella moment. Rob had looked no further than the walls of his office to surprise her. The sequins on the dress sparkled a little less brightly.

'I see,' she said, wondering when she could get her hands on a drink and feeling tears rise up. Tears, and a whole lot of anger. She'd missed the carol concert for *this*?

A stern-looking waiter came and took a drinks order. Laura hadn't even seen a menu. Rob ordered for the table.

A glass of white wine came, and she took a sip. It tasted musty and fizzy.

'Well, here's to a wonderful partnership,' Rob said, in a toast.

'And a very merry Christmas,' added Laura, trying not to think of Jasmine and her colleagues having fun at the carols, probably singing their hearts out right now, fuelled by mulled wine.

'I'm not sure about this wine,' said Laura quietly to Rob. 'It tastes a bit off.'

Rob smiled at her and laid a hand on her knee. 'It's organic, a natural wine. The taste and texture are a bit different but you'll get used to it, and then you really do appreciate it.'

Wasn't that actually always the way? Laura had to get used to whatever Rob wanted. Well, she was just about sick of it. This was meant to be *her* night. Hadn't Felicia taught her to speak up? She just had to do it for herself.

She raised her hand and called over the unsmiling waiter.

'Excuse me, I'm not really a fan of this,' she began.

Rebecca and Andre exchanged glances. Well, they were welcome to their pond water.

'Of course, madam,' said the waiter. 'What would you prefer? I could make you a cocktail?'

They agreed on a lychee martini which, when it arrived, was much more up Laura's street. She slurped it down, and felt the alcohol go straight to her head, and then waved for another. She deserved it, didn't she? After the day she'd had. And wasn't this meant to be a night for her? Emotion bubbled up in her throat.

'So, what shall we eat?' said Rebecca.

Rob reached for the menu and began to scan it. 'Let's take that, and then a few of these – I love the sound of the sea bream, and then some of the deconstructed ribs, and then perhaps some of the frozen pea mousse?'

'Can I have a look?' asked Laura, but Rob just patted her again on the arm.

The meal ordered, after much toing and froing on technical terms with the waiter, conversation resumed.

'We really are terribly excited to have you on board,' purred Rebecca to Rob. 'We can't wait to see what your plans are.'

'All in good time,' said Rob, but Rebecca continued to gaze at him expectantly, her smile poised, until he continued. 'Well, I could perhaps show you a few of our ideas for the logo, later on?'

Laura gritted her teeth. Was she honestly expected to sit through a presentation?

'So, Andre, where are you from?' she said, in a bid to steer the conversation onto normal ground.

'Paris,' he said. 'Have you visited?'

'No,' she said. 'Rob was meant to take me, actually. But it's never materialised.'

Rob looked round at her at the mention of his name. 'What's that?'

'Just saying how you've never taken me to Paris.' Was she talking too loudly? A few people at the next table had turned around. She stifled a hiccup.

'But you must come!' said Andre. 'Come when we have the launch there. We'll take you to all the most glamorous spots.'

Rob beamed. 'Well, how about that, Laura?'

'Lovely,' she said. 'That's so kind of you.' Furious as she was with Rob, she didn't want to be rude to Andre.

'And you, Laura, do you also work in advertising?' asked Andre.

She shook her head. 'No, not any more. I work at Battersea Dogs and Cats Home. I find new homes for the cats that get brought to us.'

Andre clapped his hands. 'My dear, how quaint!'

'I love it,' Laura continued. 'That feeling of giving a cat a second chance, and a human too, most of the time. One of my favourite cats was rehomed today, she's called Felicia and she's just wonderful. Look—'

She pulled out her phone to show him a few pictures. Rob leant over and whispered to her, 'Not now, please, Laur.'

Laura gazed down into her lap. An image of Felicia was on the screen, as if she was perched on Laura's knee in miniature, giving her strength.

'We'll just slip outside for a quick cigarette before the food arrives,' said Rebecca, getting up with Andre.

Once they were gone, Rob turned to Laura with a huge grin on his face. 'How about this then, Laur? Pretty cool date night, huh?'

Laura shook her head. 'A date night where it's a client dinner, and I tag along in one of their dresses?'

His face fell. 'Laura, it's the most exclusive restaurant in London at the moment. The waiting list is six months! I wanted you to see it, to do this together. It's meant to be a once-in-a-lifetime dining experience. People have flown from New York just to try to get in.'

Laura pressed her lips together. 'But a date night where I can't order anything for myself, I can't even talk a little about myself? Just have to listen?'

Rob sighed. 'This is my work, Laur. And, yes, some of this is that I have to keep these clients happy, so if Rebecca wants to see the designs, she has to see them. But you and me can go for a drink after, just the two of us. That'll be nice, won't it?'

She nodded unhappily. The food came; it was exquisitely prepared – each plate like a miniature work of art. The other three oohed and aahed over each teeny morsel, about the flavours, the skill of the chef, and Laura smiled and nodded. She barely uttered another word, but she did sink a few more martinis and wished for something substantial and stodgy – a baked potato, laced with cheese and beans, perhaps.

Before their desserts – several of which they'd been told didn't contain any sugar, thus ruining the point, in Laura's opinion – she went to the loo. It took her a while to find it, the door perfectly disguised in a faux rockface. She gazed at herself in the mirror and barely recognised what she saw. A glamorous girl in a very tiny gold dress, her hair enormous, her face perfect, her eyes empty. Laura pulled out her phone and texted Jasmine.

'How's the Christmas carols?'

But Jas didn't text back, no doubt too busy enjoying herself to check her phone. Laura sighed, and wondered for the millionth time how Felicia was getting on. She imagined her in that cosy sitting room, on Enid's knee, and her heart gave a pang. Would Aaron be there as well?

She braced herself to walk back across the restaurant and rejoin Rob and the others. Just a few bites of some sugar-free pudding to get through and then hopefully she could go home.

She trudged over to their table, and asked if she could have another martini. Rob glanced at her nervously.

'Maybe some water, darling.'

'Well, there's barely been enough food to soak up a drop of booze. Isn't it meant to be Christmas? Eat, drink and be merry? Not much of any of that going on in here.' The words were out of her mouth before she could stop them.

'I think someone's had a bit too much to drink,' said Rebecca with a patronising smirk. 'Here, you can have my bread – I didn't eat it.'

Laura pounced on a piece of bread that appeared to be the size of a 50p piece, while Rebecca and Andre looked away discreetly.

'What's got into you?' muttered Rob.

'Loads of martinis,' Laura announced. 'Maybe if I'd actually been allowed to speak, I wouldn't have had to find something else to keep me entertained.'

She gave a small hiccup.

The desserts arrived. One of them was sticks of celery with raisins glued on with honey.

'We call this frogs on a log,' said the waiter, and Laura erupted into a cackle.

'Are you kidding?'

'No, madam. Frogs on a log is made from the finest locally sourced celery and honey from London bees.'

But Laura had seen a twitch of amusement round his mouth.

'Can I get something proper, please, like a massive chocolate brownie or a mince pie?'

He hesitated. 'I'll see what I can do.'

'I'll leave you all to your frog bog,' said Laura. Her cheeks felt awfully hot. She gulped at some water and tried to focus on the conversation.

'Here you are, madam,' said the waiter, returning with a wink. He'd done her proud. An enormous brownie, covered in chocolate sauce, practically swimming in it.

She smiled what was her first real smile of the night. 'I can't thank you enough.'

'I do apologise,' said Rob. 'We fully understand that the chef wouldn't prepare dishes like this—'

'On the contrary,' interrupted the waiter smoothly. 'This comes with the compliments of the chef, who said to tell you she enjoys eating precisely the same thing as often as possible.'

He gave a small bow and retreated, and Andre grinned at Laura. 'Good for you, Laura, ordering off-menu! A true connoisseur!'

Laura tucked into the brownie, which was absolutely delicious – melt-in-the-mouth, gooey and chewy all at the same time. And it would hopefully soak up a few of the martinis.

She offered a spoon to Rebecca. 'Fancy a bit, Becky?'

Rebecca hesitated and then, unable to resist, snatched the spoon and took a big mouthful. 'Oh, that is *divine*.'

Andre tried a spoonful too, and was similarly in raptures, but Rob declined, sticking to frogs on a log.

'You got any pets, then?' Laura asked, running the spoon round the bottom of the bowl in order to catch any last droplets of sauce. She heard Rob give an exasperated sigh. Well, whatever. She'd sat through twenty minutes of identical-looking logo designs earlier on.

'Yes,' said Rebecca, smiling. 'We have a cat who keeps us company in the design studio. She's very much a street cat – she comes and goes as she pleases, but we make sure she's fed and watered and take her to the vet if she's poorly. Actually, we were thinking of naming a dress after her – the Colette.'

Laura smiled. 'I love that!'

'Well, it's the one you have on. It's meant to be edgy and unpredictable, but also feline and loving.'

Laura thought Rebecca was talking gobbledegook, but it was somehow hilarious. The room span a little bit. 'I completely agree. That's exactly how I feel in this dress. Unpredictable.'

Rob looked nervous. 'Right, we should probably be heading for home.'

'Oh, just one more drink here?' said Andre. 'They're meant to have a wonderful selection of spirits.'

Laura looked at Rob. He'd said they would at least have a drink just the two of them. He glanced at her for a moment and she raised an eyebrow. There was no way he couldn't understand what she meant.

'Of course,' said Rob. 'Just the one.'

After they'd had some Japanese liqueur – so strong that Laura could barely stomach a sip – talked more, paid the bill, said their goodbyes, Laura and Rob were alone in the street. Hit by a wave of freezing air, Laura suddenly felt incredibly sober.

'Right, so shall we go home or do you, erm, want to try to find somewhere for that drink?' said Rob, looking sheepish.

The realisation hit her like a lightning bolt. She didn't want another drink, but she didn't want to go home with Rob. She wanted to go somewhere where she felt loved and accepted and understood. And, with this date night that had been all about him, where she was dressed up, playing a character that certainly wasn't her, she realised she didn't belong. Not in Le Cave – and not with him.

Tears formed in her eyes. Was she really going to do this?

'Laur, for goodness sake, I don't know why you're so upset,' he said, trying to sound jolly. 'I know I messed up a bit tonight, but I'll do better next time. Do you know how many girls would love to be in your shoes, heading out on a night like this?'

'Are you serious?' she said, feeling tears stream down her cheeks. 'You can't even understand a little bit why I'm upset? The date nights were meant to be about you and me, about doing things for the other person that they like.'

'And you didn't like the food? You didn't like the fancy drinks? All the treatments earlier today?'

Laura shut her eyes and told herself he was reacting like this because he was hurt. 'I *did* like them, who wouldn't? But it's not me! I would have preferred to go to the Battersea concert in my tatty old fleece, with you by my side. That would have been my perfect date night.'

He sighed, exasperated. 'Laura, let's just go home.' He turned around and walked a few steps away from her, before looking back. 'Laur. Come on.'

But Laura's feet wouldn't move. She was sick of following on behind him.

'Rob,' she began, her voice wavering. 'Rob, I can't do this any more. It's just always on your terms. Me fitting in. Me tagging along. I need someone who's on my team. I . . . I . . . I think this is over.'

A group of men in Santa hats passed by, shouting to each other. Laura shivered, wrapping her coat tighter around her.

Rob stared at her. 'Are you serious?'

Laura nodded.

There was a moment of stillness between them, a moment where Laura remembered the love she used to feel for him, how she couldn't believe that a man like Rob would be interested in a woman like her. She almost reached out her hand, almost stepped towards him, but why couldn't he do that for her? Why couldn't he come back and walk by her side?

Then the spell was broken. 'Fine,' said Rob in a tight, hard voice, and he turned around and walked quickly out of sight.

Chapter 17

Laura's eyes were raw from crying. Her resolve in the street had wavered as soon as she'd seen Rob march away from her, and realised just what it would mean to lose him. Had she been overreacting, tipsy from all the booze? She was upset at how quickly Rob had walked away, leaving her alone in London, without uttering a word to try to persuade her they should stay together. She told herself it was because he was hurting, of course he was, but she was hurting too. She closed her eyes briefly, feeling them sting, and hoped she could just slip off into an oblivious sleep for a bit.

'Here, Laur,' said Jasmine, her voice low. 'I've brought you the spare duvet. You sure you're okay on the sofa? I can kip out here and you can take my bed if that's better?'

Laura shook her head as Jasmine covered her up with the duvet.

'Goodnight, Laur. I hope you sleep. Things will seem calmer in the morning.'

Jasmine had been amazing. Shivering in the middle of London, Laura had rung her to explain what had happened. Jas had come home straight after the Christmas carols earlier that night, to check on the cat she was presently fostering, and when Laura had called her, crying and tipsy, she'd ordered her to get straight into a cab and come round to hers.

'And you'll stay here for as long as you like,' she'd said. 'What are foster carers for?'

There was a cat staying with Jasmine who had been very nervous in the cattery – Missy, whose owner had been unable to keep her due to council property rules. Missy was all set up in Jasmine's spare room, and Laura insisted she couldn't be moved. She'd be fine on the sofa.

She'd poured her heart out to Jasmine, over a hot chocolate and dressed in a spare pair of pyjamas – thank God she was finally out of that dress. She explained the date night with Rob and how she'd suddenly realised that her needs would come second, always. That she'd fit in with *his* life, and not vice versa. Or that's how it had seemed. Now she was alone, she wondered what on earth her life would look like without him.

Laura awoke slowly the next morning, feeling groggy. The duvet was warm around her, but there was something else – she twisted round and realised that Missy had crept in for a cuddle. She was down at the bottom of the sofa by Laura's feet.

Laura smiled and called to her softly. The little black cat crept slowly up the duvet, Laura feeling the light weight of her paws, and then came to snuggle up by her neck, purring.

'Well, at least I'm not waking up alone,' said Laura. 'Thanks for keeping me company, Missy.'

She couldn't believe the events of the previous night. It seemed like some bizarre dream. She checked her phone, suddenly longing for a text from Rob. Surely he wouldn't let her go without a fight? But there was nothing from him. She remembered how quickly he'd left last night, that he hadn't even tried to reason with her, and swallowed back tears. More than two years together, and he let it go like that? Yes, she was being irrational in a way – it was her who had broken up with him – but it still hurt.

'Morning,' said Jas, peeking round the door with a steaming mug of tea. 'How you feeling?'

Laura wriggled upright, careful to keep Missy snuggled up in the duvet. 'Slightly hungover. A bit scared.'

'That sounds normal.'

Laura nodded. 'I had a whole life with Rob. The thought of that going . . . I mean . . . It's a lot. I was thinking we might be headed for marriage and babies. Fat chance of that now that I broke up with him in the middle of Soho right before Christmas.'

'If you truly think something between you could be mended, then that's one thing. But if it's just about being scared of the new, then it's time to be brave. I'm going to hop in the shower first, and look you out a towel.'

Laura drank her tea and stroked Missy, letting Jasmine's wise words sink in. It occurred to her that she felt more comfortable on the sofa in Jasmine's house, with piles of ironing waiting to be done and books strewn everywhere, a cat purring by her, than she did in Rob's house. *Our* house, she tried out, but it didn't ring true. Rob wasn't a bad guy – she knew some girls would love getting dolled up and being taken to a fancy restaurant, but that wasn't her. And it had never been her. Still, she shivered at the thought of being alone, just in time for Christmas. She was starting to realise just how much her life, apart from Battersea, had revolved around him. The Battersea Christmas Carol Concert had been the only date in her calendar that had felt like hers. The rest of December had been taken up with seeing Rob's friends; she'd even missed a meet-up with her uni chums in order to see some of Rob's crowd instead.

Jasmine came down and dropped a clean towel at her feet. 'Come on. There're cats to be rehomed.'

Laura groaned. 'Can't I just stay here and snuggle Missy?'

'Nope. It'll do you a bit of good. Keep your mind occupied while things become clearer. And I've found you a clean shirt as well.'

Chapter 18

Lights.

Noise.

People, asking questions.

Too much.

Jack Waite shut his eyes and hoped it would soon stop. He got overwhelmed so easily these days, after the injury. Everyone expected him to be the guy he'd been before. He'd seen pictures of this guy – good-looking, confident, sat astride a motorbike. He'd been told about the crash, the crash that should have killed him, but instead had shaken his brain about and damaged the delicate organ in ways that the doctors still didn't fully understand. He'd been in a coma for several weeks, before he'd regained consciousness and seen his worried parents gazing at him.

Everything was difficult. From tying his shoelaces, to walking, to remembering what he was meant to be doing. Apparently, he'd had a job as an area sales manager, been a popular boss to a whole team, always ready with banter, but he couldn't imagine that now. He got tired so easily, sleeping for hours at a time. Lights and movement were often overwhelming. His favourite thing at the rehabilitation centre was the swimming pool – floating in the blue water with his ears submerged, he could just about feel peaceful.

He was in an occupational therapy session that morning, designed to test how he could cope in the kitchen. The rehab centre had a kitchen where they could practise these kinds of basic tasks, so they wouldn't go home and set everything on fire or starve to death, one of the other patients had joked.

'Jack?' the therapist was saying. A nice woman. He couldn't remember her name. 'Jack? Do you think you can try opening the tin for me?'

Jack stared at the tin of beans as if it was his mortal enemy.

'I don't like beans.'

That was a lie. He *did* like beans, preferably accompanied by sausages and eggs, but he wasn't sure he could manage this.

'Well, you don't have to like them. It's just to see if you can do it,' she said patiently, and Jack felt bad. Everyone was so patient with him nowadays. The worst thing, and he felt guilty for thinking this, were visits from his family and friends. He knew he was lucky they came. But he found it too much, the weight of their hope that he would return to being the great guy everyone had known before. They came bearing their anecdotes, their photos, reassuring him that he'd be back to normal before he knew it.

Jack knew that wasn't going to happen. The doctors had explained he would most likely live with some of the effects of the injury for ever. He would adapt, and some of his functions would improve, but as for being the man he was before? Forget about it. And he couldn't bear to disappoint all these people who loved him. He got sick of being nagged to do his rehab exercises, simple tasks that before he'd have done like lightning. A lot of the time, he just gave up without even trying that hard. It wasn't worth the flurries of rage and frustration that erupted in him. He'd heard that Old Jack was easy-going and calm – well, New Jack certainly wasn't.

The therapist pushed the tin of beans gently towards him.

Jack wondered how much time he'd have to waste before their session was up. He picked up the tin opener, willing his fingers to work properly. It felt heavy and awkward in his grip. He had to use two hands to move it to the rim of the tin. Frustration rose up in him. He just wanted to chuck the tin through the window.

'That's good,' murmured the woman. 'Remember, you couldn't do that last week.'

'Some progress,' he said, sarcastically, but she just smiled and nodded.

'Now, can you try to fix it on the tin?'

Jack looked at it, feeling panicked. How the hell did this work? He must have done this thousands of times in his old life. Oh, Old Jack, what an idiot you were not to appreciate what you had. Jack felt his emotions bubble up, bitterness, regret, pain. This was another feature of the injury, apparently. His emotions fluctuated wildly. So much for the laid-back guy he'd been before. He was aware he was sweating, and almost laughed – he couldn't manage a tin of beans, when before he'd been spending hours in the gym.

He tried to prise the opener apart, just a little, to fix it on the tin. It clattered to the floor.

'Take a minute,' said the therapist. 'You're doing so much better. I know it doesn't feel like it, but you'll get there.'

Jack closed his eyes and willed the world to stop.

A knock at the door.

Luke peered round the doorframe. Luke was one of the specialist nurses at the rehab centre, and Jack liked him. Luke never made him feel like a disappointment. He brought Jack music to listen to, when his brain was up to it, and they sometimes talked about songs and bands they liked. This was something Jack clung to. His love of music was still the same as before. He and Old Jack would have that in common, at least. All the classic stuff – The Rolling Stones, Led Zep, The Who.

'Hi, Jean,' Luke said. 'Okay if I take Jack now?'

She frowned, then her expression cleared. 'Oh, yes! The visit to Battersea.'

Was that today? Well, fine, thought Jack, if it meant he could escape the ordeal by beans. What were they meant to be doing again?

'Enjoy it,' said Jean. 'And I hope you find the perfect cat for us. The beans will still be here when you get back.'

Ah yes! Jack remembered now. They were going to choose a cat for the rehabilitation centre. He or she would live in the grounds of the beautiful old hospital building. Luke had explained how the cat would be a therapeutic cat, for everyone to benefit from. Jack didn't really get it, but Luke had asked him to come with him and help, and Jack knew he needed to start getting out into the world again.

'You okay?' asked Luke as they made their way into the cold air.

'Not sure I like beans,' said Jack.

'Fair enough, mate,' Luke said with a laugh, and for a moment Jack felt almost normal again, like they were two friends bantering in a pub.

Luke explained that he had rung in advance and that Battersea's staff had already come to visit the grounds, so today they were going to meet a cat they thought might be suitable. Luke said they were going at a time in the morning when the centre would be quiet, but the journey over was still difficult. Navigating public transport was a nightmare. Luke helped him buy a ticket, that was okay, but there were still plenty of people darting up and down the stairs, and the noise of the train was the worst. It clattered through Jack's skull.

'Here, put these on,' said Luke, pulling a pair of head-phones out of his bag. 'They're noise-cancelling.'

Jack took them gratefully and put them over his ears. The noise of the train faded away and he felt like he could breathe again. He nodded at Luke and gave him a thumbs-up, before shutting his eyes. Luke understood when he needed his space, and only gave him a gentle nudge when they were arriving at the station.

'Here we are,' said Luke, as they arrived at Battersea's gates. Jack had already spotted two big billboards nearby, featuring a dog and a cat. They were buzzed through and walked across and into reception.

'This is Laura,' said Luke, introducing him to the woman who waited for them there.

She smiled and shook his hand. Was he imagining things, or did she look sad, somehow? Sometimes Jack thought that because the injury had slowed him down so much, he occasionally took in more about people than they wanted to give away. But maybe that was just wishful thinking. The world now tended to pass him by in a noisy blur, people keeping up with the rush at warp speed.

They climbed the stairs into a cosy cattery, with cats safely in their pods. It reminded him slightly of the hospital – that sense of being looked after, of being cared for, of recovery.

Now they were standing in front of a cat's pod, with the lady who had greeted them – Laura, was it? He tried to focus on what she was saying. Things went in and out of his head without registering much these days.

'This cat is called Pie,' she said. 'And he's very calm. He came in to us as a stray, but he's settled very well.'

'Do you want to go in and meet him, Jack?' said Luke.

Jack nodded. It had been hard following the conversation between Laura and Luke. He imagined that Old Jack would have done so with ease, asking questions and cracking jokes. He felt sad. Better to be away from the humans for a while.

Jack went into the cat's pod and sat down. It was quite chilled in there, really. An environment he could cope with. He was exhausted from the beans earlier in the day, and from the journey to Battersea, despite the noise-cancelling headphones. Despair rose up in him. This was who he was now. Knackered from a morning of failing to open some beans and getting on the tube. There was no sign of the cat, either. Pie. Was that what Laura had said it was called? Silly name for him. Jack didn't get the whole fuss about getting this cat. Other people in the centre had been really excited, but not him. A cat couldn't mend his broken brain, could it, or turn him back into Old Jack. He wondered if Old Jack had liked cats. Probably. Old Jack seemed to like everything and everyone. Sometimes he wanted to punch Old Jack right in the face, for being so happy and bloody perfect.

A movement caught his attention. A cat, peeking out at him from the bed. A tortoiseshell pattern. Then the cat unrolled from the cosy, curled-up ball he had been in, stretched extravagantly and strolled down to investigate Jack.

He reached out a hand to the cat, who sniffed his fingers tentatively. Then the cat came a little closer, before hopping delicately onto his lap and curling up. And that was that. No fuss.

Suddenly, Jack felt differently about the cat. He wanted him to stay there, on his knee, so much. Very gently, he placed his hand on top of the cat's little head, and gave it a stroke. He was rewarded with a soft purr, like a tiny engine.

What was this feeling? Jack cast about for the word to match to it. With the cat on his lap, he was calmer. But that wasn't this feeling.

Acceptance.

That was it. This cat accepted him completely, exactly as he was now. The cat didn't look disappointed and make him think how much better Old Jack's knee would have been to sit on. No, the cat was just fine with Jack right here and now, exactly as he was.

Jack sat in there for a bit, letting the feeling wash over him.

After a while, he noticed Laura and Luke smiling at him through the glass door. They crouched down to speak to him.

'How's it going?' asked Laura, softly.

'Good,' said Jack. That hardly covered it, but it was as much as he could muster right now.

'Well, that's good,' she replied. Jack liked her. Like Luke, she was a person who didn't crowd him or rush him. She let people be who they were.

'So, what do you think?' asked Luke. 'Shall we take him?'

Jack looked down into the cat's face. Their eyes met. Was it just him, or did he detect a gleam of roguishness in the cat's eyes? He found himself smiling.

'Yeah. Yeah, I reckon we should.'

Chapter 19

Back at Jasmine's after work that day, Laura was relaxing with a cup of tea and a snuggle with Missy, and trying hard not to get trapped in a swirling torrent of thoughts. She'd wondered about telling her mum about her and Rob, but she wasn't quite sure she was ready to. It made it all too real. Plus, she didn't want to ruin her parents' Christmas break by having them worry about her. Ditto her other friends: they'd be wrapped up with their own boyfriends and families. Laura shivered and cuddled Missy a bit closer, comforted by her soft, warm fur and gentle purr. Jas arrived back then, having braved Oxford Circus for some last-minute shopping.

'Just getting you a stocking,' she smiled, holding up a felt stocking with a tabby cat on it.

'Oh, Jas,' said Laura, 'I don't want to impose on you for Christmas Day, though.'

'You're not imposing. To be honest, it's nice having you here. You can join me at Battersea! Plenty to be done there.'

Laura thought about it. Her parents were away on their cruise for Christmas, and she could hardly loiter around Rob's flat on her own while he was down with Malcolm and Izzy. After his silence, she'd texted him, reasoning that he was too proud and hurt to do it himself. She'd sent a long message, hoping that he was okay, and saying maybe they could talk some more if she called round to get some clothes, and he'd sent a cold reply, saying simply, 'Come round after midday tomorrow, I'll have gone to my parents by then.' That had stung. He didn't seem to care, at all. She had still wanted to talk things through, to apologise for how it had happened, to explain herself, to see what Rob thought. But clearly, for him, it was completely done. She'd decided not to go round – she could restock on toiletries and pick up some clothing basics. She was overdue a shopping trip anyway.

How could it be the 23rd already? Christmas Eve was almost upon them, even if Laura didn't feel very Christmassy.

'If you're sure, then I'd love to,' she said.

Jasmine smiled. 'Brilliant. Then that's all settled. And look, I've moved Missy's bed out of the spare room, so you can kip in there tonight. She's pretty settled in now anyway.'

'Tempted to keep her?'

Jasmine raised her eyebrows. 'Yeah, if I'm honest. What a pity you couldn't adopt Felicia, Laur. I was thinking what a hard day not to have her for a cuddle.'

Laura's heart sank. She'd seen Felicia's empty pod that day, cleaned already and waiting for a new arrival. Of course, she wouldn't have had it any other way, and she'd kept her promise to get Felicia a home for Christmas, but she longed to snuggle up with the cat and forget about her heartache.

*

Christmas Eve wasn't that much brighter. Indeed, Laura felt her spirits droop even further as everyone around her seemed to be laughing and happy. She hid herself away in the office for most of the day, feeling very sorry for herself. Even the cattery, decorated with tinsel and cards, did little to cheer her up. She'd seen a picture of Rob on Instagram, back with his parents for Christmas. He looked happy, smiling into the camera, and she was glad that he was with them, adored and supported. She could have been in that picture, too. Seeing it made her miss her own parents more. She knew they loved her, that they'd be back in the UK soon, but she sometimes wished she had a close-knit family who were homebirds like her.

Snap out of it, Laura, she told herself firmly, but it didn't work.

She heaved on her scruffy coat at the end of the day, and prepared to head back to Jasmine's. Jas was having Christmas Eve drinks with some old friends, so Laura would be alone for the evening – well, apart from Missy. Jas had said she could join them, but Laura didn't feel up to a rowdy evening of socialising with people she didn't know. So much for finding her confidence and speaking up for herself. She was realising just how much of her life had revolved around Rob – when was the last time she headed out with friends of her own? They were all busy with their own lives now. That little insecure voice popped up time and time again, telling her she couldn't make it on her own.

After a busy journey home – London was emptying out as everyone headed back to their families in all corners of the country – Laura shut Jas's front door firmly behind her. The house was silent. Laura knew that Missy could be shy, so it was no wonder she wasn't running to greet her. Laura couldn't help but think of Felicia's friendly greeting, and the way her tail would twitch in the air when Laura approached.

She slumped on the sofa in the dark, and went to reach for the chocolate advent calendar before remembering Jas had cracked open the remaining doors the night she'd broken up with Rob, declaring it an emergency.

Laura sighed. She couldn't even be bothered making it to the kitchen. Here she was, then, single, homeless – or soon to be – and without Felicia. She knew she was having a pity party, but somehow she couldn't help it. She drew her knees up to her chest and wept.

Then, her phone buzzed. She glanced down at it. An email, sent to her Battersea account, entitled 'Feliz Navidad!'

Laura clicked it open.

'Hola Laura!' it began.

It was from Carlos, the little boy who had adopted Skittle.

I know you said to let you know how Skittle's first Christmas was, but, for us, the celebrations start on the 24th, so here we go! Actually, Skittle is going to be very lucky as we are going to celebrate today AND then do my dad's traditional celebrations tomorrow – my brother and sister and me want to experience a real English Christmas dinner!

Soon we are going to start eating a big Christmas Eve dinner, and open a few presents. Skittle has his own special bowl and we have bought him a fluffy toy to chase, although at the moment, he is enjoying chasing the wrapping paper more.

I can't thank you enough, Laura, for helping us choose Skittle. Before he came to join the family, I didn't have any friends in England and I missed Spain a lot. But now I have the BEST friend in Skittle! He is always there when I get home from school, ready to play and cuddle, and he always cheers me up. Mum said he had to sleep in his own bed but that didn't last a night, and now he cuddles up with me. Finally, he has had the chance to meet my big brother and sister, and they love him too. I am going round to Tilly's house, whose dad adopted Amber, and she will visit Skittle over the holidays, so hopefully soon I will have a friend in school as well.

We all wish you a Bon Nadal! (Happy Christmas!) and hope you eat lots of delicious food and have a wonderful time. In case you ever want to try it, we are attaching a recipe for a Catalan speciality – crema catalana.

There were a few photos attached, and Laura downloaded them. One of Skittle playing with the ball of wrapping paper, standing on his back legs and batting it in mid-air. Another one of the whole family, Carlos beaming at the front and holding Skittle in his arms.

Her heart warmed suddenly. She'd played a part in that! It brought her great joy to think of the cats she'd helped find new homes in the last month enjoying their first Christmas with a new family. Laura imagined them in various homes across the country, their new stories starting – just like hers was. She tried to cling to a feeling of excitement and optimism. Now was the time to be strong.

She got up from the sofa and put on the Christmas tree lights. There! That was better. Then she turned on the radio, and tuned it to Magic FM, to get some Christmas tunes on. 'Jingle Bell Rock' was playing, and Laura couldn't resist a quick boogie – thank God the curtains were drawn.

Missy looked cautiously round the door.

'Don't worry, girl!' called Laura. 'Just getting into the Christmas spirit!' The cat quickly darted away again.

She glanced at the recipe from Carlos. Hmm. The ingredients list looked a bit complicated, but it had given her an idea. She'd bake cookies as a Christmas surprise for Jas. Laura went through to the kitchen and pulled out the ingredients from the cupboards.

A couple of hours later, she was covered in flour and had eaten rather a lot of cookie mix, but she felt a whole lot happier and a whole lot more Christmassy. She'd made plenty of cookies so they could take some into Battersea and feed the volunteers. She'd found a cat-shaped cookie cutter in one of Jasmine's drawers, and she'd even shaped the leftover bits into paw prints.

Laura glanced at her watch. It was almost eleven, and no

sign yet of Jasmine. She left her a cat-shaped cookie and a glass of water with a sticky note saying, 'Drink this! Happy Christmas!', and went to bed. As she drifted off to sleep, her mind ran over the cats she'd helped find new homes that month. There were some that stood out more than others, where people had shared their stories with open hearts. There was Carlos and Skittle; Lucie and Bumpkin; Wanda and Teddy; Mark and Amber; Alison and Brandy; Jack and Pie; Casey and Notch; Rufus, Alan and Santa Paws – and Enid and Felicia. And Aaron.

Nine cats, nine shared lives. Nine Christmas Days. Nine new beginnings.

Chapter 20

'Wake up, sleepyhead, he's been!'

One thing that baffled Laura about Jasmine, for all the time she'd known her, was her remarkable resistance to ever being hungover.

It was 7.30 a.m., and Jasmine had bounced into her room like she'd had twelve hours' sleep, not attempted to creep in at 2 a.m. and accidentally woken Laura with her giggling.

'Are you not even a tiny bit hungover?' croaked Laura, reaching for the cup of tea Jasmine had brought her.

'Nah, not really! Reckon your little kitty cookie sorted me out,' said Jas, beaming, her skin somehow radiant. She put a stocking bulging with presents on Laura's bed.

'Right! Open this, and then we need to get off to Battersea before too long.'

Well, what girl, no matter her age, didn't perk up at the sight of presents?

Laura opened her stocking with glee. A chocolate orange, some knickers and socks, a new scarf and hat, and a book of poems about cats. She embraced Jasmine in an enormous hug.

'I'm lucky to have a friend like you,' Laura whispered. 'Look, I didn't have time to do something amazing like this, but I did find these in a little shop.'

She handed Jasmine a small box, and her friend unwrapped a pair of earrings – tiny origami cats, made from pretty patterned paper.

Jasmine gasped. 'I love these, Laura! You plonker! You didn't have to get me anything.'

Laura grinned. Jasmine only ever called her a plonker when she was really chuffed about something. 'I wanted to. You've been such a good friend to me.'

The girls hugged again, before Jasmine chivvied them into the shower and out of the door, handing Laura a pair of glittery cat ears to wear.

'Seriously?' said Laura.

'Very seriously. They're your pair from the carol concert you missed. We'll take the car – there's no public transport today, so you don't have to worry about the jealous gazes of other commuters.'

They drove through the streets of London, which were practically deserted. They spotted families strolling through the streets, kids playing with their new toys and windows lit up with pretty festive lights.

Laura inhaled and tried not to wonder what Rob was doing. She'd decided not to text him on Christmas Day, leaving him to get on with enjoying his family. No doubt Izzy would be delighted to hear they'd broken up. No, she focused instead on the nine lives, and wondered how Mark and Amber were getting on . . .

*

Across London, Mark had been up since 6.30 a.m. He knew he was ridiculous, as he still woke up early every Christmas (sometimes earlier than his own kids), but there'd been an even earlier riser than him. Amber. His fuzzy ginger alarm clock.

Those first few days with her had been a wonderful roller-coaster ride. He'd played with her for hours, laughing delightedly at her antics. She'd chase her feather toy around frantically, flopping onto her side and then getting up again as soon as she had her breath back, before eventually collapsing into a purring slumber on Mark's knee (or sometimes neck). He loved to watch her round tummy rising and falling as she snoozed, and it was even better when she was dreaming – her little face would twitch, and sometimes even her paws, as if she was scampering even in her dreams.

Having another heartbeat under the same roof was simply wonderful. He wasn't home alone any more – and being at home now had a purpose apart from getting work done. The kids adored Amber too – she brought energy and joy into every encounter, and she smoothed over any interactions with Jess, his ex. She'd always come in for a cuddle when she dropped off the kids, and had brought round some old fluffy jumpers to make Amber a little bed.

For this, her first Christmas, Mark had made her a stocking. The kids had helped – they'd picked out toys for Amber from Battersea, including a pink mouse, and a smart collar for Amber to wear when she was ready to go outside. They'd made her cards as well, wishing her a very 'Miaowy Christmas' in her new home, and saying how much they loved her.

Amber had woken him up at six-thirty by jumping on his head, which had given Mark the fright of his life and made him laugh hysterically. Amber had then got a fright at his laughing, and had hopped down the bed, arched like a witch's cat, her tail all frizzed up.

'Come here, poppet,' Mark had said, scooping her up and carrying her downstairs. 'We'll make a little Christmas video for the kids to wake up to, shall we?'

He set the video rolling on his phone. Amber instantly pressed her nose to the screen, creating an intense selfie, and Mark was laughing again. God it felt good to laugh. He could see the difference every time he looked in the mirror. He was lighter, in some way.

Somehow, he managed to orchestrate Amber's 'Christmas Message and Stocking Unwrapping'. He finished the Christmas video, and sent it to the kids, ready for when they woke up. Then he had a thought. Hadn't the lady at Battersea, Laura, asked him to let her know how Amber's first Christmas was? The video was incredibly silly, but surely she'd understand. And if it made someone else giggle on Christmas morning, all the better.

*

Nothing like a bit of poop for clearing the mind, thought Laura as she emptied another litter tray. It was impossible to dwell on your recent ex-boyfriend when you were trying to prevent a lively cat either from darting out between your legs as soon as you opened the pod door, or from thinking that cleaning out the litter tray was the start of a hilarious game. She gave the tabby cat in the pod a little game with a toy on a stick, before stepping out.

There was a buzzy, happy atmosphere in the cattery that morning. Over fifty volunteers and staff had come in, to ensure that the cats had a taste of Christmas cheer. They all mucked in with cleaning and grooming, and each cat even had a Christmas stocking hung on their door, filled with treats and toys.

She took a quick break, to grab a cup of tea and a mince pie, when her phone buzzed. Another email notification. This time titled 'Merry Kitt-mass!' She clicked on it and found a video. Laura pressed play and was greeted by Amber's face and loud purr.

'Say "Happy Christmas!"' Mark's voice could be heard in the background.

Amber let out a miaow and Laura cracked up laughing.

'Now, it's your first Christmas,' said Mark. 'And do you think you've been naughty or nice?'

Amber let out another miaow and made a jump at the screen.

'Naughty AND nice, that sounds about right! Well, I think you deserve a Christmas stocking then . . .'

He then proceeded to help Amber open her presents – sending her skittering after the paper each time, before she returned to see what was inside. A rainbow feather mouse, a jangling ball, a smart collar, and a bowl decorated with her name.

Laura smiled. She remembered how much Mark had wanted to be needed. He looked a different man in this video, his voice full of laughter.

'Merry Christmas, Mice and All!' the video finished, with Mark holding Amber up to his face and giving her a kiss on the head.

Laura noticed a little message from him in the email. 'Laura, hope you don't mind me sharing this very silly Christmas message, but Amber insisted. As I hope you'll see, we are having a wonderful first Christmas – and we hope you are too. I can't thank you enough for putting us together.'

Laura felt another surge of Christmas contentment. She wondered if she'd hear about any more of her nine cats – each time she thought of them, it gave her wounded heart a boost. How was Felicia getting on, in particular? And Enid? And Aaron? She willed them to send her a message.

After a morning spent playing with the cats and their new toys, they all sat down for a Christmas lunch in the café, accompanied by Christmas carols on the radio and a bit of prosecco. Rumour had it there would even be a visit from Father Christmas.

'Merry Christmas!' Jasmine and Laura toasted each other. Jasmine gave Laura an encouraging wink. Laura knew Jasmine would understand how she felt. Yes, she had been the one to break things off with Rob, but her heart was still bruised. Realising the truth of her relationship had been very painful. And she was hurt that, for Rob, it seemed to be so easy to let her go. She still hadn't told her parents, deciding she'd do so after Christmas, when she'd come to terms with it all. They'd sent her a Christmas message, a picture of the two of them on a white-sand beach, grinning happily and holding two large cocktails. Laura couldn't help but smile. How could she puncture that tropical Christmas cheer? She'd look forward to seeing her parents when they were back. Maybe she could put in the odd extra trip up north as well.

A white envelope dropped into Laura's lap. She glanced up to see one of the security guards.

'This got dropped off for you last night, Laur, just after you'd gone,' he said.

'Oh?'

'Yeah, tall, good-looking guy.'

Laura's heart began to pound. Her imagination ran wild. Could this be Rob, wanting to talk or finally fight for her? Or, wait, might it even be Aaron? Did he have feelings for her after all?

She turned the envelope round, amused to see a pawprint 'seal' on the back, and tore it open.

'Dear Laura,' the card read, in spindly handwriting,

I hope that by the time you read this, you are tucking into a delicious Christmas dinner and are pleasantly drunk. Rest assured, Felicia and I will be doing the same – although she will be off the booze, don't worry! She is currently curled up on my knee, and has made herself right at home in a very short space of time. In fact, it feels like she has been here for ever, and I adore her more every minute. Aaron will soon be cat-proofing the garden, so she can stroll around in spring.

I could see how much Felicia meant to you and I want to thank you for caring for her so beautifully, and being generous enough to let her find a home with us. Do you know that the name Felicia actually comes from the Latin for 'happy', and I think there are happy times ahead for all of us.

Laura wasn't quite so sure about that.

I have a little secret to let you in on. When I was a young girl, I volunteered at Battersea! It was very different in those days – I've enclosed a photo so you can see.

Wishing you a happy Christmas, dear Laura.

Love,

Enid and Felicia

Laura looked at the photo. It was indeed Enid, much younger, grinning toothily in front of Battersea's old cattery. Laura smiled. How amazing that Battersea could keep uniting so many people and animals across generations. She'd ring Enid after Christmas, and see how Felicia was getting on. She'd also mention the Knitting Kittens group that they ran once a month – maybe Enid would like to come and join in, and play a part in Battersea's community once again.

A loud 'Ho ho ho!' rang out, and Father Christmas lumbered into view, a sack over his shoulder, to giggles from the volunteers.

Yes, he might look a little bit like one of the security guards, but that didn't matter as he handed out a chocolate mouse to each of the volunteers.

'And what would you like for Christmas, young lady?' said Santa to Laura.

'Well, Terry – err, Father Christmas, I mean . . . I'd like . . .' Laura paused. She had no idea what she wanted now. Her Christmas wish had been for Felicia to find a new home. And she'd thought she had everything she wanted in Rob. But that hadn't been true.

Jasmine, sensing her discomfort, dived in. 'Well, she wants world peace for all kittens, but in the meantime I'm sure a bottle of Baileys wouldn't go amiss.'

They all chortled together, before Santa moved on. Laura gulped. She wasn't looking forward to January. Christmas was one thing, when she was distracted and everyone was on holiday, but the reality of her new single life would hit her before long.

Soon enough, the end of the shift rolled around. Jasmine and Laura bade their farewells to the other volunteers, and headed out to the car.

'How you doing, Laura?' asked Jasmine, as they started the engine and she tuned the radio to carols.

'I'm okay,' said Laura. 'It helped being with everyone in Battersea, cuddling the cats. Keeps your mind off things, all the hustle and bustle.'

Jasmine nodded.

'How about you, though?' asked Laura in return, aware that for Jasmine as well Christmas was bound to be a raw time of year.

'I just keep thinking how much better I'm doing now than this time last year,' said Jasmine. 'And I am. But there's still the odd moment when I just think, wow, my life looks different from how I thought it would.'

'I can relate to that,' said Laura. 'I guess that's just life, eh? You think you've got everything sorted, then, bam – it all changes.'

'It certainly does,' said Jasmine, easing the car out. 'Let's get home and put a cheesy Christmas film on. There's still plenty of chocolate to get through.'

'Sounds like a plan to me,' said Laura. 'Distraction is the name of the game.'

And distraction worked well, for a bit. Cuddled up with Missy, with *Love Actually* playing on the telly – they both knew the dialogue off by heart – and scoffing chocolate, Laura could feel almost normal. But she had no idea what lay ahead.

Chapter 21

Dear Laura,

I'm sorry not to write to you in time for Christmas Day, but I hope that you had a brilliant Christmas and I wish you a happy New Year!

I hope you remember me – I came in with my mum, very miserable, and we adopted a little cat, Notch, together. Maybe your colleague Jasmine told you (and please say hi to her, she helped me so much) but I'd just gone through a horrible break-up.

Casey paused and broke off from her writing. The anxiety was rising up again. She glanced round the cosy living room at her mum's and saw Notch, curled up and asleep in her fleece bed that hung over the radiator. The soft rise and fall of the cat's tummy calmed her down.

I wasn't in a good way. I'd been really hurt by my ex, and I couldn't make it into work or anything. My life had been pulled from underneath me, that's how it felt. Mum pretty much had to drag me to Battersea that day.

I'd been dreading Christmas Day. But having Notch with us helped so much. She is a shy girl, and has taken plenty of time to settle in. She needed lots of places to hide and feel comfortable, and we would just let her be – not fuss over her, just let her take things at her own pace. Gradually, day by day, she started to trust us more and more. Sometimes now, she'll even come for a little cuddle. She gives me something else to focus on, something to love.

Casey had been particularly grateful on Christmas Day. She'd made the mistake of looking at Instagram and caught a glimpse of Fern's Christmas Day post, picture-perfect, her swelling belly just visible in a knitted dress. All her emotional trauma had surfaced again. But, then, she'd seen Notch tentatively peeping around the door. She'd put down her phone and beckoned the cat towards her. Sometimes she felt like Notch had a sixth sense for when she really, really needed her. There'd been more than one occasion when Casey had felt her anxiety rising up again and then Notch had padded quietly over to be near her. She knew that the cat wasn't particularly confident or sociable yet, so she was even more grateful for those moments. Later on Christmas Day, she'd shut her Instagram account entirely. She'd also taken out the present she'd bought for Adam in the sales and decided what to do with it. She'd stitch the jumper together differently, and make a luxurious bed for Notch.

In fact, our little cat has given me the strength to move on. To stop looking back. I think to myself, if she can do it – come and build a home with us and trust people again after all she's been through – then so can I.

It's hard work and I'm not going to pretend things are always easy – but they're a lot easier with our cat here. Thank you, Laura and Battersea, for saving us both.

Casey signed off the letter, and went to look for an envelope. She laid a hand gently on Notch's head as she went past, careful not to disturb the slumbering cat too much. Her next step was to get ready for work the next day. With her mum's support, she'd finally confessed to the school what had happened to her, and the issues she was having.

Her boss had been really sympathetic. They had worked out that Casey would come in three days a week in order to help her adjust. The first day had been difficult, with all the hustle and bustle of a new term, and boisterous kids after Christmas, but Casey had taken things a few steps at a time – breaking down her tasks so she didn't get over-whelmed, and spending her lunch break walking in the small park nearby as a rest from so many people. She thought frequently of Notch during the day, and looked forward to getting home to her. Now, they were introducing the cat to the outside. Watching Notch take her first tentative steps into the garden, glancing back around as if for reassurance, was another source of inspiration for Casey. Little by little. Step by step. That's how new beginnings were made.

*

Christmas and New Year were over and Laura had just finished reading Casey's letter. It was a horrible January day, with rain lashing down outside. She was grateful to be in the cosiness of the cattery. Casey's letter had made her think about her own situation. The rest of the Christmas break had been difficult, and Laura had actually come back into Battersea as early as possible, in order to avoid thinking too much. She'd gone out with Jasmine on New Year's Eve, but had come home soon after midnight. She'd cried herself to sleep more than once, thinking of all the good times she and

Rob had shared, all the positive things about him, looking back at old selfies of them grinning into the camera, heads pressed together. Had she been too hasty? Could they work things out? These questions had tormented her.

She'd barely heard from Rob at all. She'd sent him a few messages asking how he was doing, and if he wanted to talk more, and he'd replied simply saying, 'Fine, not really.'

But now, inspired by this letter from Casey, she knew she needed to stop looking back. It was time to be brave.

Taking a deep breath, she pulled out her phone.

Her first text was to her mum. 'Hi Mum. Bit of sad news from me. Me and Rob broke up. Would be good to talk to you soon.'

And then she sent another text.

'Hi Rob, I think I should come and get my stuff. And it would be nice to say goodbye, properly.'

*

That weekend, Laura turned up nervously on the doorstep of her old home with Rob. She was going to move into Jasmine's for the foreseeable future – along with Missy, who Jasmine had decided to adopt formally. 'A double adoption,' Jasmine kept teasing. 'Couldn't leave my little waifs and strays out on the street.' And so it was time for her to pick up her things and start making a go of her new life. That didn't stop her stomach being knotted with nerves. Rob had been civil in his reply, and she wondered how it would be to actually see him.

She rang the doorbell, even though she still had her keys, and heard Rob's familiar footsteps coming to answer. He opened the door, in a T-shirt, jeans and bare feet, handsome as ever.

'Hi, Laura,' he said. 'Come in.' There was no antagonism in his voice, but not much warmth either.

She walked into the house they'd shared together, suddenly feeling like a complete stranger.

'So, how are you then?' she asked him, once they were in the kitchen. She wondered if she should put the kettle on for a cup of tea. They'd spent several years together; it seemed a shame to just leave it on such a formal note.

He shrugged. 'I'm okay. Good to be back at work.'

'I know that feeling. I've just been burying myself in work, really.'

'With all your cats.' He smiled at her.

She smiled back. Finally, a bit of the tension eased off.

'Yes, still completely covered in cat hair, I'm afraid. So, how are you doing? Are you . . . okay?'

Rob raised his eyebrows at her. 'I think I am, really. It was a shock when you did it, but perhaps we weren't right all along.'

That stung. Laura felt her cheeks burn. 'Oh. Well, there were plenty of times when I thought we were very right together. I know it didn't work out, but I still care about you, Rob. I'm still grateful to you for all the good times.'

There was a painful silence before Rob's expression softened. 'And me to you, Laura. You're a special person.'

They looked into each other's eyes for a moment. *I thought I would marry this man*, Laura found herself thinking, and a lump rose up in her throat. Silently, Rob opened his arms and she fell into them, pressed tightly against his chest. Tears rolled down her cheeks. This was harder than she'd thought it would be.

'I'm sorry,' she choked.

'Shhh,' Rob soothed her, and memories flicked through her mind of all the times they'd spent together, all the kind gestures between them, all the hope and optimism there'd once been. After a few moments, he spoke again. 'Laur, I think it's best if you get your things. I don't want this to be harder on us than it needs to be. I moved your stuff into the office, I hope that's okay?'

She nodded and wiped her nose. 'Right. Yes. I'll just have a look in the kitchen cupboards.'

'I think I got most of your stuff already, but have a look, of course,' said Rob.

She took a peek in the cupboards. Yes, he was right. There was hardly anything of Laura's left – none of her chipped, battered, favourite mugs standing out against his sleek ceramics; none of her baking bowls getting in the way of his steel kitchenware.

Next, she went upstairs to the office. Rob had neatly packed up her clothes, folding them into a suitcase. The same with her toiletries – she was glad that he hadn't included any of the FruitySoap freebies. She took a quick look round their bedroom, holding her breath as her heart gave a pang. She found one or two books, and the odd pair of socks, but, other than that, Rob had done a thorough job. It was almost like she'd never lived there at all.

'I'll give you a hand out with the boxes,' Rob said, coming up the stairs behind her.

She nodded, and together they carried out the cardboard boxes and suitcases to Jas's car – a sad reversal of when she'd moved in.

When the last box was done, it was time to say goodbye. Laura took a deep breath and turned to face Rob, then remembered.

'Oh! Rob, there's a quilt in the spare room that's mine. I'll just get it.'

He frowned. 'It's okay, I can go.'

'No, no, easier if I do it – I'm not even sure where it is.'

She turned around and went back up the stairs, and opened the door to the spare room.

Instantly, a small cat shot out, giving her the fright of her life.

'Rob!' called Laura. 'Rob! There's a cat gotten into the spare room!'

She heard Rob coming up the stairs behind her.

'How on earth did it get in there, maybe through a window? But how . . .'

Laura's voice trailed off when she saw Rob holding the cat in his arms, a guilty expression on his face.

'Laura, meet Silky.'

The cat blinked up at her with slanting blue eyes. A Siamese, sleek, skinny, young-looking.

Laura goggled at him. 'Hang on a minute. This is . . . *your* cat?'

She peered into the spare room, where there was a multitude of cat toys, a scratching-post tree and a cat bed.

Rob nodded.

Laura was almost speechless. 'What? I mean . . . You said you *never* wanted a cat! You refused, point-blank, to even discuss it!'

Silky gave a typical Siamese high-pitched yowl in Rob's arms and glared at Laura. Laura had never met a cat she didn't like, but she sensed it might just be possible with Silky.

Rob sighed. 'Well, I know. It's just that one of the girls at work was getting rid of her, couldn't cope, and she showed me some pics, and well . . . she just goes so beautifully with the décor.'

Laura couldn't speak for a moment. Then she burst out laughing. 'Are you seriously telling me that's the only reason you got her? Because she matches the sofa?'

The cat's creamy-white and chocolate-brown markings did indeed blend beautifully with Rob's neutral colour scheme.

He looked embarrassed. 'No, not the only reason. Thought it might be good for me to have a bit of company. She's a great stressbuster, when she's not trying to claw the rug.'

Laura could only stare and take in the scene. She quickly found her quilt. What more was there to say? She couldn't believe it. She'd longed for a cat for years, Rob knew how much she'd wanted to give Felicia a home, and she'd only been gone five minutes and he'd gone and got one – and not just any cat, a Siamese, one of the most demanding and attention-seeking breeds possible. Words bubbled up in her throat, anger, resentment, and she was about to launch a tirade against Rob, but then, suddenly, they melted away. And she was left with nothing but a light feeling as she looked at him for the last time, Silky in his arms. This had never been her forever home.

'I think I should get going.'

She turned and walked downstairs, Rob following behind.

'Goodbye, Rob,' she said firmly, but not unkindly, on the doorstep. 'Thank you for the good bits. I wish you, and Silky, the best of luck with everything.'

And, with that, she turned around and marched to the car, not looking back. Step by step. That's how new beginnings were made.

Chapter 22

On into January, Laura continued to bury herself in work. She had accepted she and Rob were over, and it was for the best, but she still found adjusting to single life hard. Her parents had been very sweet – her mum was checking in with her every few days. Laura had also decided she'd be the one to arrange the next catch-up with Rachel and Carys, and was in the process of fixing up a date with them. But, even so, her daily life looked very different. The nights when Jasmine was out with her pals, or weekends when she was away, were difficult times to bear. Some things felt a lot more difficult on your own. If Jasmine was around, the two of them would often cook together, but when it was just Laura – well, there'd been a few too many instances of her scoffing a packet of biscuits in front of the TV instead of making a proper dinner.

One Tuesday, she prepared to ring around a few of the adopted-cat owners she hadn't yet heard from. Top of her list – Enid. Laura tried to ignore the wriggling butterflies in her stomach as she dialled her number, praying that Aaron would answer.

'Hello?' came Enid's distinctive voice.

Laura tried not to be disappointed. 'Hi, Enid! It's Laura from Battersea, just ringing to see how things are – and say thank you for your lovely Christmas card and photo.'

Enid chuckled. 'I'm glad you enjoyed it, dear. Quite the looker, wasn't I? Well, all is well here. Do you want to speak to Felicia? I'll just put her on.'

There came some rustling and then Laura could hear the sound of an unmistakable purr. Her heart leapt.

She cooed down the phone to Felicia, who gave a miaow back, before Enid returned to the receiver.

'She knew it was you!' said Enid. 'She was sitting on my lap and she pricked up her ears as soon as you spoke.'

'So she's settling in well?'

'It's like she's been here for ever. Right from the first night, she was curled up by the fire, leaving us in no doubt who ruled the roost. And we're both on a strict exercise regimen. I have her chasing around a few times a day, I promise you!'

Laura laughed. 'I'm delighted to hear it. So, do you need our support with anything?'

Enid paused, and Laura found herself hoping she might have an excuse to call her again.

'She's not going outside yet, but we'll take our time with that. Horrible weather anyway. So I think we're doing just fine, actually, dear.'

'Oh. Okay. Well, that's wonderful. Oh, there was one other thing I wanted to mention. We hold a knitting group here once a month, where people make the toy mice and blankets for the cats. I wondered if you might be interested? It'd be a lovely way for you to get back involved with Battersea.'

'That's ever so kind, dear, but I'm just not sure it's my cup of tea. And I'm ever so busy these days – I'm doing these dance classes down at the leisure centre! But thank you.'

'Well, if you ever change your mind, the door's always open,' said Laura, reluctant to say goodbye. 'We have a saying: once a Battersea cat, always a Battersea cat – and I think it applies to our humans as well.'

'It certainly does,' said Enid. 'Now, dear, I'd better go – Aaron's popping round for lunch and I need to prepare myself for whatever health-food horror he's inflicting on me today.'

Laura's heart jumped at the mention of him. She wondered if Enid would mention she'd talked to her.

'Oh, how's Aaron doing?' she said, attempting to be casual.

'He's very well indeed. Busy planting all the time, and studying. We're going to give the garden a bit of a makeover, actually, make it more cat-friendly for Felicia. And cat-proof, of course, ready for her to explore safely.'

With that, the two women said goodbye. Once the phone was put down, Laura felt flat. That was it, then. Felicia was on into her new life, and it was all going marvellously. Laura told herself she was just being silly with this left-behind feeling.

Her next call, to Alison, revealed a few more issues as Brandy settled into her new home.

'Do you want me to pop in?' offered Laura. Alison's place wasn't too far away from her own home, and, as she'd soon be starting as a volunteer, Laura thought it might be nice to pay her a visit and start to build up a friendship.

Alison opened the door with a big smile.

'Laura! Come on in.'

Alison was far more self-assured than Laura had seen her before. She was dressed in a bright, patterned jumper, and she chatted away confidently to welcome Laura in.

'So, tell me what the issues are,' said Laura, when they were both sitting down with a cup of tea.

'Well, at first everything was going well,' said Alison. 'We got her home, she settled in well, actually – much better than we'd anticipated. We were having lots of fun, and even Christmas seemed to be all right – we were a bit worried about how she'd cope with Fiona being back, but the two of them got on famously. There was lots of playing, lots of cuddles, then Fiona went back to university. But then, after that, it seemed that things got a bit worse. It's not awful, just the odd little accident outside her litter tray, and she perhaps seems not quite herself sometimes. She's not been going outside yet – we want to make sure she's settled here before we try that.'

Laura nodded. Alison had clearly been listening to Battersea's advice – they recommended cats stayed indoors for two to six weeks before being introduced to the outside world.

'Is she around?'

'She normally snoozes in the living room this time of day.'

They went through and found the cat dozing in her bed. She woke up when they came in.

Laura observed her for a couple of minutes. Cats were good at disguising when they were stressed, and it was often quite hard to pick up the signs. She could see that Brandy looked healthy, but some of her behaviours did indeed look a little agitated – her ears twitched back and she would groom her front paw often.

'See, she keeps doing that, and she definitely didn't at first,' said Alison.

Laura nodded. 'Can I have a look at her set-up?'

Alison brought her through to the kitchen, where Brandy's water and food bowls were kept. Laura couldn't see a problem there – the water was clean and fresh, and the bowls were positioned in a corner, with no sign of the litter tray in sight. Cats, being scrupulously clean creatures, often didn't like using a litter tray that was near their food source.

Brandy's litter tray was placed separately, in the utility room, right by the washing machine.

Could that be part of it? wondered Laura. If the cat had been frightened by the noise of the washing machine at some point, that would give her an aversion to the litter tray.

She voiced her theory to Alison, who nodded in agreement.

'It's a good point. I didn't think of that. And, we're near the neighbour's garden on this side – they have a dog who barks quite a bit when he's out.'

Together, they moved the litter tray into the quieter downstairs bathroom.

Laura also told Alison she could try plugging in some pheromone sprays to help calm Brandy down.

'Thanks so much for your advice, Laura,' said Alison. 'And for popping by. It's going to be good to have a friendly face when I start at Battersea. Now, how are you? Did you and Rob have a nice Christmas?'

Laura's face fell. 'We actually broke up, just before Christmas.'

'Oh, I'm so sorry, what an awful time of year for it. How are you doing?'

Laura shrugged. 'I'm not really sure. I feel like I might be in a kind of limbo state with it all.'

Alison placed a hand on her shoulder. 'I hope you don't mind me saying, but when I saw you both together, I wasn't sure it was a match. You gave so much of yourself to him.'

'I know,' said Laura. 'It's just in my nature to be like that.'

Alison paused. 'I'm the same. But it's important, too, to make time for yourself. To learn to live for yourself a bit. If there's anything I'm learning from Brandy there, and from cats in general, it's the importance of a bit of independence.'

Laura thought about that after she'd left. Alison was right. Look at how much she'd benefited from throwing herself into a new opportunity with Battersea – and that was before she had even started. Laura was sure that once she was actually in the role, she'd go from strength to strength. Should she challenge herself, throw herself into something she'd never thought she'd be able to do?

It was New Year, and time for a whole New Independent Laura. No more mooning over Aaron and Felicia; no more what-iffing about Rob. No more having digestives for dinner. It was time for change. She should be more like Jasmine, who was always out and about, always socialising and trying new things. She needed to get out of her comfort zone.

And that was how, the following Thursday night, she found herself at a salsa-dancing class on the outskirts of London, in a lively bar. She'd messaged Alan and Rufus to apologise for missing the New Year's drinks, and explained that she and Rob had broken up. They'd been very sympathetic, and had invited her to join them at their weekly salsa class. 'Nothing too serious,' Rufus had promised. 'To be honest, we go for the margaritas and to have some guilt-free nachos after.'

Her instinct had been no, she had two left feet, but she forced herself to try it. She needed to start picking herself up and getting on with things. Who knew, maybe this could be the start of a glittering new hobby, she might get really into it . . .

'Laura, other way!' hissed Alan, halting her spin.

'Whoops, yes,' said Laura. She'd been daydreaming as usual.

The instructor, in a shimmering shirt unbuttoned far too low for January and tighter trousers than Laura could ever get away with, called out another indecipherable instruction that everyone else understood. They all had that sassy back-and-forth step down perfectly.

Laura tried to watch them and do the same, but ended up stamping on Alan's foot.

'Jesus, Laura!' he said, hopping in agony. 'I'm getting another margarita to try to numb my toes again.'

They both walked over to the bar and slurped on their drinks.

'I don't think I'm exactly a natural at this,' said Laura, thoughtfully.

'I hate to put anyone off dancing, but I kind of agree,' said Alan. 'If I'm ever going to walk again, perhaps we could sit the next one out.'

That was Thursday night. Jasmine was away visiting family that weekend, so Laura made sure to jam-pack her time full of activities. If she was going to be a whole new woman, she had to get used to organising her time properly and making good use of it.

On Friday, Laura went speed-dating, muttering something to herself about how she needed to get back on the horse. The evening wasn't much of a success. The men were either horribly overconfident or terribly nervous, and Laura ended up treating the nervous ones as she would new arrivals at Battersea – speaking slowly and calmly, with no rapid movements, and she gave them a few matches just to boost their confidence. Even this approach earned her only one match. Frankly, it was something of a relief given the company, but Laura couldn't help but feel rejected. She'd even put on her red lipstick!

On Saturday morning, she dragged herself out of bed early to go on a run, which involved a freezing-cold circuit of the park, a cup of tea to warm up, and then another freezing-cold circuit of the park.

She spent the rest of the day in bed, warming up and trying to learn Spanish – which she had decided would be one of 'Brand New Laura's' hobbies. Then she could confidently head there in the summer, sit in a plaza and sip sangria to her heart's content. With Aaron beside her. No! This was about being a whole new Laura, a fabulous independent woman. She erased the image of Aaron offering her patatas bravas and replaced it with a copy of a book, one of those long, worthy ones. But she dozed off before she'd even managed to learn how to introduce herself in Spanish.

Saturday night was a film – she'd reconnected with an old friend of hers, Sarah, from the agency days. It didn't go as well as planned. During a wine afterwards, Sarah just kept asking her why she'd broken up with Rob, as if Laura was completely mad. She also kept asking how long ago it had been, and whether either of them was seeing other people yet – clearly, she was completely smitten with him. Laura sighed. She suspected Rob's taste of the single life would be rather different to hers, given the number of devotees he had in the office.

Sunday morning – another run, trying to ignore her aching calves.

Sunday afternoon – preparing healthy meals for the rest of the week; trying to meditate, uninterrupted by Missy pawing at her; doing some sit-ups.

'Laura, you look like death,' said Jasmine, pulling no punches as Laura arrived in the office on Monday morning. Jasmine had travelled in straight from her aunt's home in the countryside, and looked fresh-faced and rested.

She groaned. 'I'm exhausted.'

'What have you been doing in my absence?'

'It's a whole new me, Jas. I need to learn to live for myself.'

Jasmine looked doubtful. 'Right. And how does this involve you looking like death on a Monday morning?'

'It's just all the self-improvement, it's exhausting.' She listed all the things she'd been doing and Jasmine burst out laughing.

'Laura! This is crazy! I'd be exhausted doing all that.'

'But that's the point, I thought I needed to be more like *you* – you're always off doing interesting things, seeing people.'

Jasmine shook her head. 'Half the time, I want to be more like you. Calm and kind and happy in my own company, not dashing around all the time and annoying people by talking too much. Oh, a card came for you.'

Laura opened the envelope to reveal a painting, a simple rendition of a little cat. It was Pie, the cat who had gone to the rehab centre, and was accompanied by a note.

Dear Laura,

I wanted to send you this picture to brighten up the cattery. The painting is part of my rehab – it helps me improve my motor control, although I'm not sure I am going to be the next Picasso.

Pie has helped me more than I can say. Or should I say Zep, as we renamed him, after the great Led Zeppelin. I didn't believe a cat could make a difference – I was wrong about that. He has helped me accept who I am, right now. Not what I was or what I might be in the future. He has helped many other patients at the centre feel the same way. Our lives are not easy, but he makes the journey a bit more joyful.

We are very grateful he found a home with us. He is happy and very loved.

Sorry not to write more, it's extremely difficult for me. Please come and visit whenever you like, to see Zep at work.

Jack

Laura read the short letter again, letting the power of its words sink in. The cats who went on to do this kind of therapeutic work were very special animals indeed. She could only try to imagine the devastating effects of Jack's accident and his struggle to adjust to a new life. And what an amazing lesson Jack was learning from Zep. Animals were wonderful that way. They just accepted you, as you were, in that moment.

It wasn't just a lesson for Jack, she realised. She needed to get some perspective on her own life situation. She'd been heading up the wrong path with this self-improvement obsession. In future, she'd be open to trying new things, but she didn't need to become a whole new person. She needed to accept herself, imperfections and all, just as she was. She leant over to Jasmine.

'Jas?'

'Yeah?'

'What are you up to tonight?'

'No plans.'

'Want to join me for digestives and *Cash in the Attic*? I've recorded it.'

Jas looked at her and grinned. 'Cancelling whatever new hobby you had planned?'

'I think that my ballet career can wait, yes.'

Chapter 23

Although Laura had abandoned her project to turn herself into Superwoman, she did recognise that she needed to focus her energies in some direction – if she didn't, she worried she'd start dwelling on everything. She thought about what she liked best about her life, and about her job, and realised that – aside from cuddling cats – it was *stories*. In particular, the stories of the cats and the people who came to own them. She thought of all the amazing stories behind her own 'Nine Cats of Christmas', how the cats she'd rehomed had benefited people's lives, and her mind started to turn over. Could she do something where she followed up on how they were getting on and the effects the cats were having on people's lives? She'd already heard from several of them. It was Valentine's Day next month and she wasn't looking forward to it, but the thought of doing something that celebrated the bonds between people and animals, and involved the stories of how their lives had changed following an adoption – now that was something that appealed. Battersea could even use the stories to appeal to other potential rehomers.

Excited, she began to brainstorm possible ideas for her little campaign. She came up with the name 'Perfect Pairings' – make that 'Purrfect'. She'd write to each of the nine people she'd helped adopt cats before Christmas, and ask if they'd mind her coming to do a little follow-up story, or using what they'd already told her. Not all of them would respond, she was sure of that, but she hoped she might get a few good stories out of it. And, she told herself, she'd try taking a few photos. In terms of new hobbies, photography appealed. She had a fairly good camera from years ago, which had been neglected recently. It would be nice to take some photos that weren't quick snaps on her phone.

She shared her idea with Jasmine later on.

'I love it, Laura! Such a good idea. Then we should have a little event to say thank you for their time, right?'

'Like what?'

'Well, you and me could organise a fundraising night ourselves – I've always wanted to do that, and it's better than moping about on Valentine's Day. What if we invited your interviewees along, and encouraged other people to attend and donate?'

'It's a good idea, Jas.' She thought for a moment. 'Hey! What about a cheese and wine tasting event? Surely people would be willing to pay a bit of money towards that?'

'Who doesn't want some cheese and wine in February?' smiled Jasmine. 'A perfect pairing if ever I heard one.'

Laura nodded, feeling excitement light up her face. Finally, a project to focus on.

*

In the next few days, as well as concentrating on her usual rehoming duties, Laura started to plan their event. She found a cosy local pub where they could rent a room and organise a tasting, and, of course, she and Jasmine just *had* to go and sample a few of the wines in advance.

She'd had a quick reply from Alan and Rufus, who said they'd be delighted to help with her project and she could come and see them whenever she liked. She'd also heard back from Lucie, a subdued note, suggesting that Laura come round for a chat and proposing some dates and times – she was going to start letting Bumpkin out in the garden, she said, and it might be nice if Laura was there to see that.

A few days later, Laura pulled up the collar of her coat and shivered as she waited for Lucie to open the door of the maisonette.

Eventually, she arrived, pulling open the door and saying 'Hi' to Laura. The girl looked pale and thin, hunched in a grey sweatshirt.

'Lucie, how are things?' said Laura, fearing what had happened.

'Come in,' said Lucie, shivering.

Inside, there was an empty bed in the living room. Bumpkin was curled up, dozing on it.

'I don't have the heart to get rid of the bed yet,' said Lucie, and Laura turned to look at her, her eyebrows gently raised.

Lucie nodded. 'Yeah. Granny passed away just after Christmas.'

Laura said nothing, but just embraced Lucie's thin frame in a hug.

The girl pulled back after a few moments and wiped her eyes. 'Let me get you a tea,' she said.

Laura went through with her to the kitchen as the kettle boiled.

'Are you okay to talk to me today, Lucie? If it's too much then please don't worry at all.'

'No,' Lucie replied firmly. 'I want to talk to you. And you can use any of this in your story, by the way. It's really important other people know how much a cat might help them.'

They went into the living room and sat on the sofa. Bumpkin raised his head, and came to sit on Lucie's knee, purring. The girl visibly relaxed.

'So, Bumpkin here is the best nurse ever. After we got him home, he settled right in. He was purring on Granny's lap within about half an hour.' Lucie smiled at the memory. 'She loved him. How could you not? And I know people say cats are selfish or they aren't loyal or whatever, but that's just not true. Bumpkin knew Granny was ill, he knew when she was having a good day or a bad one. He'd always be gentle with her, he never pounced on her feet like he likes to do to mine, don't you, boy? And we had an amazing last Christmas together. Granny was mostly in bed by then, but she managed to get up and dressed and sit at the table for a bite of Christmas dinner. We set Bumpkin a place as well, I have to admit. And Mum was here too. That made it extra-special. She's going to stay around for a bit.' Lucie smiled gently at this, and Laura was relieved she wouldn't be alone.

Lucie continued talking about Christmas. 'Then we just opened loads of presents. I went really overboard for Granny. I know it's crazy, but I just wanted her to have everything. Lovely soaps to smell, her favourite perfume, a new scarf. They comfort me now that she's gone. And we really spoilt Bumpkin as well. His first Christmas with us – his only one with Granny – and we wanted him to remember it. He got more toys than he knew what to do with! And a little taste of chicken.

'Then, after Christmas, Granny went downhill, fast. We had nurses coming in to care for her and keep her comfortable. They were amazing. And Bumpkin was constantly with her. I used to wait up with her, check that she was sleeping and comfortable. I didn't want her to be alone when . . . when it happened.'

Lucie paused and wiped a tear from her eye. 'Then, one day, I got in from work and Granny was sleeping – she was fine. Peaceful. Mum was out, doing the food shop. I pulled the blanket up and gave Granny a kiss on the forehead, and I thought I'd just take a moment of snoozing in my own bed – I'd been down on the sofa most nights in case she needed anything. And I got up, about an hour later, and I came back downstairs – and she'd gone. She'd just slipped away while I was sleeping upstairs. I felt like I couldn't forgive myself, for not being there. Then I heard that it happens a lot. That people just slip away when their relatives are out of the room. Maybe it's easier that way, who knows? But then it occurred to me. She hadn't been alone. Bumpkin had been on her bed when I'd checked on her, and he was there when I came back in. In fact, Granny's hand was resting on his head, just gently.'

She stroked the cat's ears. 'So, I will be for ever grateful that Bumpkin has been here for us. And I don't know what I would have done without him these days. Now it's me he's gentle with, always coming for a snuggle, always snoozing with me at night. Mum feels the same. He's a great comfort.'

'I'm so glad he's here with you both,' was all Laura could say.

The cat lifted his head and gave a small miaow, before stretching out on his back to have his tummy rubbed.

Lucie turned to her and grinned. 'His comic timing is pretty good as well. Honestly Laura, that's something to put in your story about how he has affected me. He makes me really appreciate the little moments. Granny too. Even when she was in pain, he could make her laugh. Shall we see how he gets on outside? I've been putting it off a bit – the thought of him going far away is terrifying, but it'll be easier with you here.'

'Of course,' said Laura. 'Is this just before a feed time?'

'Yeah,' said Lucie. 'I read all the stuff online. He's due some food in about ten minutes, the greedy thing. I've been tapping his bowl as well, to get him used to the association of that sound with food.'

Together, the two girls opened up the back door and waited. It was important that Bumpkin take this at his own pace. He was instantly curious – soon at the threshold of the door but a little more tentative about stepping out. He looked at Lucie as if for reassurance.

'There's a good boy,' she said. 'You can come back in whenever you like.'

Cautiously, Bumpkin left the flat entirely. He paced delicately across the lawn, stopping to sniff each individual blade of grass.

'Look, that's what I mean,' said Lucie. 'He just savours every moment.'

Together, they watched the cat pad a bit further in his explorations. His fur was a little bit puffed up against the cold, but he looked quite relaxed. He saw a leaf skitter across the paving stones and pounced on it, causing Lucie and Laura to laugh. Then he went over to a particular tree, its branches naked in midwinter. He sat by it, before rubbing his body around the trunk, as if in greeting.

'Weird,' said Lucie. 'That was Granny's favourite tree. The almond blossom. She always used to wait for it to flower in spring.'

'Looks like it's Bumpkin's new favourite too,' said Laura.

'We'll plant another, together. I want to be reminded of Granny, even as I make the place my own.'

Soon, the ten minutes were almost up. Lucie called Bumpkin in for his food, and he came almost instantly, cantering towards her with his tail up in the air, as pleased to see her as if he'd been away for ten days, not ten minutes.

'Come on then, my little explorer,' said Lucie, gathering Bumpkin up in her arms and warming them both up with a cuddle. Her face broke into a genuine smile.

Laura took a few photos and decided to leave them to it. She'd head home and appreciate the little things. She'd give her mum a call. She'd reach out to some more friends she hadn't spoken to in an age, and invite them along to the Purrfect Pairings evening. Before she left, she mentioned the event to Lucie and left her a little flyer she'd made about it.

'No pressure, though,' said Laura.

Lucie considered it. 'Thanks for the invite. I just need to see how I'm doing, day to day, if that's okay?'

'Of course,' Laura reassured her, before saying goodbye and shutting the door behind her. Laura was so glad that Lucie had Bumpkin to be with her through her grief. Sometimes, little things added up to be awfully big.

Chapter 24

Laura's next visit was a weekend trip down to Alan and Rufus, where she was received in style.

'Can I interest you in another glass of fizz?' said Alan, proffering the bottle to Laura. 'We have to toast Santa Paws – sorry, I should use her official new name, Chloe, in her new abode.'

She was hardly going to say no. Thank goodness she'd abandoned 'whole new Laura' and dry January. She just had to remember to actually get some words out of them about how Chloe had affected their lives, and not just lose the entire afternoon getting tipsy and playing board games. She asked them how they were getting on.

As per usual, Rufus launched in. 'Well, she's just simply marvellous, isn't she? We love her to pieces. Couldn't wait to get her home.'

Alan laid a hand on his knee. 'Shall I talk for a bit?'

'Sorry,' said Rufus. 'I'm a bit nervous.'

Alan turned to Laura. 'I know that Rufus explained how we got Evie just before I lost my mum.'

Laura nodded.

'There's a bit more to it than that. I've had struggles with depression since I was a teenager. I had a really bad episode after Mum died. I mean it when I say that I wouldn't be alive now had it not been for Rufus' – he took his husband's hand and kissed it – 'and, even though this sounds silly, for Evie. Rufus took care of me, wonderfully. And so did Evie.

'So when she died, I was really worried about another bad episode. Actually, it was one of the factors that made me decide we should get another animal. I didn't want to put Rufus through something like that again, not if there was any possible way I could help myself. The pressure on a couple when one of you has mental health issues is immense.

'And I'm so glad we did get Santa Paws – I mean, Chloe. Ever since we got her home, she's given us something to focus on. We chat to her, all the time. We chat in these silly voices that no one else will ever hear. It breaks up the tension, it makes me laugh – she really is a lifesaver. To be loved, unconditionally, and to love like that in return. That's what life is about. That is what a pet – although that seems far too little a word for what Chloe is to us – will always remind you. People will say that we rescued her – but I feel like she's rescued us.'

'Beautifully put,' said Rufus quietly, giving Alan's hand a squeeze. 'Who rescued who?'

'Can I see Chloe herself?' asked Laura. The cat had played a part in her own story too, she realised. The day when Laura had struggled up to London with her in that enormous carrier – looking back now, she could see how symbolic that was of her relationship with Rob. When she'd needed help, he'd not been there for her. He'd not been on her team.

'Of course,' said Rufus. 'She's probably sleeping by the radiator in our bedroom. She's showing very little interest in going outside in this chilly weather.'

Laura padded upstairs and saw the sleeping cat, her flanks rising and falling contentedly. She grinned. How satisfying to see Chloe in her new home – she just should have picked this chimney in the first place.

'How are you doing after the break-up?' said Alan, when she came back down.

Laura sighed. 'I'm all right, I think. It gets a bit lonely.'

'Of course it does. But just remember what I told you, Laur. What we learnt from the cats who rescued us. It's about love, and being loved back. That's what you deserve. And you'll get it, mark my words. There are so many people who adore you.'

Rufus nodded. 'Including us,' he said with a wink.

She laughed. 'I'm just trying to plough my energies into work and new projects. I think I forgot who I am a bit, after so long with Rob. On which note, I'm planning this night on Valentine's Day – you don't have to come, of course, but it should be fun and it'll raise money for Battersea. I'm hoping to make some of these interviews into little pieces, maybe with a portrait or two.'

She showed them a leaflet for the Purrfect Pairings event. She'd written it to encourage people to bring not only romantic partners, but other people who mattered in their life – family, friends, or even colleagues. She'd also said it would be lovely if people could bring pictures of their cats or pets, along with a line or two about how their perfect pairing complemented them.

Alan and Rufus looked at each other. 'Well, will you be my date, then?' asked Rufus.

'I can't think of a better way to celebrate Valentine's than this,' said Alan. 'Count us in! I love a good wine on a special occasion.'

Rufus snorted. '"Special occasion" being most nights.'

'Every night is a special night with you, my love, and Chloe too, of course.' Alan batted his eyelids dramatically at Rufus.

'He's only being so charming because you're here,' said Rufus, ruffling Alan's hair nonetheless. 'Here, you should get going, Laura. I don't want you missing your train – there's a fair wait until the next one. We'll give you a lift to the station.'

As she hopped in their battered little MG sports car, Laura felt warmth spreading through her. Here she was, building up a new life. People were liking the idea of Purrfect Pairings! She'd shared the idea with her colleagues, and loads of the volunteers seemed up for it too. Rachel and Carys had messaged her back, saying they'd love for that to be their next meet-up. She'd asked for a £10 minimum donation, and plenty of people were signing up for more than that. Everyone seemed keen to have something in the diary to look forward to, after a grey and miserable January.

There was just one thing. She hadn't heard back from Enid yet. She'd sent her a letter, but hadn't had a reply. And she could hardly go and call her up – if she was honest with herself, Enid had sounded perfectly happy and had said that things were going well with Felicia, and she wanted to enjoy her new lease of life. Laura didn't want to be a nuisance, and she certainly didn't want to pressure Enid into something she didn't want to do. She'd just have to focus on enjoying the stories that she was able to hear.

*

For some reason, Laura hadn't expected to hear back from Wanda the witch, but she sent her an enthusiastic email saying she'd love to come to Purrfect Pairings, and inviting Laura to come over and talk about how she and Teddy were getting on.

'I could even dress up in some of my ceremonial robes, and you could take some pictures!' she offered.

Given how ornate Wanda's outfit had been when she came to Battersea, Laura was distinctly intrigued to see what she'd wear for a special occasion. *Why not go?* she thought. She was enjoying how her project was getting her out and about, and connecting with people again. As well as Lucie and Bumpkin, and Rufus, Alan and Chloe, she'd already paid visits to Mark and Amber, Casey and Notch, and Carlos, Skittle and the family, and she had a visit to the rehab centre to see Jack and Zep booked for the following week. So that was how she found herself, at the weekend, hopping on an early train and heading down to the south coast. It beat another lonely day of self-improvement, that was for sure.

She took a bus to Wanda's village, and found what had to be her cottage. It was adorable – with a thatched roof and crystals and pretty wind chimes hanging outside the door. She was about to pick up the knocker – shaped like a cat's face, she noted with amusement – when Wanda flung open the door.

'I knew you were here!'

'Is that your sixth sense?' Laura said, impressed.

Wanda laughed. 'It's more Teddy's extra-sensitive hearing. He starts yowling whenever he hears anyone nearby – he's better than any guard dog.'

Teddy was indeed yowling and twining himself around Wanda's legs, then Laura's. He was a typical Siamese. Laura sometimes struggled to get on board with the breed's pushy, talkative nature – laid-back cats Siamese definitely were not. She wondered briefly how Rob was getting on with Silky, before pushing the thought away from her mind.

Wanda picked him up and he nestled in her arms, his blue eyes gazing intelligently at Laura. With Wanda's stunning silver hair, pale-grey eyes and silvery robes, they made quite the pair, thought Laura. She'd be able to get some amazing photos. With Teddy chattering all the way, they went into the kitchen, which opened up to a conservatory at the back of the house. It was a beautiful space, just as Laura had remembered it from the photos at Battersea. In real life, it was filled with the delicious fragrance of sweet herbs and scented candles.

'Can I make you a tea?' asked Wanda, and Laura gladly accepted. She was chilly after the journey.

'Would you mind holding Teddy? He'll only start yowling if I put him down.'

Laura took the cat from Wanda, and he put his paws on her shoulders, almost like a human child. Siamese cats were a bit uncanny, thought Laura. She didn't quite dare look at Teddy's eyes – was he capable of putting a spell on her? Then the cat butted her cheek gently and began to purr, as if telling her not to be so silly.

Wanda made tea, and they sat down together – Teddy springing loyally back to his mistress's side. Laura reached into her bag and pulled out a present, wrapped with a large bow.

'What's this?' said Wanda, surprised.

'Consider it a little thank-you gift for helping me out,' replied Laura.

Wanda tore open the wrapping to reveal the cat statue that Laura had intended as Rob's Christmas present. Laura waited to see if her heart gave a pang, but she just felt happy at the beaming smile on Wanda's face.

'Thank you so much! I love it!'

Teddy gave a miaow as if he approved too, as Wanda set it proudly on a shelf.

Laura snapped a few photos on her phone and they looked amazing. Wanda looked like some fantastical winter queen, attended by her loyal cat.

She told Wanda that's what she thought, and the witch giggled.

'I think it's more the other way round – I'm generally attending to this one's every whim.' She stroked Teddy and beamed.

'So, why do you think you're a perfect pairing?' asked Laura.

She'd perhaps been expecting Wanda to talk about her spells and how Teddy helped with that, but she said something simpler.

'Well, we're opposites, really. But that's what makes us a perfect match.'

'How do you mean?'

Wanda paused for a moment. 'Well, how can I explain it? Teddy is such an extrovert. He's always running off to investigate what a sound is; whenever anyone comes to the house – like you today – he can't wait to meet them. It's the same with any clients. He's always curious about things – he's always investigating. Sometimes it's a bit too much, as he has worked out how to scale the wardrobe and climb along the top, and has made a bed in my good linens,' Wanda finished with a smile. 'Oh yes, and he can open the kitchen door by jumping up and hanging on the handle.'

Laura smiled too. This didn't surprise her – Siamese were notoriously intelligent.

'Anyway. I'm different to Teddy. I know everyone sees me in the crazy robes, with the hair, but, actually, I'm pretty shy. When I go out in this stuff, it's like a form of protection. I was horribly bullied in school, for years. I was a classic outsider kid – a geek, not interested in boys, weird-looking, bad skin. It's actually how I got into the witchcraft stuff. I wanted to cast spells to protect myself from the bullies.'

Laura's heart went out to the young Wanda. She seemed so strong and confident now, it was hard to imagine her as a shy teenager.

'I think perhaps that stuff stays with you a bit. It scares me to think about going into the outside world as just me. To think about being judged by other people, or mocked. So I get dressed up, I act a certain way – all to protect myself.'

'So how does Teddy fit into all this?' asked Laura.

'Teddy reminds me to connect with people. He reminds me to be curious. Everyone who comes to me for treatments – they always comment on him, and then I get talking to them on a better level. He provides a way for me to connect. And now, because most people in the village have seen him wandering around outside – you can't really ignore Teddy, and he's been guilty of inviting himself into a few houses where he's not wanted – people know he's mine and they talk to me more. They ask what he's up to, and what I'm up to, and, suddenly, I'm being asked to things. I'm being asked to the pub, I'm being asked if people can come round and play with him. And now I'm thinking, what more can *I* be curious about? All these things that maybe I've wanted to try before, but haven't had the guts to. You know, the other weekend I went caving!'

Laura personally couldn't think of anything worse than heading down into a cave, especially in this weather.

Wanda caught her expression and laughed. 'I know, I know. But I've always been fascinated by them – I told you I was a weirdo. They're meant to be powerful centres of healing and spirituality. But, anyway, the point is – I went! I went and did it, and I knew Teddy would be at home waiting for me, and I only bloody loved it.' Wanda positively beamed.

'So that,' she finished up, 'would be the best part of mine and Teddy's perfect pairing. He teaches me to connect and be curious.'

Chapter 25

Before Laura knew it, February had rolled around and Valentine's Day was upon them. The Purrfect Pairing fund-raiser had loads of people signed up to it, and Laura's stomach gave a nervous flutter when she thought about the evening ahead. She'd spent the past week typing up versions of her interviews and designing some beautiful posters of the portraits she'd taken. She'd also visited Jack at the rehab centre, to hear more about how Zep was getting on. Jack had said it would be too overwhelming to come to the event, but was keen to talk to her about the impact Zep had had on his recovery. As well as the important gift of acceptance, he said the cat was teaching him responsibility again. On the days when he was in charge of feeding Zep, he had to engage with his rehab tasks. Opening a tin might take ages, but it was worth it to satisfy a miaowing cat. Laura had left feeling a glow of satisfaction from seeing Zep at work, and with a beautiful photo of Jack laughing as Zep tucked into his food.

'Are you excited?' asked Jas over breakfast on Valentine's morning.

'A bit nervous, if I'm honest.'

'You should be really proud, Laur. You've pulled this off in so little time and you're going to raise loads of money for Battersea. And off the back of a break-up too!'

Laura paused for a moment. Yes, she supposed she *should* be proud of herself. She'd been amazed how her life had blossomed over the past few weeks. Going to see her Nine Lives – well, most of them – and chatting to them, organising the event; speaking to people who might want to come – that was very different to how she feared the single life would be. She'd been surprised at how much she and her parents had talked, too. She was planning on going up to York as soon as they were back. There were more and more entries in her calendar, invites and events she'd organised with friends old and new. There were times when she missed Rob, of course, but now she was looking forward to the future.

She was going to leave Battersea a bit early in order to prepare the pub, and get herself ready, and, as she was only on emailing duty that morning, she'd skipped washing her hair, pulled it back into a bun and then dashed out of the house with a piece of toast in hand, otherwise she was going to be late. It was probably a good thing she didn't have a boyfriend this Valentine's Day, as she was growing a massive spot and had been scratched down the face by a mischievous kitten the day before. But there was something liberating about not caring! She imagined what she would have been getting up to with Rob and cringed – that night in the restaurant had been terrible. She was more than ready to spend Valentine's night celebrating Battersea's Purrfect Pairings, accompanied by a decent amount of cheese and wine.

Laura spent the morning happily slurping on tea and biscuits in the office, and writing bios for their new arrivals. She'd had another idea, and that was to promote the cats who needed to be rehomed as pairs under the Purrfect Pairing tag. They had a couple of them in at the moment: sibling kittens from the same litter, a mother and son, and two older cats who'd been kept as a pair by their owner. She was keen to write some lively copy and get them up on Instagram as a Valentine's Day post, and she was pretty pleased with the results by lunchtime. She'd pop out and get a sandwich, and then it would soon be time to head to the pub and start decorating, before nipping home to get showered and changed. She had a pretty jumper with a sequin trim she'd been saving to wear.

As she passed through the reception, a lively gang was sat knitting – mostly women, of all ages, plus the occasional brave man. Ah, yes, it was the Knitting Kittens' Valentine's Day special meeting! They were knitting mice in various shades of pink and red, which would go to the cats as toys.

'Happy Valentine's Day, Laura!' called out a lady named Myrtle. 'How many did you get, then?'

Laura laughed. 'None, I'm afraid.'

'Still time!'

'Unless one of the cats is going to surprise me with a dozen red roses, I think not,' Laura joked, heading out to the café.

She was on her way back in with a fresh tomato soup stain down her fleece – her oldest one, she probably should chuck it – when her heart leapt into her throat.

Aaron.

He was with Enid, helping her walk down to the cattery reception.

'Please no, not today of all days,' moaned Laura softly.

As per usual, he looked completely gorgeous, in a well-worn blue shirt, his skin glowing from so much time spent outside.

There was absolutely no way to avoid them. Laura forced herself to smile, after briefly attempting to cover up her spot with her hand and realising it would probably just draw more attention to the offending blemish, which was probably about the size of Mars anyway. Oh, well. Sod it. He wasn't interested anyway.

'Enid! Aaron! How lovely to see you!' she called, waving confidently.

'Hello, dear!' called back Enid, while Aaron raised his hand in greeting and then looked at his shoes.

'Everything all right?' asked Laura when she was by them. *Please don't let something have happened to Felicia*, she thought with sudden alarm.

'Everything is wonderful!' said Enid, beaming. 'I wanted to give this knitting-group malarkey a try, I do love knitting. Young Aaron kindly brought me along.'

'That's me,' said Aaron, before blushing as well. Laura felt better that she wasn't the only awkward one in this situation.

'Will you show us where to go?' asked Enid.

Laura brought them through into the reception area, where she introduced Enid to Myrtle, who got her a chair and settled her in.

'When will you be ready, Nana?' asked Aaron.

'Oh, a good hour or so, at least,' replied Enid. 'It'll be wonderful to be knitting again! The click-clack of the needles and all that. And plenty of time for you to take Laura here to see Felicia.'

'Oh gosh, I mean, I don't think so,' began Laura.

'Yes, she's probably far too busy,' said Aaron.

'Nonsense!' said Enid sternly. 'Aaron, you need to show Laura the lovely new garden we've made for Felicia. The poor girl will have been dying to know how she's getting on. Off you go, the pair of you – I'll just wait here until you're done.'

In silence, the two of them turned around and walked out into the fresh air.

Once they were out of sight, Enid turned to Myrtle.

'You're going to have to show me the ropes, I'm afraid. I can't knit a stitch!'

Myrtle goggled at her. 'Well, of course! But what was all that about loving knitting?'

'It's the only way I could think of to get those two together,' confided Enid. 'Had to pull my innocent old lady act. Kids today – no idea how to actually get together! My poor grandson, I've never seen him like that over anyone.'

Myrtle cackled. 'I like your style! Now, what colour mouse do you want to make?'

*

Once they were away from Enid's forceful influence, Aaron turned to Laura. 'Honestly, Laura, if you don't have time, don't worry. When she gets an idea into her head, she won't take no for an answer.'

'I'd like to see Felicia, actually,' Laura confessed. 'She was a very special cat to me.'

Aaron smiled. 'Thought that might be the case. I've got the car so we'll be quick.'

Laura hopped in the passenger seat of his battered car. Now they were close together, alone, the radio playing as rain gently drizzled on the windscreen. It was easier to chat without looking into his gorgeous brown eyes, Laura decided. She could just about hold a conversation.

'So, how was your first Christmas with Felicia? Enid sent me a card, which was very thoughtful.'

'It was wonderful,' he said, with a smile. 'Nana's like a new person! She's up every morning to feed her, she plays games with her, she goes out and finds Felicia new toys to play with. She's determined the two of them will be healthy – although I do have to watch her feeding Felicia treats a bit.'

'Yes, that cat can be a bit of a dustbin,' said Laura fondly.

'She's a real treasure. You can tell how much love she has to give.'

There was a silence, broken only by the sound of the indicator.

'How was your Christmas, then? Your colleague – Jas, is it? – told me about you heading off for some very glamorous night, the day we picked Felicia up,' said Aaron.

Was it just her, Laura wondered, or did this sound very much like fishing? She swallowed. It was time to be honest. She caught a glimpse of herself in the wing mirror of the car. Spot, scratched cheek, hair pulled back – well, this was her.

'Ah. Well, it was a glamorous night but not a very happy one. I broke up with my boyfriend.'

'I'm sorry to hear about your break-up,' said Aaron.

Was it just her, or did he not sound sorry at all?

He cleared his throat and tried again. 'Very sorry indeed. How are you doing?'

'Well, it's not been easy. But it was definitely the right decision. So, I've just been figuring out how life looks on my own, throwing myself into a few work things – it's been good, actually.'

Should she mention Purrfect Pairings? She guessed that he would have already seen the invite she'd sent to Enid, and must not be interested. Besides, she didn't want to come across as desperate. She asked Aaron how he'd been, and he was soon talking about plants and the work he'd done to the garden. Laura didn't have that much of a clue what he was talking about, and decided not to mention that she couldn't even keep a cactus alive, but she loved hearing him talk.

Soon, they pulled up near Enid's house. Laura was so excited at the thought of seeing Felicia once again.

'I'll show you the garden first, we can creep round the back,' said Aaron. 'We've not let Felicia out yet. Wanted to make sure she was really settled in, and I've been cat-proofing the fence.'

Really, thought Laura, she could not have wished for a better home for Felicia.

Aaron walked her down the side of the house to a beautiful little garden. He pointed out what he'd done, the enthusiasm rising in his voice as he talked about plants.

'We planted a few more shrubs to give her a bit of coverage, plus put in those wooden boxes so she can have somewhere to hide and shelter in if the weather is bad. The fence now has that overhanging mesh at the top, so she can't get out – although I'm not sure she has much reason to try, bless her. She seems mighty content by the fire. And look, by the back wall.'

Laura saw a charming table and two chairs, along with a wide shelf fitted to the wall.

'The chair and table are for Nana – and me, if I'm in her good books – and the shelf is for Felicia to perch on. I was reading that cats like to be up high.'

Laura nodded, her hands clasped. This garden was a cat's paradise.

'It's been brilliant for Nana,' continued Aaron. 'She's been helping me plant everything; look – we've got catnip here. Nana never complains about her knees when it's all for Felicia, who likes to watch what we're up to from the window.'

'Overseeing everything,' Laura said with a smile.

'Yes, she doesn't miss a trick, that one. Here, you're cold. Let's go and see your Felicia.'

Aaron turned and opened the conservatory doors. 'She'll come running when she hears your voice, I'm sure of it.'

Laura couldn't wait to see her. This was the best Valentine's treat she could have wished for.

'Felicia,' called Laura. 'Here, girl! You've a visitor!'

They paused, waiting to hear her approach.

'Try again,' said Aaron. 'She could just be sleeping.'

Laura called again. No sign of Felicia. Had the cat forgotten her already?

Aaron frowned. 'That's weird. She always comes running. Here, help me look for her.'

Searching the house didn't take long. Aaron looked upstairs in the bedrooms and found no sign of the cat, and Laura looked downstairs, in the kitchen, living room and little bathroom.

'Aaron,' she called. 'The bathroom window's open!'

He ran down the stairs and looked, groaning. 'Oh no. I always tell Nana to get that lock fixed. Felicia must have pushed it ajar – that gap is easily big enough for her to get through. Laura, we have to find her. She's not been outside from here before. If anything has happened to her . . . If she's found the main road, if next door's dogs . . .'

Laura could sense his panic rising. She touched his arm. 'Aaron, keep calm. We'll find her. Can you get her food bowl and some treats?'

Aaron grabbed them from the kitchen, and they went out into the street, too worried about Felicia to notice the cold or the drizzle.

'Felicia!' they called in unison, banging on her food bowl and rattling the treats bag. 'Felicia! Come here, there's a good cat!'

'Come here, my little fur-noodle!' called Aaron, and Laura's heart melted.

After twenty minutes of calling, there was no sign of her and Laura was starting to get worried too. All sorts could have happened to her.

Aaron ran his hands through his hair, agitated. 'Oh God, Laura, where can she be?'

Laura was thinking. 'If she's got a fright, she could have darted somewhere to hide. It's very possible she might be stuck somewhere, or lying low until she thinks the danger has gone.'

They'd walked around the block a few times by then, and the rain was getting heavier.

Aaron looked at her. 'Laura, you're getting soaked. Go back inside and I'll keep searching.'

'No, I'm staying with you,' Laura said firmly.

Just as they were trying to decide where to look next, they heard a faint, peeping 'miaow' through the rain.

'Did you hear that?' Aaron said, turning to her.

She nodded. 'Felicia!'

Another miaow came. They looked around, and then up, to see Felicia stuck in the crook of a tall tree, right on the border between the pavement and a garden.

'Felicia!' said Laura, a wave of relief pouring over her.

'She's well and truly stuck, isn't she,' said Aaron. 'What should we do?'

Laura would normally have advised waiting a bit longer to see if Felicia made it down on her own, but the cat looked wet, miserable and thoroughly unhappy. If a cat wasn't used to being outside, it could often climb higher than it was comfortable jumping down from and get stuck.

'We need to help her get down.'

They called out encouragement and shook the treats at her, and Felicia got up and looked for a moment as if she was coming down, but then she backed away from the attempt, staring at Laura with helpless golden eyes.

'Let's knock on the door, see if they've got a ladder,' said Laura. They went through the gate and up the path, but there was no answer at the door.

'Laura, I'm going to get my ladder,' said Aaron. 'I'm just five minutes away. We can put it against the tree from the pavement side, so it's hardly trespassing. Can you stay here and keep an eye on her?'

Laura nodded, and Aaron jogged off in the rain.

'I hope you're happy with yourself, young lady,' said Laura. 'All this attention just for you!'

Felicia gave a miaow.

'How am I? Well, thank you for asking. I'm doing all right. I've got a new home now too. Me and Rob broke up.'

Felicia cocked her head to one side, as if listening.

'I just hope there's someone who's more suited to me out there.'

Felicia miaowed loudly, and Laura turned to see Aaron returning with the ladder. It was a full-on Mr Darcy moment – the rain had soaked his shirt and Laura didn't know where to look. Felicia kept miaowing loudly, as if to say, 'There he is!' Laura blushed furiously. Why did Aaron have to see her like this, today of all days? Couldn't she have been slightly more glamorous – perhaps not the full sequin dress works, but at least with washed hair and a touch of mascara?

Aaron leant the ladder against the tree and asked Laura to hold it steady. He climbed nimbly up, and could just about reach to Felicia. The cat scuttled over to him, and, in an awkward manoeuvre, he got a hold of her – Laura saw him wince as the cat clung to him with her claws. He tucked her firmly under one arm and slowly descended.

'Well, that's quite enough adventure for one day,' he said, passing her over to Laura. Laura clutched the soggy cat to her, who was now purring wildly and chirruping, delighted to be rescued.

'Oh, Aaron, your arm!' In her fright, Felicia had clawed red marks down Aaron's wrist.

He grimaced. 'I'll live. But do you mind if we pop into

my place? It's on the way back to Nana's, if we walk another way, and I can take the ladder back.'

'Of course,' said Laura. She held Felicia tightly against her as they walked, elated to see the cat safe and sound.

Aaron's flat was beautiful. After the homely clutter of Enid's, she had perhaps been expecting something similar, but it was a simple space, painted cream, with house plants dotted everywhere and seedlings sprouting up in any available spot. Facing a little fireplace was a cosy sofa, laden with colourful cushions.

'I'll put the fire on,' said Aaron. 'Then just get myself showered and cleaned up – and you need to warm up, fast.'

Laura was freezing. The rain had soaked her fleece through, and it was a struggle to stop her teeth from chattering.

'I'm fine,' she tried to say, but Aaron threw her a look. He went out of the room and came back with a towel and a jumper.

'Here. The bathroom's just down the corridor if you want to dry off a bit. I need to move some of my seedlings as well, so you can actually sit down.'

Laura padded down the corridor and into the bathroom, taking off her wet fleece, towelling herself dry the best she could and slipping into Aaron's jumper. She treated herself to an inhale. Freshly laundered. Her stomach flipped. Might he . . . be interested in her? She glanced in the mirror and was greeted by a drowned rat – it was a wonder Felicia hadn't tried to pounce on her. Sighing, Laura wrapped her hair in a turban and vigorously scrubbed at it, before returning to the living room.

There was no sign of Aaron, just a steaming mug of tea and a crackling fire. Felicia had taken up residence on the hearth and had made herself at home. She got up and ran to Laura as soon as she came back in the room.

'Well, you're looking pretty pleased at how today is turning out,' murmured Laura, sitting down on the floor and resting her head against the sofa arm. Felicia came and snuggled on her lap, and they both enjoyed the warmth of the flames.

A feeling spread over Laura as she sat in Aaron's living room, listening to the rain lightly patter the window, Felicia snoozing on her lap, a mug of tea warming her hands. She shut her eyes, just for a moment.

Home. That was the feeling.

*

'Oh my God, what is the time?'

Laura jerked awake, looking round in embarrassment and scrabbling to see her watch. She'd been fully asleep, Felicia cosied up against her neck like a furry scarf.

'Don't worry, you've only been snoozing for about half an hour. I didn't have the heart to wake you,' said Aaron, carefully watering some plants.

'I wasn't snoring or anything, was I?'

Aaron hesitated. 'I think Felicia might have been purring a bit loudly,' he said, with a playful smile.

Laura groaned. 'Oh no, I'm sorry. And I have to set up for Purrfect Pairings.' She rubbed at her face, feeling groggy and mortified that Aaron had heard her snoring. Aaron came round and sat on the end of the sofa.

'Perfect what?'

'It's a fundraising night I've organised. To celebrate all the amazing pairings in life – cats and people, and people and people, but all sorts. Not just, you know, couples.'

She dropped her eyes when she said 'couples'. Then Aaron was reaching towards her face. Oh my God, was this it? Was he about to kiss her? He brushed her cheek gently with his fingers and Laura shut her eyes and leant forwards.

'Money spider,' Aaron said.

Laura opened her eyes again. Aaron had a tiny little spider running across his fingers.

'I didn't want to freak you out, don't know if you're scared of spiders.'

'I'm not,' said Laura. Felicia opened her eyes and miaowed with interest at the little spider.

'I'll put him in the plants,' said Aaron, going over and placing the spider carefully in a house plant. Laura couldn't help smiling. He was so gentle and kind.

'So, about this perfect pairings,' Aaron said, coming back over. 'It sounds great. Nana would love it.'

'I sent an invite,' Laura explained. 'And then didn't hear back, so I presumed she wasn't interested. She's very welcome, of course. There're going to be lots of people there who rehomed cats at around the same time, and it's a bit of a celebration of that as well. Or it will be, if I can actually manage to organise it in time.'

She checked her phone and saw a raft of missed calls and messages. Panic rose up in her.

'There's so much to be done,' she said, getting up and dislodging Felicia, who gave a disgruntled mew, as if she hadn't caused the day's drama.

'Look,' said Aaron. 'Your rucksack is still at Nana's. Let's go round, return Felicia, and then I can give you a lift back to Battersea. I'm sure Nana is sick of knitting by now. And I'm not doing anything, so I could even help you set up the pub. If you like?'

Aaron looked tentatively at her.

'Aaron, that would be amazing! Let's go!'

They moved fast. Aaron nipped back to Enid's and brought the cat carrier back, into which Laura bundled Felicia. They settled her in at home – she was delighted to be back – and shut the bathroom window tightly.

'Now that the prisoner is secured,' said Aaron, 'let's get you back to Battersea.'

'I wonder what happened to the invite,' said Laura.

'Hmm. Nana does have a bit of a habit of screwing letters up and throwing them to Felicia.'

Aaron reached down and picked up a few balls of paper, Felicia thinking that he was starting a game. She batted one in particular with her paw, and Aaron uncrumpled it.

'As I thought,' he said, laughing. 'Here's our invite.'

Felicia miaowed loudly, looking happy with herself, glancing from Aaron to Laura.

'Do you fancy coming along, then?' asked Laura, twisting her fingers together and holding her breath.

'Seeing as I'm helping you set it up, I don't think I have much of a choice,' said Aaron, smiling. 'And yes. I'd love to. Come on, let's get going.'

They drove back to Battersea, to find Enid and Myrtle gassing away in the café.

'Sorry we took so long, Nana,' said Aaron.

'Did you?' replied Enid. 'It feels like you've been gone five minutes. Me and Myrtle here, we're planning on a trip to the V&A.'

'That's great,' said Aaron. 'Listen, I promised Laura I'd help her set up the pub for this event they're doing tonight. A Purrfect Pairing cheese and wine tasting, to raise money for the cats. Lots of people are going, who adopted cats around the same time as us. I can run you home first and then come back and help Laura, and then come and pick you up again if you want to come with me to the tasting?'

Enid looked at them both. 'You know, dear, I think I'm perfectly capable of getting the bus back. I need to start putting that pass to good use again. You help Laura. And, as for tonight, I might rest up with Felicia and leave the two of you to it.'

Myrtle gave Enid a not-so-subtle wink.

'Well, if you're sure, Nana?' said Aaron.

'Oh, I'm sure.'

'Laura's also doing a project where she talks to people about what adopting a cat has meant to them, if you wanted to talk to her about that?'

'Aaron, I am perfectly sure you can string a word or two together about that, given the amount of time you and Felicia spend rolling around on the floor together,' said Enid, mock sternly, causing them all to laugh.

Chapter 26

A couple of hours later, Laura glanced around the room with satisfaction. If she did say so herself, it looked pretty great. The dark wood interior of the pub was lit with fairy lights, and she'd printed out big posters of the adopters and their cats, along with a few words about what rehoming a cat had brought to their lives. She'd had so much fun setting up with Aaron. He'd had her laughing constantly, with stories about growing up with Enid, including how he'd been so into plants when he was little that he'd tried to plant *himself* one summer, asking Enid if his toes would take root if he stayed still long enough. He also did a wicked impression of Lettie Maddox as a YouTuber – Laura had caved and told him the identity of the celebrity who'd upset her, only for Aaron to look blank and say he had no idea who that was anyway. He'd insisted on watching a video or two, and now had a perfect imitation of her style that had Laura in stitches.

'Okay, my babes, I think you are totes ready for a glass of wine, right?' he said, pouting at her, Lettie-style, in a way that Laura found both hilarious and weirdly attractive. She'd find anything Aaron did attractive, however.

'I guess I have to abandon any idea of getting changed,' Laura sighed. Aaron came over to stand by her side, looking at the final portrait they'd hung up.

'Into that gold dress of yours?' said Aaron. A corner of

the portrait came away. They both reached up to fix it at the same time, their hands brushing.

'No, not the gold dress,' said Laura. 'Thank God.'

Aaron smiled. 'Good. I like you much better in my jumper,' he said, his voice soft. He lowered his hand from the picture and, hesitating, brushed her arm lightly.

'Do you want the glasses here, then?'

Laura almost leapt out of her skin with shock. Her heart had been pounding already at Aaron's touch, and the barmaid's sudden entry, complete with banging down a tray of glasses, gave her a terrible fright.

'Yes, that's fine,' said Aaron. 'Just on the table over there.'

He gave Laura's arm a squeeze – hmm, that felt more matey than anything flirty – and went to help unload them.

'And two glasses of red, please,' he finished. The barmaid nodded and fetched their drinks.

Laura tried to compose herself. 'Thank you so much, Aaron, for all your help today.'

He passed her a glass of wine and clinked his glass against hers. 'Honestly, Laura, it was nothing. All the work is yours. And doesn't it look amazing! You did it!'

'*We* did it. It's been a roller-coaster of a day.' She took a sip of red wine and allowed herself to relax, just a little, staring at their handiwork.

'Tell me about them,' said Aaron.

'Well, this is Lucie,' she said, showing him the first picture. 'And I met her when she was very rude to me at a make-up counter.' Lucie's portrait was a beautiful one. Her face was sober, unmade-up, and she stared at the camera with great emotion in her eyes. Bumpkin sat upright on her lap, as if guarding her.

'Take joy in the little moments,' Aaron read out loud from her story.

Laura nodded. 'She had a very hard Christmas. Her granny passed away.'

Aaron shook his head. 'I'm sorry. That's so hard.'

They moved on around the room, looking at the portraits. Aaron listened intently to everything Laura said, often asking questions about the rehomers, or indeed about the cats themselves.

'And so you found her up the chimney?' he said, laughing, when it came to Chloe, aka Santa Paws.

Laura nodded, telling him how she got the cat back to Battersea.

Aaron frowned. 'On your own?'

'Yeah. On my own.'

Aaron's expression said it all. Laura didn't want to start dwelling on Rob, so she moved on to the next portraits.

Casey's read, 'A fresh start'.

Wanda's, 'Be curious and connect', along with a stunning portrait of the two of them, their ethereal eyes gazing directly at the camera lens.

Carlos's, 'A friend every day', alongside a picture of him playing with Skittle, who was leaping into the air.

Alan and Rufus had the caption: 'Love and be loved in return'. Theirs was a portrait of them side by side on the sofa, hands intertwined, looking at each other and laughing. Chloe was curled up beside them.

Jack's said, 'Acceptance – and taking responsibility'.

Alison had gone for 'The importance of independence'. In her photo, Alison was beaming at the camera, sitting up straight with Brandy beside her, every inch a woman ready to face the world.

Mark and Amber's caption was 'Be silly'. This was along with a very cute photo of Amber pushing her nose into a giggling Mark's cheek.

'These are beautiful, Laura,' Aaron said. 'Seriously. They're amazing.'

'Thank you,' said Laura, simply. Before, she'd have brushed off Aaron's compliment, saying it was nothing, that anyone could have done it, but now she realised she was right to take pride in her work. And the way Aaron had looked at it all so carefully, had praised each piece and really listened to her, had boosted her confidence no end. She pulled her shoulders back and held her head high, ready to enjoy the night.

She just had one regret. Laura would have loved to have included Felicia in the event, as she was such a special cat to her. Plus, she could have got an amazing photo of Enid and Felicia, two absolute divas. She turned to Aaron.

'What would you say Felicia brought to you?'

Aaron blushed bright red. 'Well, err, she's certainly given my nana a new lease of life. Weight loss, being active, all that . . .' he stammered.

'I meant to *you*,' said Laura, curious as to what he would answer.

Aaron looked at her for a moment and was about to start speaking, when –

'Oh my GOD, Laura, you've worked miracles!'

Jas arrived in a whirlwind, flinging her bag down and catching Laura up in a huge hug.

'You like it then?' laughed Laura.

'I LOVE it! Laura, we have to use some of these more widely, they're beautiful.'

Jasmine caught sight of Aaron then. 'Hey! Don't I know you?'

'Yeah. I'm Aaron. My nana adopted Felicia. Or rather, she adopted us.'

'Of course!' said Jasmine, shaking her head. 'Brain like a sieve. Well, welcome. You're a bit early.'

'Oh no,' said Laura. 'Aaron helped me set up.'

Aaron gave a little smile and looked at his shoes.

'Right then,' said Jasmine, clearly trying desperately to suppress a grin. 'Well done, Aaron. Laura, can I just have a quick word? About some paperwork.'

'I'll just give Nana a quick ring and check she's okay,' said Aaron. 'Back in a minute.'

As soon as he'd gone, Jasmine turned to Laura, her eyes glinting with delight. 'Laura Summers, WHAT is going on?'

'You mean with the paperwork? What's it about?'

Jasmine rolled her eyes. 'Honestly, Laura, there's no paperwork! You and Aaron! I *knew* he liked you – he looked really crestfallen when he came in that time and you weren't there, and then when he saw you heading off on that terrible date night with the flash git!'

'My ex-boyfriend,' said Laura, but she couldn't help but laugh.

'Yes, exactly. I reckon he was going to ask you out. He was marching back in with a very determined look on his face. No man ever looks that determined about fetching another toy mouse.'

'Really?' said Laura, her heart thumping. *Had* Aaron been going to ask her out, that night before Christmas?

'Well, what matters, Laur, is that he's here now and he's staring at you all the time. Get in there! It's Valentine's Day! And here's your very own perfect pairing!' Jasmine was practically hopping from foot to foot.

'Calm down,' hissed Laura. 'He has to think we're talking about paperwork when he comes back in.'

She explained what had happened earlier that day.

'He rescued her from up a tree!' said Jasmine, her eyes boggling at Laura. 'Laura, if you don't snap that man up, I swear I will. This is your night! Enjoy it, you're a star.'

At that moment, Aaron came back in along with the first few guests. He directed them in from outside and took their coats from them. They were a mixture of volunteers and staff from Battersea, some with friends and partners in tow, and Laura went over to say hello.

Laura caught sight of Lucie, hovering nervously at the entrance, and went to greet her. She knew how hard it was to socialise when you weren't feeling up to it.

'I'm so glad you came,' she said, giving her a warm hug. 'Come and look at your portrait.'

Reading Lucie's words was Casey, looking much happier and brighter, with her mum by her side too.

'Is this you?' Casey asked Lucie gently. 'What beautiful words. I'm so sorry about your loss. Here, I'm Casey.'

The women introduced themselves and quickly began chatting about the cats they'd adopted. Laura smiled. She had the feeling that the night would result in many more connections.

'Hey!' came a tap on her shoulder, and Laura turned around to see Rachel and Carys, her friends from university.

'Thanks so much for inviting us,' said Rachel. 'This is wonderful! It's like a whole exhibition!'

'Agreed. So great to get away from the kids for a night. Did you take the pictures as well?' asked Carys, and Laura nodded, delighted to see her friends again and show them what she'd been up to.

She excused herself to welcome Mark and show him the portraits, and then saw Wanda arrive out of the corner of her eye. She wanted to go over and say hello – she remembered what Wanda had said about being shy socially – but then she saw Aaron go to welcome her with a glass of wine. He turned back to Laura and gave her a comforting wink, and she beamed back at him.

People were turning up thick and fast now. She saw Rufus and Alan arrive, Rufus in a paw-print-patterned jumper.

'I begged him not to wear it,' said Alan dramatically, as he kissed Laura on both cheeks.

'Well, it was this or my tiger-print onesie,' Rufus retorted, sticking out his tongue. 'And who, Laura, is the man who keeps gazing at you like I sometimes do Alan, when he's not criticising my dress sense?'

Alan gave Rufus an affectionate kiss on the cheek. 'You know I think you're gorgeous in anything. But Laura, yes, who is that man?'

'He's called Aaron,' she said, trying to keep the smile from her face. 'He adopted Felicia, in the end. Or he and his nana did.'

'Hello, Laura! Who are your friends? Don't I recognise you from that party before Christmas?'

Laura turned around to see Alison had arrived, with her husband John, and was addressing the last part of her greeting to Rufus.

'Yes, that's right,' said Rufus. 'I'm afraid I wasn't very sociable that day.'

'Me neither,' said Alison. 'But let's make up for that now. I'm Alison, and this is my husband John.'

Laura had to marvel at the difference. Here was Alison, confidently introducing herself to Rufus and Alan, and getting on splendidly.

The room was filling up fast now, and Aaron came to find her, picking his way through the throng of people.

'Thought you might want a quick glass of water,' he said, handing a glass to her.

She nodded. She was parched with all the chatting, and relieved to stand with him for a moment.

'Do you think it's okay?' she asked him.

He smiled. 'I think it's more than okay. I think everyone is having a great time! We might want to start off the wine tasting while the sommelier can still get a word in edgeways. Want me to tell them we're ready?'

'Please,' said Laura, as she turned to welcome another group arriving.

The sommelier tinged a glass to signal the start of the wine tasting, and they gathered round to try their first pairing, a delicious pinot noir and gooey brie. Time flew by, aided by free-flowing wine and plenty of laughter. After the tasting, Laura took a moment to survey the scene – Mark chatting to Casey (they'd figured out she worked at the same school his kids went to); Wanda inviting Lucie to come and see her country cottage; Rufus and Alan chatting to a giggling Alison and John. The atmosphere was happy, cosy, warm. People were really engaging with each other – the stories on the wall had proved to be real ice-breakers, and everyone seemed keen to swap tales of their own beloved cats. Laura sighed happily. She loved to see the connections being made.

'Taking it all in?' said Aaron. 'I could do a quick YouTube video about it, if you like?'

Laura giggled. 'Oh, absolutely. This will count as top-quality content for our brand.'

Then came another ting-ting of a glass, and Jasmine stepped forward, rosy-cheeked from the alcohol.

'I just want to say an enormous thank you to a very special cat lady who has brought us all together,' she said, to be greeted by a round of applause.

'GO, LAURA!' shouted Alison, swinging her handbag around, before John shushed her. Alison had proved to be the life and soul of the party. Rufus had declared her a true partner in crime, as her husband had tried to give her some tap water.

'Laura is not only a brilliant colleague and friend,' continued Jasmine, 'but she's responsible for many of the matches we can see around the room tonight – both in portrait and in person. So, here's to you, Laura! And here's to more perfect pairings!'

'To Laura!' everyone shouted, and Laura blushed furiously, as people called for her to speak.

She was about to decline, when she felt Aaron give her hand a reassuring squeeze. This was *her* moment. She should take it. She stepped forward.

'Well, thank you all so much,' she began. 'This evening is to celebrate connections, so I can hardly take credit for it as an individual. Thank you all for your brilliant support.' She paused to gather her words. 'One of the questions I asked the amazing interviewees was what rehoming a Battersea cat had meant to them, and what it had taught them. And then I asked the question of myself. What has working at Battersea taught me?' She caught Aaron's gaze and looked back at him, remembering how it had felt to be with him that afternoon.

'It's taught me about home,' she said, her voice steady now. The room had hushed. 'It's taught me what home truly is. Home isn't just a place, four walls and a roof, and lots of pretty furnishings. Home is about being loved. Being accepted. Knowing you have a place. Home is a feeling. So, here's to us all, finally feeling at home.'

She raised her glass one more time to lead a toast, before stepping back by Aaron's side. He reached quietly for her hand once again, and this time their fingers intertwined.

She was exhausted. Happy, but exhausted. Gradually, people started to peel away, saying goodbyes, sharing journeys home. A few livelier ones – Jasmine, Alan, Rufus, Alison and John – decided to head on to another bar and keep the Valentine's party going.

And then, after the whirlwind, it was just Laura and Aaron again.

He began to carefully take down the posters, rolling each one up neatly.

'You don't have to do that,' said Laura. 'You already helped me so much setting up.'

He looked surprised. 'I want to do it, Laur. Sit down and have a last drink.'

Laura's feet were aching. She was glad to sit down for a moment and nurse a drop more wine. Aaron kept working. She felt the same peacefulness creep over her that she had that afternoon in the flat.

'Come and sit with me,' she said, patting the space next to her.

Aaron looked round and grinned. 'How could I resist?' He sat down beside her, close to her.

Laura took a deep breath and raised her eyes to his. 'You never answered my question,' she said, 'about what Felicia brought to you.'

Aaron smiled. She thought he wasn't going to say anything, and then he took her hand in his own, twining their fingers together again. 'Laura. She brought me *you*. Or so I've been desperately hoping, ever since I first saw you in the cattery.'

Laura's heart was pounding. 'Me?'

Aaron brushed a strand of her hair away from her cheek. 'Yeah, you.'

And with that, Aaron drew her closer and kissed her.

Epilogue

Christmas Day, ten and a half months later

'Aaron Sanderson, if you have another one of those chocolates you will pop,' said Enid, balling up a piece of wrapping paper and throwing it at her grandson.

He deflected it neatly. It plopped near Felicia, who was lying on her back with her legs stuck in the air and barely moved a muscle, a perfect embodiment of how Laura felt post-Christmas dinner. Her parents had left about half an hour ago. Laura had been thrilled at their decision to stay in the UK for Christmas. In fact, she'd seen much more of them throughout the whole year, as they'd stayed much closer to home. 'We always just thought you were so busy with your life in London,' her mum had said, on one of their now regular outings together, and Laura had given her a tight hug.

She and Aaron had stuffed themselves with all sorts of festive goodies. Enid had been more restrained, helping herself to a few slices of chicken and plenty of vegetables – she'd slimmed down dramatically in the last year, and had even taken up yoga.

'Largely so I can nag Aaron to do it,' she'd confessed to Laura. 'He can barely touch his toes.'

Since Valentine's Day, Laura and Aaron had been very much A Thing. The Valentine's night kiss had turned into a date that weekend, ostensibly to return Aaron's jumper, which Laura had conveniently forgotten. 'Returning the jumper' had been the excuse for their next few dates, after which Aaron had said, 'Look, Laura, I don't really care about the jumper but can I adopt you officially? Or does Jasmine need to interview me first? I don't mind, but I need to know you'll be snoring on my sofa on a semi-official basis from here on in.'

And that was that.

There had been weekends away together, laughing like she'd never laughed before; a trip to Spain in the summer, where she had indeed sat with Aaron in a sunny square with a jug of sangria; helping in the garden – although Aaron teased her that she had the kiss of death when it came to keeping plants alive. This, their first Christmas together, had been wonderful. They'd spoilt each other rotten with thoughtful little presents and outings throughout December – ice-skating, Sunday walks, pub lunches, and they'd once even got dressed up and gone out for a fancy dinner, not quite Le Cave, Laura was relieved to find, but a delicious Italian restaurant. They'd also gone to the Battersea Christmas Carol Concert, along with Enid and Laura's parents, and Aaron had proudly worn a pair of cat ears alongside Laura. They had seen many familiar faces there, with lots of people asking Laura if Purrfect Pairings was going to happen again.

Laura caught Enid surveying them both happily, as they sprawled on the sofa together. She had given Laura a pair of gloves that she'd knitted herself – there was a thumb missing on one of them, but Laura said it was far more useful to be able to poke her thumb through anyway. Enid's confession about how she had pretended to knit in order to force her and Aaron together had kept them laughing – and grateful – for months. She still teased them that they owed everything to her, which she didn't hesitate to deploy as blackmail when she wanted a cup of tea made. And Enid had struck up a friendship with Myrtle, who had forced her to learn to knit more or less properly, in between their various escapades around the country. That was just one of many friendships that had sprung up through Battersea. Alison was now a firm fixture on nights out with Jasmine, and had thrown herself into volunteering. Laura caught up with Alan and Rufus for a delicious dinner or country walk every few months. Casey and Lucie had become friends too, and Laura had even spotted Casey out holding hands with Mark a few weeks ago – she didn't want to be nosy, but she suspected a romance might be on the cards there.

'Now what did I tell you last Christmas, Laura?' said Enid.

Laura cast her mind back. 'Errr. I can't remember, Enid.'

'I don't want any more comments about how I'm losing my marbles when you and Aaron have got brains like sieves. In the card I sent you.'

Laura shook her head. 'I'm none the wiser.'

'I told you that Felicia meant happy.'

Laura grinned. 'So you did. And, save your breath – you were completely right.'

Felicia thumped her tail on the floor, as if in agreement.

'And, with that,' Enid said, 'I think we two old ladies will leave you young ones to it. Come on, girl.'

Enid got up and headed up the stairs, Felicia following loyally behind.

Aaron reached for another chocolate.

'Oi!' said Laura, snatching it away. 'That's my favourite!'

She scoffed it before he could protest otherwise.

'That's what I love about you, Laura, your generous nature,' teased Aaron. 'I must say, you appeared quite different in the cattery.'

'Completely fooled you, didn't I?' said Laura through a mouthful of chocolate.

Aaron kissed her on the nose. 'Yes, absolutely.'

Laura glanced around the room, not believing how this year had turned out. Enid's house was as cosy as could be, a Christmas tree twinkling in the corner, handmade decorations strung up, the TV turned down low, in a companionable chatter. Her life was full. It wasn't just Aaron, a man she loved more and more each day. Her life was full of connections, with family and friends too. Relationships she treasured and nurtured. And, of course, life wouldn't be complete without lots of cats too. There'd been so many rehomings that year, more than she could remember, and she loved to think of Battersea cats as little glowing dots of light and love, all around the country.

Aaron nudged her gently. 'What are you thinking about?'

'Cats,' Laura said truthfully.

Aaron laughed. 'I should have known. Listen, I've been wanting to ask you something.' He turned to look at her. 'Would you . . . would you move in with me?'

Her heart leapt. It made perfect sense. They spent almost all their time together anyway, and, while Laura had loved living with Jasmine, she was ready to come home.

There was just one question she had to ask him first.

'Can we get a cat?'

THE END

Acknowledgements

A huge thank you to Phoebe Morgan and Sam Eades at Trapeze for their wise and creative counsel, and good cheer throughout the writing of this book – I'm very grateful to you both. I'd also like to thank the fabulous team at Orion for their support of the project, a full list of whom can be found in the back of this book.

I'm indebted to the lovely staff at Battersea for allowing me to visit (and cuddle a few residents!) and for answering all my questions about the work they do. Particular thanks go to Sarah Van Kirk, Rosa Steele, Ellie Chitty, Sophie Ottley, Claire Davies and Jenny Dainton.

Finally, thank you to each and every reader for buying the book and helping support the vital work Battersea do.

Credits

Trapeze would like to thank everyone at Orion who worked on the publication of *The Nine Lives of Christmas* in the UK.

Editorial
Phoebe Morgan
Charlie Panayiotou
Jane Hughes
Jo Whitford

Copy-editor
Lorraine Jerram

Proof reader
John English

Audio
Paul Stark
Amber Bates

Contracts
Anne Goddard
Paul Bulos

Design
Rachael Lancaster
Lucie Stericker
Joanna Ridley
Nick May

Finance
Naomi Mercer
Jasdip Nandra
Afeera Ahmed
Elizabeth Beaumont
Sue Baker
Victor Falola

Marketing
Amy Davies

Production
Claire Keep
Katie Horrocks

Publicity
Alainna Hadjigeorgiou

Sales
Jen Wilson
Esther Waters
Rachael Hum
Ellie Kyrke-Smith
Viki Cheung
Ben Goddard
Mark Stay
Georgina Cutler
Jo Carpenter
Tal Hart
Andrew Taylor
Barbara Ronan
Andrew Hally

Dominic Smith
Maggy Park
Elizabeth Bond
Linda McGregor

Rights
Susan Howe
Richard King
Krystyna Kujawinska
Jessica Purdue
Hannah Stokes

Operations
Jo Jacobs
Sharon Willis
Lucy Tucker
Lisa Pryde